Summer Under The S

Catherine Ferguson

Published by AVON
A division of HarperCollins*Publishers* Ltd
1 London Bridge Street
London SE1 9GF

www.harpercollins.co.uk

A Paperback Original 2019

A catalogue copy of this book is available from the British Library.

ISBN: 978-0-00-830251-1

Typeset in Birka by Palimpsest Book Production Limited,
Falkirk, Stirlingshire
Printed and bound in UK by CPI Group (UK) Ltd, Croydon CR0 4YY

This book is produced from independently certified FSC™ paper to ensure responsible forest management.

For more information visit: www.harpercollins.co.uk/green

For Matthew. You make me so proud.

Chapter 1

It's the third Saturday in May and I've booked to take Mum to the theatre for her birthday.

Her all-time favourite musical is running for two weeks.

Oklahoma!

I remember being over the moon when I realised it coincided with Mum's special day. It seemed significant somehow. I booked the tickets straight away – the best seats available.

I'm imagining her swaying in time to 'Oh What a Beautiful Morning', a delighted smile dimpling her face and lighting up her brown eyes. She's going to have the best birthday ever.

There's only one problem ... I can't for the life of me remember where I put the tickets.

Recent events have muddled my brain like never before, so I suppose it's not surprising my mind has gone temporarily blank. But I'm certain I put them on the hall table along with all the other post, and they're clearly not there.

'Rachel?' I yell for my flatmate. 'Rachel!'

She appears in the hall, a look of alarm on her face, holding her hands aloft as if about to conduct an orchestra. 'Daisy? What's happened? Are you okay?'

I carry on scrabbling through the pile of mail, even though I've been through it three times already.

'I can't find the tickets,' I wail, trying to ignore the horrible panicky feeling rising inside.

'Oh.' Absently blowing on her newly varnished nails, she contemplates me with the slightly worried frown I've grown used to lately. 'I put them in the kitchen drawer when I was clearing up. I ... um ... wasn't sure you'd be going. What with ... everything that's happened.'

My eyes flash with impatience. 'Of *course* I'm going. It's Mum's special day and this is her birthday treat. You know she loves musicals. Especially this one.'

Rachel nods, murmuring, '*Oklahoma!*'

'Precisely, and I need to get a move on,' I call, haring through to the kitchen and pulling open the messy drawer where all the miscellaneous items live. 'Or else I'm going to be late. The performance starts at two.' Finding the tickets, I sigh with relief.

'Are you getting the bus in?' Rachel is hovering in the doorway. 'Shall I come with you?'

I turn away from her to close the drawer, suppressing a sigh and flicking my eyes to the ceiling. 'There's really no need, Rachel. But thanks for offering.'

I love Rachel to bits. But I wish she wouldn't fuss so much. I'm absolutely fine, and I've told her that over and over again, but she obviously thinks I'm lying.

Rachel and I have been friends ever since we worked as reporters on the same local newspaper when I was fresh out of journalism school.

Our career paths have diverged a little since then. We're both thirty-two. But while Rachel has worked her way up to be chief sub-editor at a well-known glossy magazine, saving enough to own this house, I spend my days writing about flappers and float valves. This sounds more boring than it is. Actually, scratch that. It's exactly as tedious as it sounds. But it pays the rent.

Writing for a plumbing trade publication called *Plunge Happy Monthly* is not my dream job if I'm honest. But on the plus side, anything I don't know about spigots and galvanised steel piping really isn't worth knowing about.

Another advantage is that I don't have the unsociable early mornings and late nights that Rachel has in her senior position, so therefore I've got more free time to focus on writing my book. That's the theory, anyway.

I've been working on my book – a quirky romance, with an accident-prone heroine called Hattie – for the last five years, on and off. Mum keeps saying I'm too talented a writer not to finish it and I keep promising I'll get it done but it never seems to happen. I suppose I'm worried that when I've finally finished it, everyone will laugh and think it's terrible, and say things like, *Who on earth does Daisy Cooper think she is? Imagining she can write a book people would* actually *want to read?*

I've made a decision, though, that now is the right time.

I will stop critiquing the chapters I've already written and making little changes to the opening, and instead, I will push on till the end. Mum will be so proud of me.

Riding the bus into town, I sway from side to side, my thoughts drifting to the last time I went to see one of the old-style musicals with Mum. It was her birthday that time, too, and the musical in question was *West Side Story*.

Even *I* was excited about that one. I'd grown up singing the songs from *West Side Story* because the soundtrack was on in the house all the time. We used to do the housework on a Saturday morning, singing along to 'America' because it has such energy. And I clearly remember whirling around the living room, clutching cushions like dance partners and trilling 'I Feel Pretty' at the tops of our voices. We collapsed, hot and laughing hysterically, on the sofa and Mum drew me in for a hug and declared that when I wrote my best-selling book one day, it would be even more fabulous than her favourite musical. I wanted to be a writer even then, when I was about ten. It's funny the things you remember.

It was just Mum and me at home because my dad died when I was four, soon after we moved up north from Surrey, and our only relatives – Dad's sister and her family – live in Canada. Mum's oldest friend, Joan, lives down in Surrey – they met at primary school down there – and she goes down to visit Joan, but not very often. It's not surprising, I suppose, that Mum and I have always been really close. I'd say that, as well as being the most brilliant mum I could ever have, she's also my best friend. We talk about absolutely everything and she's always so supportive, even when she doesn't entirely agree with my decisions.

As well as owning the soundtrack to *West Side Story*, we also had the film version on video when I was a kid – it's probably still there in a box somewhere – and we watched it together so many times that, even now, I'd probably be word-perfect if you asked me to write down the lyrics. Beautiful actress Natalie Wood played the lead role. She died in a mysterious boating accident several years before I was even born and I remember being haunted by the sad tale of her losing her life at such a relatively young age. She was just forty-three.

My eyes mist over, taking me by surprise. Life is so horribly fragile. It can be over in a split second.

But I swallow on the silly lump in my throat, telling myself this is going to be a happy day.

When I reach the theatre, it appears I was wrong about the happy bit.

A huge sign hangs above the doors.

Performance cancelled due to illness.

My heart plummets into my shoes. This can't be true, surely. Not today of all days. Maybe the sign is still up there from yesterday and they've forgotten to take it down ...

In the theatre, I walk up to the desk and stand in a queue with other disappointed musical lovers to find out what's going on. When finally it's my turn, I can't help the snippiness in my tone, even though the very nice woman on duty explains that, sadly, the cast have been struck down with laryngitis.

I give a bitter laugh. 'What, *all* of them?'

'Well, no, the lead and her understudy.'

'Well, that seems a bit odd. I mean, laryngitis isn't infectious, is it? Not the kind you get from straining your voice.'

Confrontation is not my style as a rule, but agitation makes the words burst out.

The woman blanches slightly. Maybe I'm speaking too loudly. Or looking too desperate.

Lowering my voice, I lean a little closer. 'Look, I know it's not your fault it's been cancelled. But this was meant to be a treat for my mum's birthday. She's sixty-one today and she's been looking forward to it for ages.' I'm starting to shake slightly and I can feel the tears welling up. 'She circled the date on her calendar with a red marker pen, like she always does when she's excited about something. It can't possibly be cancelled.'

'I'm so sorry.' The woman's face softens with sadness. 'I

know it's not quite the same but an extra day is being added to the show's run. Can I put you both down for two seats on the thirty-first instead?'

She scans the entrance hall, presumably expecting to spot someone who looks like she might be my mum.

I swallow hard.

If I tell this nice woman the truth, her face will fall in shock and I don't want to make her feel uncomfortable.

'Yes. Two seats on the thirty-first would be perfect.'

'Lovely. Let me just organise that for you.'

I nod, blinking furiously as the tears threaten to spill over. I can't bring myself to tell her that, actually, only one seat is required.

Because my lovely mum died eleven days ago.

I can hardly say those words to myself, never mind a stranger.

It won't sink in that she's gone. I keep thinking it's all been a bad dream and that, any moment, my phone will ring and it'll be her, wanting to know if I'd prefer chicken or beef for the big Sunday lunch she always makes for us, and laughing about some TV show she's been watching.

I suppose I've been in denial ever since that terrible day when I had to say my final goodbyes.

The woman looks up from amending the booking with a big smile.

'I'm sure your mum will still enjoy her birthday treat. Even if it *is* just a little bit late ...'

*

Afterwards, I walk straight to the nearest pub, go up to the bar and order a double brandy. I don't drink much as a rule.

A glass or two of wine at the weekend is all. I don't even particularly like pubs. But numbing the raw pain with alcohol suddenly seems like a very good idea.

It's mid-afternoon and the pub is fairly deserted, which I'm thankful for. It means I can sit at my table in a shadowy corner for as long as I like, with no curious eyes looking over, wondering about the identity of the sad person sitting all alone, drinking double after double.

All I want is to feel numb. I want to reach that stage of intoxication where you're wrapped in a warm glow and anaesthetised against reality.

But unfortunately, it doesn't seem to be working.

No matter how much brandy I down, thoughts of Mum – and how I'm going to manage without her – continue to march relentlessly through my exhausted brain.

If only Mum hadn't had a fear of doctors and hospitals, she might still be here. But she'd ignored the tiny lump in her breast, not even telling me about it because she knew I'd march her straight along to the GP. She kept telling herself it was nothing and, by the time she eventually decided she should probably get it checked out, it was already too late.

Sitting there, all alone with just my drink for company, frustration and anger at Mum for not going to the doctor sooner mingles queasily with my grief.

I need to go!

I stand up – *whoa!* – then promptly sink back down again. I feel like I'm on a whirling merry-go-round. I appear to have lost control of my legs, which is not good. Not good at all.

How will I get home?

Toby.

It's after seven so he'll probably be finishing up for the day.

My boyfriend is a busy fund manager at Clements & Barbour, based in the City – just around the corner from here, in fact. A lift would be perfect. (The idea of trying to board the correct bus in my helpless state – climb on *any* bus, for that matter – is not an appealing one.)

I scramble in my bag for my phone and start panicking, convinced I've lost it, before realising it's right there on the table in front of me. I stab at his name.

It rings for ages but, finally, he answers.

'You're there!' Relief floods through me at the sound of his voice. 'It's Daisy. Could you – could pick me up, please, Toby? I'm in The Seven Bells and I'm – er – a little bit squiffy.' A loud hiccup escapes. 'Oops. Sorry.'

There's a brief silence. I can hear papers rustling on his desk.

'Can't you get the bus?' he asks at last, and my heart sinks. Tears spring to my eyes from nowhere. I hate being a bother. Especially when Toby works so hard and such long hours.

I swallow hard. 'It's just I've had the worst day and the alcohol has gone straight to my head.' *And I really want you to scoop me up and take me home and tell me everything is going to be all right!*

'Okay. Well, if you give me five minutes, okay? *Five minutes*.'

'Five minutes,' I repeat, but he's already hung up.

I sink back in the seat, feeling wretched and guilty, like a teenager who's sneaked out on a school night and is now in the doghouse waiting to be picked up.

I glance expectantly at the door every time it opens. But forty minutes later, Toby still hasn't arrived. Some emergency must have come up, delaying him ...

People are giving me funny looks. I need to get out of here.

Then I think of Rosalind, Toby's mum. She lives just a short walk from here.

Somehow I manage to make it across two main roads in one piece, and then I'm knocking on Rosalind's door. I can hear screaming and wailing from inside and I nod, reassured. Definitely the right door. It's just a normal day in the life of the chaotic but lovable Carter family.

Toby doesn't know how lucky he is to be part of such a large brood.

Rosalind takes one look at me and pulls me against her large, pillow-like bosom, almost squashing the breath out of me. 'Oh, you poor love. What's happened?' she murmurs into my hair.

Her familiar warmth is too much, and the tears I've been trying to suppress all day start leaking out.

'Come on in.' She pulls me over the threshold.

'It's Daisy!' yells one of Toby's ten-year-old twin brothers and the screaming suddenly stops. Several pairs of small feet thunder along the corridor to greet me. I'm called upon to admire a model of a jet aeroplane, and a paper bag of sticky red sweets is thrust under my nose from another direction.

'Let me talk to Daisy, you lot,' commands Rosalind, shooing the kids away good-humouredly and ushering me into the kitchen. 'Honestly, what's this place like? A total madhouse!'

I breathe in the smell of home baking and feel my shoulders relax.

'It's perfect,' I say, sinking down at Rosalind's scrubbed wooden table with a sigh.

Chapter 2

I first met Toby when we bumped into each other – quite literally – in the centre of Manchester one day.

I noticed this dark-haired man hurrying in my direction, engrossed in his phone, and I prepared to step aside to avoid a collision. But he looked up, saw me and swerved the same way, which resulted in us doing the awkward 'dancing' thing, shifting one way then the other. We apologised and laughed – and I noticed he had the most startlingly blue eyes.

The encounter was all over in a few seconds, but as I watched him striding off, I suddenly realised he'd dropped something. A book. I picked it up. It was a slim volume entitled *Mergers & Acquisitions*.

I started hurrying after him, eventually catching up at the entrance to a large, glass-fronted building with a plaque announcing, 'Clements & Barbour Financial Analysts'.

'Excuse me.'

He was about to go through the swing doors but he turned.

'I think you dropped this.'

He looked at me with those piercing blue eyes. Then recognition flared as he saw what I held.

'Hey, thanks.' He looked genuinely delighted to be reunited with his book. 'It was really nice of you to come after me.'

'No problem. It was on my way,' I lied with a casual shrug. 'The book looks – erm – interesting.'

His eyes widened. 'You think so? Most people glaze over at stuff like this.'

I shrugged. 'It's always nice to learn about something new.' *Especially if your teacher is handsome and intelligent to boot!*

He nodded. 'Listen, I've got to dash into a meeting but if you'd like to know more, we could meet later for a drink?' He held up the book.

'That would be lovely.' I smiled knowingly. It was as good an excuse as any to get to know each other.

'Toby Carter,' he said, and we shook hands.

'Daisy Cooper.'

When I walked into the pub later, he was already there. *Mergers & Acquisitions* was on the table in front of him, along with several other thick tomes with mysterious titles.

I quickly realised he'd taken me quite literally when I said I liked learning new things, and his guided tour through the financial implications of mergers and acquisitions was somewhat of a surprise. I didn't mind, though. It meant I had a legitimate reason to stare into those gorgeous blue eyes!

'I'm boring you, aren't I?' he said at one point.

'No, no,' I rushed to reassure him.

'I tend to think everyone must be as fascinated as me by this stuff,' he said with a sheepish look that made me really warm to him. 'My brothers say I'm a nerd.'

I smiled and asked how many brothers he had.

His reply left me temporarily speechless. 'You have *seven brothers*?' I gasped at last.

He nodded. 'I'm the oldest. Mum and Dad kept trying, hoping for a girl, but it never happened.'

'That's amazing. I mean, it's almost a whole football team! Gosh, you'll never have to worry about being lonely, will you?'

He smiled rather wearily. Clearly I wasn't the first person to look gobsmacked by the copious amount of male siblings.

'Do you still live at home?' I asked, trying to imagine what it would be like to have such a big family. I couldn't help thinking it sounded perfect.

'No, thank God. I've just moved into my own place. We lost Dad last year and Mum's not so great at the old discipline thing, so the younger kids were becoming far too loud and unruly. It was a relief to get my own space, to be honest.'

'I'm sorry about your dad,' I said, wondering how I'd cope if anything ever happened to Mum. 'But you're lucky to be part of such a lovely big family. I'm an only one. And if I've got brothers and sisters, I don't actually know about it because I'm adopted!' I smiled broadly to let him know I was perfectly comfortable with this.

'Oh.' His eyes widened. 'Have you – have you ever tried to find your real mum and dad?'

I shrugged. 'As far as I'm concerned, the mum and dad I've always known *are* my real parents. And I'd hate to upset Mum by going looking for my biological mother, so I never have.'

He looked a bit surprised by my revelations. I was fairly taken aback myself, to be honest. I didn't make a habit of talking about my adoption to relative strangers.

I've known I was adopted ever since I was small.

Mum and Dad grew up in Surrey and, after they married and found out they couldn't have children, they decided to adopt and I arrived. Then, when I was four, we left our home in Surrey and moved north to Manchester, where I've lived ever since.

I've never been able to establish exactly why we left Surrey. I always felt I never got a proper answer from Mum when I asked her. She talked vaguely about there being better job opportunities for Dad, but he worked for the same sort of engineering company up north as he did when we lived in Surrey, and her explanation didn't quite ring true. So I just stopped asking.

Whatever the reason, Mum and I have always been happy in Manchester ...

There was a slightly awkward pause and I cast around for a change of subject. 'You've got lovely eyes.'

'Oh. Thanks.' Toby smiled and leaned closer across the table. 'Listen, Daisy, do you fancy grabbing something to eat?' He glanced at his watch. 'I've got to prepare for a presentation tomorrow but I could give you ... um ... fifty minutes?'

I nodded. 'Great.'

It wasn't the most romantic proposition I'd ever received but I was intrigued.

Toby Carter was clearly passionate about his work and I'd always found that sexy in a man.

We started dating, seeing each other once or twice a week. Toby often had to work late, so he'd phone me when he was finishing up and I'd hop on a bus into town and we'd go for something to eat in the pub round the corner from Toby's work. He'd tell me about the people he worked with and the places he'd been to on company business, like New York and Paris and Geneva. And I'd stare into his gorgeous blue eyes, loving the fact that I was spending time with a real grown-up man – not some overgrown teenager like Mason.

Mason had been undeniably sexy; a fabulous kisser with twinkly eyes and great one-liners. But he was strangely resistant to changing his underwear, and his idea of the perfect night was to loll around on the sofa in his favourite baggy sweatpants, drinking cans and eating pies from tins. His flat was a tip. It always looked as if it had just been ransacked by intruders, and during our very brief relationship, I'd avoided staying over because that would have meant venturing into the scary wilds of his bathroom.

Mason ambled through doors ahead of you, but Toby held them open. And his bathroom, when he took me back to his flat for the first time, was spotlessly clean.

I wasn't sure if it would be a long-term relationship. We got on well and the sex was good but he seemed strangely averse to me meeting his family.

Then finally – three months into the relationship – his mum invited us for tea and I realised why Toby had been hesitant about taking me to his old family home.

'The place is a bloody shambles with kids everywhere arguing over nothing,' he groaned in the car, before we went in. 'Honestly, Daisy, it was such a relief to get my own place and move out. Are you sure you don't just want to grab a pizza? Mum won't mind. She's very easy-going.'

'But I've been looking forward to meeting them,' I said, smiling encouragingly. 'And I'm sure it's not half as chaotic as you make out.'

Actually, it was. And then some.

But I loved it.

I'd never been to a house like it. There were people all over the place: in the kitchen, chatting over tea and biscuits, and in the living room, apparently watching a horror movie. Toby was the oldest and his brothers ranged in age from twenty-one-year-old Tom – who was apparently there with his girlfriend, Becky – right down to eight-year-old Josh. Two boys of about ten, who I assumed were the twins Toby had told me about, charged down the hallway, shouting, 'Can we go out, Mum? Just to the park?'

'Yes, but don't be long,' called their mum from the kitchen.

Toby groaned as they fled past us. 'Daniel and Harry. Sorry about that.'

I shook my head. 'It's absolutely fine.'

It was only ever Mum and me at home. I'd always wondered what it would be like to have a big family.

I smiled at the pairs of trainers, wellies and shoes lined up along the wall of the hallway. It looked as if a shoe shop was having a stocktake. There was something quite cheering about it.

'Let's see if we can find you a seat.'

As we walked into the kitchen, the young people gathered around the table looked up curiously, and a plump woman with masses of curly auburn hair heaved herself out of a rocking chair and bustled over to us. Her radiant smile lit her face, all the way up to her friendly blue eyes. They were the exact same shade as Toby's.

'This is my mum. Rosalind,' said Toby. 'Mum, this is my new friend, Daisy Cooper.'

I smiled shyly at her and held out my hand. 'Pleased to meet you, Mrs – um – Rosalind.'

'Likewise, Daisy Cooper.' She gave a throaty chuckle and, ignoring my hand, pulled me into a big warm hug.

Chapter 3

Mum was always the biggest champion of my writing. My most adoring (and my only) fan.

She kept pressing me to finish writing my book but I always considered it pie in the sky, the idea that I could make it as an author. It just didn't happen to ordinary mortals. Publishing was such a competitive industry. You had to be super-talented to be in with a chance. I couldn't imagine something so miraculous as a book deal ever happening to me, so why would I waste my time trying, when the inevitable result would be crushing disappointment?

But one day, about six months after we received the devastating news of her cancer, I arrived at the house and she waved a magazine at me with an excited little smile.

'A short story competition,' she said, her eyes gleaming. 'I think you should enter.'

I started to shake my head but she got quite stroppy, which was unusual for her. She was normally so easy-going about everything.

'You need to stop prevaricating and just do it, Daisy! If I had my time over again, there's lots of things I'd do. I'd train to be an optician for a start!'

'Really?' I stared at her in astonishment. Why hadn't I known this?

'Yes.' She shrugged. 'I've always been fascinated by the way eyes work and it seems like a good, steady job. But what I'm saying is: stop pussyfooting around and *do what you love!* For *me*! Because life is much too short!'

We stared at each other through a blur of tears. And then, silently, I took the magazine, folded it up and put it in my bag.

I went home and stayed up late into the night, turning over ideas in my head. And then by morning, I had my plot. The advice was always: *Write what you know*! So I decided I'd make my lead female character a high-flying magazine editor, like Rachel. *Unlike* Rachel, however, my heroine had sworn off love after one disappointment too many (I knew enough about that to write all too convincingly) – until the new and charismatic head of marketing arrived and made her rethink everything ...

It took me a week to write it.

During that time Mum suffered a chest infection that hit her really badly and she ended up in hospital. I was frantic with worry, but it helped me cope, having the short story competition to focus on and being able to tell Mum about my progress.

Once the story was written, I spent two weeks rewriting and agonising over whether it was good enough to send, during which time Mum was allowed home but then readmitted to hospital a few days later. The infection had apparently returned with a vengeance.

I told myself she was strong and would triumph over this

latest setback. But the night after she was readmitted, I finally stopped prevaricating, closed my eyes and hit 'send'. My story flew off into the unknown and I sat back, feeling exhausted. There was nothing more I could do. If the story was bad, it didn't really matter. At least Mum would know that I'd tried ...

A few days later, the house phone rang early one evening and Rachel knocked on my bedroom door, saying it was for me.

My heart leaped into my mouth and, for one wild moment, I dreamed it was the magazine phoning to say I'd made the shortlist.

But it wasn't the magazine.

It was the hospital.

Mum, who was already very weak, had now succumbed to pneumonia. She was slipping in and out of consciousness and I was quietly advised that time was running out.

I drove to the hospital in a state of shock.

How could this have happened? The doctor had said she thought Mum had months to live. Possibly even a year. And we'd been planning all sorts of lovely things to do together that didn't involve too much strength on Mum's part. So to suddenly find she might not even have *days* ...?

Joan! What about Joan?

My heart was in my throat.

Joan was Mum's best friend but she lived down in Surrey, my home until I was four, a long train journey away. Even if Joan got on a train now, she might not make it in time. But she'd made me promise I'd tell her immediately if Mum's condition worsened ...

Running from the car park to the hospital entrance, I made

a breathless call. Joan seemed to understand the urgency immediately – probably from the stark fear in my voice – and she told me to be strong and that she'd see me and Mum soon.

'Tell Maureen I'm on my way with a bag of sour apples,' she said before she rang off.

I smiled to myself as I rode the lift to Mum's floor. 'Sour apples' were Mum and Auntie Joan's favourite sweets when they were schoolgirls together in Surrey. It was sure to give Mum a boost to hear that Joan was travelling up ...

When I entered the ward, the curtains were pulled around Mum's bed and a nurse was emerging. Her eyes softened when she saw me. I walked over to her, my heart banging uneasily.

'We've made your mum comfortable,' she murmured, touching my forearm. 'She's in no pain although she's drifting in and out. Go in and let her hear your voice.'

I nodded, suddenly terrified of the responsibility. It had only ever really been Mum and me after Dad died. I was all she had. I had to do this right ...

But how did you stay strong enough to say a final goodbye to the person who meant the whole world to you?

In the end, I couldn't hold back the tears. But it felt peaceful and absolutely right that I was there, holding her hand, telling her that she was the most wonderful mum in the world and that I would always love her.

Her hand tightened a little on mine when I said that, so I knew she could hear me. I leaned closer and whispered, 'I sent the short story off. If it turns out I'm the next Jane Austen, it will all be down to you.'

She opened her eyes and her lips moved, and I realised she was trying to tell me something, so I leaned closer.

Her voice was so faint, I couldn't make out what she was whispering at first. But then I realised. '*Wuthering Heights*.' She was murmuring the name of her all-time favourite book.

My eyes filled with tears and I nodded and kissed her hand. 'I'll bring the book in later and read it to you,' I promised her.

She looked straight at me for a moment, her eyes shining with love.

And then she was gone.

*

A month later, when I got the call saying I was one of three runners-up in the short story competition, I could hardly believe it.

I'd won a thousand pounds. But better than that by far, my story was actually going to be published in a future edition of the magazine!

When I imagined all the people – perfect strangers – who would read the words I'd written, it gave me such a jolt of disbelief and happiness.

My triumph was tinged with pain, though.

The one person who would have joined wholeheartedly in my silly dance of delight around the house was no longer here to share my joy.

I swallowed hard, steering my mind away from the memories.

Rachel would whoop with glee when she heard, though. And Toby would be amazed. He might finally see that I was serious in my ambitions to be an author! I couldn't wait to tell him ...

It seemed such a momentous thing to have happened in

my life that I decided a celebration was definitely in order. So I booked a table at our favourite restaurant and phoned Toby at work to break the news.

'I heard from the magazine. I was a runner-up,' I squeaked, as soon as I got through. 'So I've booked a table for dinner tonight. My treat!'

'Dinner tonight?' He sounded uncertain and my heart sank.

'Yes. But I made the booking for later ...' I could hear the hum of voices in the background.

'Could we do it tomorrow night instead?' he asked. 'Sorry, it's just I doubt I'll get away till after nine tonight.'

A sharp dose of reality pierced my high spirits but I forced a smile. 'Yes, of course. That's fine. Tomorrow night it is.'

'Great. Look forward to it. Hey, well done you, though. I can't believe you won it. Wasn't there a big cash prize?'

'Well, no, I was a runner-up. The prize is – erm – a thousand pounds.'

'Ah, right. Still, that's a very nice result for a few hours' scribbling, though. You never know, this could turn out to be a nice little earner. How much do they pay for magazine stories?'

'I'm not sure. But really, I'm more excited about the fact that people in the publishing industry seem to think I have some talent ...'

'Well, I've *always* known that, Daisy.'

'You have?' My heart gave a joyful little lift. Perhaps he'd read some of my stuff, after all. I was writing the first draft of my book with pen and paper, and I sometimes left my notebook lying out so Toby could peek if he was curious.

'Of course. Your creative talents are legendary, my love. No one whips up a chocolate fudge cake better than you.'

Chocolate fudge cake?

'A thousand pounds, eh? Dinner is *definitely* on you tomorrow night!'

I was about to tell him the most exciting bit – that my story was going to appear in the magazine. But before I got a chance, he said, 'Sorry, love, got to dash. See you later.'

I hung up, feeling strangely sad. The conversation hadn't gone at all the way I'd thought it would. Toby had missed the point; he seemed far more delighted about the prize money than anything else.

Then I told myself not to be so silly. Being runner-up, out of thousands of entries, felt epic to me. It was bound to after all the hours I'd spent daydreaming of becoming a published author. But I couldn't expect Toby to understand the thrill I felt when I read that email telling me I was a winner ...

Also, being so busy at work, he probably wasn't totally focused on what I was telling him. I was sure that, by the following night, he'd have begun to realise what it meant to me, and we could have a lovely time celebrating.

I might even push the boat out and order champagne!

The following night, I called at the hairdresser's on the way home from work and treated myself to a sleek blow-dry. Then later, with a tummy full of excited butterflies, I dressed in my favourite little black shift dress, which looked more expensive than it was, teaming it with patent heels and chunky pearls.

I scrutinised myself in the mirror. It was maybe a bit over-the-top for a weekday dinner but I didn't care. This was the most exciting thing that had ever happened to me and I was going to enjoy it! After losing Mum, I was due a break. Hopefully this would be the start of a whole new adventure.

Perhaps, one day, I might even dare to dream of handing in my notice at *Plunge Happy Monthly* ...

I'd arranged to meet Toby at the restaurant at eight-thirty but I was there a little early, just in case. The waiter came over and, after a second's hesitation, I ordered champagne. It arrived in an ice bucket and I smiled and said I'd wait for my dinner date to arrive. It was important Toby was here when the cork was popped! I wanted him to feel he was in it with me; that he was an important part of my success.

By nine o'clock, he still hadn't arrived, but I wasn't worried. He'd have got held up; it happened all the time. There was no point phoning. He was probably already on his way.

I ordered a soft drink and read the email from the magazine for the hundredth time.

At nine-twenty, fed up with the sympathetic looks I was getting from other diners, I dialled Toby's number.

I braced myself for multiple apologies but he actually sounded quite calm.

'Daisy? I just got home to an empty flat. Where are you? Did we run out of milk or something?'

Crushing dismay punched me in the gut. No wonder Toby was 'late'. He'd forgotten all about it.

'Daisy?' I could almost hear the cogs in his head ticking over. Realisation dawning. 'Oh God, we were meeting for dinner, weren't we? Listen, stay there. I'll be along now.'

I finally found my voice. 'No, it's too late now, Toby. I've hogged the table for long enough and I've lost my appetite. I'm coming home.' I couldn't keep the hurt from my tone and, as he rushed to apologise some more, I hung up.

I drove home with a horrible sick feeling inside. I realised I was probably over-reacting, but the forgotten dinner just illustrated what I'd long suspected – I was far more interested in Toby's life than he was in mine. He'd known ever since we met that I longed to be a writer, and although I realised he viewed my 'scribbling' – which was how he termed it – as just a nice hobby and never likely to lead anywhere, I'd nonetheless thought he'd understand how thrilled I was about my magazine success.

But apparently it was so insignificant to him that it had totally slipped his mind!

My throat hurt.

I wanted a partner who supported me to the hilt in whatever I wanted to do in life. Someone who cherished my hopes and dreams almost as much as I did myself. The way Mum did.

Was I kidding myself imagining Toby could ever be that person?

When I got home, he greeted me at the door, full of more apologies, blaming the falling markets for wiping all other thoughts from his mind. He'd laid the table and ordered Thai food, my favourite, and there was a big bunch of hastily acquired roses in the centre of the table. But I was nowhere near ready to forgive.

I ignored him, threw my coat over a chair, yanked the fridge open and pulled out an open bottle of white wine. 'You probably aren't even interested in *reading* my story, are you?' I glared at him, all the hurt tumbling out, then glugged half a glass of wine down in one go.

'Of course I am.'

I laughed bitterly. 'Well, you're hardly going to say no now!'

I was being petty, I knew, but I couldn't help it. I wanted more from a relationship than this ...

'Hey, listen. Of *course* I'm interested.' Gently he removed the glass from my hand and took me in his arms. I stood there, rigid, desperate not to respond.

'The thing is, though, I'd much rather read your story when it's printed in the magazine and your name is right there on the page in big letters! How proud will I feel then?'

I twisted away from him. 'That's easy to say.'

'It's easy to say because it's true.' He sighed. 'Look, you know I'm no good at English. The only thing I ever read is books about finance. And take-away menus.'

'That's true.'

'But when that magazine comes through the door, believe me, I'll be the first to read your *prize-winning* story.' Smiling, he put a finger to my chin and gently turned my face to his. 'You're brilliant, Daisy Cooper.'

When he kissed me, I relented and kissed him back, relief flooding through me.

The thought of us splitting up terrified me. It was too soon after Mum to cope with something else so emotionally devastating.

I might have had misgivings about Toby and I being right for each other, but the fact was, Toby and his family – especially Rosalind – had been totally there for me when Mum died. I wasn't sure I could bear the thought of doing without them now.

The doorbell rang, announcing our take-away. Toby bounded to the door, calling, 'Let's do something special for my birthday in July? I'll book a week off work and you can have me all to yourself!'

Grudgingly, I agreed. Perhaps a holiday was what we needed.

I'd book a surprise romantic trip and then we'd see ...

Chapter 4

It's a month later and I'm sitting on the floor of Toby's bedroom, sorting through the latest load of boxes I've brought over from Rachel's garage.

I always thought moving in with a man for the first time would be a mark of how responsible and grown-up I'd become. It would be a conscious, level-headed decision to move the relationship to the next stage.

But there was nothing remotely level-headed about the speed with which this latest life-changing decision was made.

Not that I'm complaining!

The past few weeks since my short story triumph have passed in a mad whirl, mainly due to the fact that Rachel's boyfriend, Adam, proposed to her right out of the blue. Rachel was ecstatic and, after we'd celebrated for the best part of a week, she told me she'd decided to sell her house and move in with Adam. So obviously I needed to find somewhere else to live.

It was the following Sunday, when we were over at Toby's mum's house for lunch, that everything crystallised into an obvious solution ...

*

I was in the kitchen, helping Rosalind make cauliflower cheese to go with the roast.

I suppose I was feeling more emotional than usual at the thought of my flat-share with Rachel coming to an end.

Rosalind seemed to pick up on my feelings.

'So how are you, my love?' she asked, her tone filled with empathy. I knew she was thinking about how I must be missing Mum and, immediately, the pain of loss – which was never far away – came crashing in.

'I'm fine. Absolutely perfect,' I said, pasting on the bright smile I used when people started asking questions that brought on the panic. I could feel Rosalind's kind eyes watching me as I stirred the bubbling cheese sauce on the hob.

'Yes, but how are you *really*?' Her voice was soft and loving, and my throat closed up. To my alarm, my hand started to tremble and I had to stir extra fast to stay in control, with the result that some of the hot sauce splashed onto my hand.

Rosalind gently took the pan from me and I ran my hand under the tap, grateful to turn away so she couldn't see the tears of panic that had sprung up when she tried to probe deeper.

Why did people always want me to talk about Mum and what had happened?

Didn't they realise that was the worst thing they could possibly make me do? I needed to get over this, otherwise I was in danger of losing my sanity, and in order to move on, I needed to concentrate on the present, not keep going over and over what I couldn't change.

Why couldn't they see that?

With an effort, I pulled myself together and turned. 'I'm

in a bit of a fix, actually,' I said. 'Rachel's selling the flat.'

'Oh, Daisy, you poor thing. So you have to move out?' Rosalind looked horrified.

'Well, not immediately. She won't even be putting it on the market until later in the year.'

'But still ... it's a bit unsettling.' Her look said: *As if you haven't already been through the mill enough ...*

I shrugged and started grating more cheese for the topping. 'Something will turn up.'

'Perhaps it already has.'

'Sorry?'

Rosalind smiled, dimples appearing in her rosy cheeks as she stood up, flushed from checking the beef in the oven. 'Toby was telling me only the other day how well things are going between you.'

'He was?' I looked at her in surprise. I didn't think Toby confided in Rosalind about such personal stuff.

She shook her head and laughed. 'Well, he was actually talking about the rising cost of living and how it was probably true that two could live just as cheaply as one. But when I cheekily asked if he was thinking of sharing his place, he didn't deny it. Quite the opposite, in fact.'

'Did I hear my name there?' Toby walked in at that moment.

'Daisy was telling me about her housing situation and I was just pointing out that a solution might be staring you both in the face, that's all.' She gave us a mischievous smile. 'Keep an eye on the roast, will you? I'm just going to make sure those kids aren't actually killing each other out there!'

When she'd gone, Toby and I looked at each other. We both laughed a bit awkwardly.

'Mum wants you for a daughter. You do realise that,' Toby said with a sheepish grin.

The idea of that squeezed my heart so that I had to look away and blink rapidly.

'It does make sense,' he added. 'I mean, you moving into my flat.'

I swallowed hard. 'Really? You'd like that?' All sorts of feelings were tumbling around inside me. A while ago, I'd doubted that we were right for each other. But then Mum got ill and I was just so grateful for Toby's support that I forgot all about my concerns that we were suited for the long haul. It just seemed important to get from one day to the next.

Could I really move in with Toby? It was such a huge commitment. Shouldn't I at least take a week to decide?

But then I thought about how the times I spent here with Rosalind, Toby and the boys filled me with new hope for the future. I always came away from these lovely family Sunday lunches feeling happier than when I arrived and that had to mean something. It was that precious feeling of belonging. It was worth its weight in gold ...

'I'm game if you are,' said Toby, and there was a vulnerability in his smile that took me by surprise and melted my heart. It wasn't the most romantic of propositions but that didn't matter. I was being given a chance to move on with my life. To start afresh and make brand-new memories with Toby.

I wanted that new start like I'd never wanted anything in my life before.

So I smiled shyly and took his hand. 'I am game.'

We were kissing when Rosalind walked in.

'Oh, please tell me you have good news?' She beamed, crossing her hands over her heart. And when we nodded, she gave one of her throaty laughs, hurried over and drew us both into one of her big hugs. Toby, never one for displays of emotion, went a bit wooden, but the tears in Rosalind's eyes were reflected in mine and I knew then that everything would be all right.

*

So at the age of thirty-two, I'm finally doing the grown-up thing of living with a guy! It feels unsettling yet quite exhilarating all at once.

It's Saturday morning and I'm trying to get unpacked. But the boxes I'm tackling are full of Mum's belongings – stuff I kept after clearing the house to put it up for sale – and I keep snagging on memories of my life with her. Everything I pull out seems to have a special meaning attached to it.

Toby, who's getting ready to go into work, pops his head round the bedroom door, holding the house phone aloft. 'It's Joan.'

Panicking, I shake my head, miming to him to tell her I'm out. Joan will want me to talk about Mum and I just can't face all that.

But Toby says, 'Yeah, she's here. Hang on a second, Joan.'

He hands me the phone with a frown. So obviously, I have to take it.

I close my eyes and take a big, bolstering breath. 'Hi, Joan. Lovely to hear from you!'

Her warm voice on the other end, asking me how I've been and when I'm going to come down and visit, squeezes my heart painfully. Joan and Mum were such great friends. The memories of spending happy times together, the three of us, immediately start crowding in, and I feel the familiar clench of panic in my chest. With my free hand, I pull my cardigan tighter around me. It's a dark maroon colour, a loose, waterfall design, with shiny maroon buttons. Toby hates it but it's really comfy.

Joan asks about Toby and I tell her it's his thirtieth birthday next month and I'm planning to surprise him with a romantic break away.

'You could both come down and stay with me,' she says. 'Use my place as a base to explore Surrey.' Then she laughs. 'Hardly romantic, though.'

'Oh, no, we couldn't impose on you like that.'

She sighs. 'It's just a shame I don't have a spare room. Ooh, I know! Why don't you stay at Clemmy's place, the two of you? Now, that would be *very* romantic!'

'Clemmy's place?'

'Yes, didn't I tell you? I definitely mentioned it to Maureen. Your mum always quite fancied the idea of glamorous camping.'

'Glamping?' I ask. 'Yes, she did, didn't she?'

'I wish Maureen could have seen this place.' Joan sighs. 'She'd have loved it.'

My throat tightens. Mum and I talked about going glamping together but we never got round to it. If only I'd realised my precious time with her was limited ...

Joan clears her throat. 'Anyway, yes, Clemmy and that lovely fiancé of hers, Ryan, have opened the most glorious glamping site on the banks of a lake. It's completely idyllic and the tents are magnificent. You'd really think you were staying in a five-star hotel!'

'Sounds lovely.'

Clemmy is Joan's niece and was one of my best friends at university, although we've sadly lost touch in the years since we left. She went back to live in Surrey, near Joan, and I returned to Manchester. I'm intrigued by the idea of the glamping site but, however much I love Joan, I don't think spending time with her during our romantic break would be the best thing to do. She would want to talk about Mum and, quite frankly, that's the last thing I want.

Why would I need to when I have all my lovely memories of Mum locked away inside?

And anyway, this romantic break away is going to be a special time, just for Toby and me. We'd finally have time to talk – *really* talk – about our future together. The magazine with my story printed in it had arrived, which was really exciting, but I'd purposely not told Toby. I was going to present it to him when we were away on holiday and he finally had the time to read it!

Glamping in Surrey is a nice idea but not for us right now ...

I don't like disappointing Joan, though, so I tell her I'll think about it.

In all the whirl of moving house, I haven't even thought where to take Toby for his birthday. But it's June already. I need to make a decision!

I get back to the unpacking, thoughts of Greece – or maybe Italy – flitting through my head; Toby and I, perfectly relaxed, languishing on a hot sandy beach somewhere, next to a sun-sparkled sea ...

I'm currently tackling a box that was up in Mum's loft and looks as if it hasn't been opened since we moved there more than a quarter of a century ago. I brush a cobweb from the front of my cardigan as a musty smell rises from the contents of the box – old books, mostly romance fiction with rather garish covers. Mum loved reading and never liked parting with her books. She was ruthless about clutter and was always boxing up stuff like clothes, shoes, old handbags and jewellery for the charity shop. But books were different. She held on to those. I've kept some of her favourites but I've carted so many off to the charity shop already.

I'm about to seal the box up again and mark it 'charity', when I spot something wedged down the side of the box. I pull it out.

A handbag.

It's a cheap-looking bag. Glossy pink plastic with a gold-coloured clasp and a long narrow strap. Appliquéd onto the front is a pink and gold pony with big eyes and a flowing mane. I can't imagine Mum would ever use something like that herself. It's definitely not her style. But someone clearly loved it because it's scuffed around the edges and well-used.

Was it mine when I was a teenager?

It's so distinctive, I would surely remember it. But I don't.

Opening the clasp, I find it's empty, apart from an ancient-looking bus ticket and a lipstick in 'shell pink'. There's a pocket inside, though, and I can feel there's something in there. Carefully unzipping it, I draw out a folded-up envelope.

Smoothing it out, I'm disappointed to find that it's empty. Whatever letter was in there, which might have brought a clue as to the owner of the bag, has long gone. But there's an address on the front of it that makes the breath catch in my throat.

Maple Tree House, Acomb Drive, Appley Green, Surrey.

I've never been to Appley Green. But I know it for one very important reason.

Mum told me it was the place where I was born.

I asked her once if she knew anything about my birth parents and where I came from. I must have been about sixteen at the time. She was ironing a shirt at the time. It's funny how you remember the little details. Mum looked across at me and, for a moment, I thought she wasn't going to answer me. Then she shook her head. 'Sorry, love. All I know is that you were born in a village called Appley Green, not far from where we lived in Surrey, and your mother couldn't look after you so she put you up for adoption. I wish I could tell you more but ...'

'So you don't know anything at all about my ... *real* mother?'

She got really flushed when I asked her that. The iron slipped and she burned her hand and had to dash through to the tap in the kitchen to run cold water over it.

I felt bad because actually, *she* was my 'real mum'. The other woman, who had had nothing at all to do with my upbringing, was only my 'birth mother'.

After that, I never asked again. I suppose I didn't want Mum to think she might some day lose me to my biological mother.

The name, Appley Green, stayed in my mind, though. I have an image in my head of what the village looks like, although it's probably not like that at all. I searched for a photograph of my birthplace online once but I drew a blank.

I glance at the date on the old bus ticket I found in the bag.

July 15th 1990.

I was born in 1987 so I would have been three years old when this ticket was issued.

I stare at the envelope. It obviously held some sort of

advertising letter because it's simply addressed to 'The Householder'. No name to give me a clue. My eye focuses on the village name. Of course it's pure coincidence that I was born in Appley Green and there it is, typewritten, on this envelope. But it still sends a little tingle of curiosity through me. The owner of the bag must have lived at Maple Tree House, Acomb Drive, Appley Green.

Maybe they still do ...

I turn the envelope over, and scrawled on the back of it, in child-like writing, is our old address in Surrey. I always remember it because Mum used to laugh about the name. Our street was apparently called 'Bog Houses', and Mum used to say it was a lot more picturesque than it sounded.

There it is, on the back of the envelope, presumably scribbled down by the owner of the handbag.

3 Bog Houses, Chappel-Hedges, Surrey.

So many questions are tumbling through my head.

Who did the bag belong to?

How did it end up in Mum's loft?

And why did Mum – who was so meticulous about getting rid of clutter – carefully box it up and keep it for all these years?

Chapter 5

The words on the blog site jump out at me.

*

Clemmy's Lakeside Glamping, near Appley Green, Surrey

Live in luxury while getting back to nature at our beautiful lakeside glamping site!

*

Going online to find out more about Clemmy's glamping site, I wasn't prepared for what I would see.

But there it is, in bold black letters.

The nearest village to Clemmy's site is ... Appley Green.

I sit back, my head whirling. How weird is that?

A little zing of excitement rushed through me when I spotted the name of the village, and my heart is now bumping along at a fair old rate. From my perch on the bed, I stare at Clemmy's website on my laptop for a long time, wondering if it might be some sort of a sign.

Glamping in a gorgeous setting could be the ideal holiday for us. Toby and I could go down there and have a lovely time together. And it would be the perfect opportunity to see Appley Green for myself and catch up with Clemmy.

I don't usually believe in signs.

But finding the handbag with the address in it? And now this a few days later?

The glamping site looks gorgeous.

The three dwellings, well spaced across an acre of grass leading down to the lake, are nothing like the tent we took with us on camping holidays when I was little. They're spacious and elegant, the cream-coloured canvas sweeping up into two dramatic peaks, giving them the look of a Bedouin tent in the desert. Toby would be sure to love them.

Inside, Clemmy has worked miracles with the space. She always did have a great eye for design. No expense has been spared on the canopied beds, and the soft furnishings are to die for. There's a gorgeous bedroom and a separate living area with a big squashy sofa, all done up in creams and golds. Then there's a shower room with loo, and even a little kitchen with all mod cons. Plus a gorgeous log burner for when the nights are cool.

A photo of an elegantly dressed couple catches my eye. They're sitting at a little table for two, just outside their tent, clinking champagne glasses and laughing. Candlelight flickers on the table and there's a rustic blue jug filled with hedgerow blooms. In the background, the setting sun streaks the horizon in glorious reds and pinks as the beautiful couple toast their future together.

There are lots more photos of the surrounding area, too.

The lakeside setting is glorious and it's clear there will be ample places to explore – from the sophisticated boutique hotel a short walk from the glamping site, to the long swathe of forest glimpsed on the far side of the lake. Toby and I could go for long walks with a picnic and, if it's warm enough, we can swim in the lake.

I stare at the two words, Appley Green, until they start to blur into one.

The oddest feeling is growing inside me, adding very frisky butterflies to my churning stomach. It feels as if everything is happening for a reason and I'm being led towards something that could be life-changing.

It only takes five minutes to book it.

Sunday to Sunday. The second week in July. Just a few weeks away.

We're going glamping!

*

'Do they have Wi-Fi?' asks Toby when I tell him we're all booked.

'Of course. They'll have everything you could possibly want. Including me.' I snuggle up to him with a flirty smile. Actually, I've no idea about the Wi-Fi. I'll have to check with Clemmy.

'Sounds lovely,' he says, smiling and kissing my forehead. 'Let me pay for it, though. I earn far more than you.'

'But I want it to be my treat.'

'Yes, but it's the thought that counts. Don't bankrupt yourself. At least let me pay a bit towards it.'

I feel a twinge of uneasiness.

It sounds like Toby's imagining five-star luxury, or at least somewhere more expensive than a glamping trip. Perhaps I should book a hotel break instead?

Am I being selfish, taking Toby there because part of me is really curious to see Appley Green?

Then I think of the pictures on Clemmy's website. When Toby sees how special it is, he'll love it, I'm sure. It will be something a little bit different that he'll always remember when thinking of his thirtieth birthday.

What could be more romantic, after all, than eating dinner under the stars, at that pretty little table with its glowing candles and fresh wild flowers. Listening to the sounds of the countryside, watching the sun go down and planning adventures for the next day.

Clemmy's glamping site looks like the perfect setting for romance.

What could possibly go wrong?

*

The following morning, I'm dozing after the alarm has gone off, when I have the weird nightmare once again.

Afterwards, my eyes spring open in alarm and I find I've been clenching my fists so tightly there are red nail marks on my palms.

Technically, they're not nightmares because I'm never actually asleep when I have them. It's more of a flashback, really.

And it's always the same.

It's dark. I'm running along a narrow lane with tall hedges on either side, and terror has me gripped in its clutches. I don't know what I'm afraid of but there's a frenzy of panic inside me and I'm crying – huge gasping sobs that hurt as the icy night air blasts my throat. It's winter. Snow is clinging to the hedges, and their ghostly shapes as I blunder past are like an army of sinister snowmen.

Looking back along the lane, I peer desperately into the pitch black, searching for something. I'm crying for the thing I've dropped. But all the time, I'm moving further and further away from it, against my will, along that spooky lane ...

More than the panic and the fear, it's the feeling of heart-breaking loss that lingers longest when the images start to fade.

Eyes open now, I stare into the early morning gloom, thinking about the pink plastic handbag I found in Mum's box the day before. Slipping out of bed, I take it out of my bedside drawer and, trying not to disturb Toby, I cross to my case that's lying open on the floor, partially packed, and I slide it in, under some clothes.

Could there be a link between my recurring flashback and that mysterious pink bag? I need to take it with me ...

Chapter 6

On the morning of our departure, as luck would have it, the stock markets decide to plummet.

It's hardly the Wall Street Crash, but it's dramatic enough to etch a permanent groove above Toby's nose as he sits in his study, urgently discussing the repercussions with his colleagues in the office.

I knock on the door as noon approaches. Toby's ear is still welded to his phone.

'Shall I pack for you?' I ask, feeling guilty for interrupting such high-level discussions.

He turns and looks at me blankly.

Then he says in a really stern voice, 'Bloody hell, no, that would be an *absolute travesty*.'

I blink at him, confused for a second. I suppose he thinks I'd pack all the wrong things. Then I realise he's still talking to his colleague.

Sighing, I slink out of the room and leave him to it.

I told Clemmy we'd be there by three and she said she'd have a picnic basket with afternoon tea waiting for us. But my vision of lounging on a rug in the sunshine with Toby, enjoying home-baked scones with jam and cream and Earl Grey tea, looks like it might not happen after all.

At last, at just after four, we hit the road in Toby's Fiesta.

It's not exactly the relaxing journey down I'd envisaged as Toby is constantly on the car Bluetooth, talking to the office. But I don't mind too much. It means I can indulge in a spot of daydreaming, staring out of the passenger window, enjoying the scenery and looking forward to arriving at what will be our lovely home for the next seven days.

I'd thought about asking Toby if we should invite Rosalind along and maybe some of the boys if they wanted to come. But I sensed Toby would probably want it to be just us.

We go round to Rosalind's every week for Sunday lunch and it's pretty chaotic, with kids running around and everyone talking over each other. Toby hates it, but to me, it's a sort of celebration. It reminds me of Christmas.

Every Christmas Eve, Mum used to invite the neighbours and her friends from the call centre where she worked for a bit of a party. It was the one time in the year we had folk round and Mum really pushed the boat out. The house was bursting with people and laughter, Christmas music and big aluminium platters of festive food.

Even as a little kid, I looked forward to that party on Christmas Eve more than the big day itself. I'd love a big family one day ...

I glance across at Toby with affection and catch his eye. His stern brow smoothes out and he smiles at me, before returning to the vexing world of market slumps.

Eventually, he winds up the conversation then turns and beams at me. 'After a day like today, this is *just* what I need. Some no-holds-barred pampering in a luxurious setting.' He sighs and rolls his shoulders in anticipation of the relaxation ahead.

I stare at him in alarm.

Why didn't I at least think to bring a bottle of supermarket champagne?

I clear my throat. 'Listen, Toby, I ... er ... there's something you need to know. This place we're going to—'

He shakes his head firmly. 'Stop right there! You said you wanted it to be a surprise, and I'm absolutely fine with that.' He smiles across at me and my heart flips. He looks so handsome with his fair hair flopping over his forehead.

'Yes, but—'

'No buts, Daisy. Just tell me where to go when we get to – Appley Green, is it?' He grins. 'And for goodness' sake, stop looking so worried. I'm sure I'll love it, wherever it is. In fact, I know I will – as long as you're there with me.'

He pats my knee and I relax slightly. Perhaps he won't be disappointed after all. Spotting a signpost, a little thrill of anticipation – mixed with a degree of trepidation – zips through me as it hits me that we're travelling nearer my place of birth with every mile. I lived down there for the first four years of my life. Would anything spark a memory?

I'm not even thinking about Maple Tree House, though.

I've tried to imagine myself knocking on the front door. But I can't for the life of me think what I'd say if someone actually answered it.

Did you used to know my adoptive mum, Maureen Cooper?

Is this your handbag?

Do you know anyone round here who had a baby thirty-two years ago and gave her up for adoption?

I break out into a sweaty panic every time I think about it.

So I've decided the best thing to do is to just enjoy the

holiday with Toby and put searching for my birth mum out of my mind.

I can obviously check out the area and maybe even visit the village of Appley Green and have a look around.

But as for walking up to the front door of Maple Tree House?

Absolutely no way …

Chapter 7

My heart is hammering as we draw near our destination – for two reasons.

With signs for 'Clemmy's Lakeside Glamping' popping up here and there, I'm wondering when the penny will drop and Toby will guess that's where we're going.

And I can't stop peering at all the dwellings we're passing, wondering if any of them are Maple Tree House. I'm trying not to look because we're here for Toby's birthday treat and I'm feeling a little guilty that I have an ulterior motive for choosing the glamping site for our holiday.

I haven't told Toby about finding the handbag with the Appley Green address inside it. I haven't told anyone yet, not even Rachel. I'm hugging it to myself for now, processing it all in my own head before I tell anyone else about it.

I had no idea how I'd feel when I actually got here.

I think I vaguely imagined that I'd go to Appley Green and have a look around, marvelling that it was here I began life. I even pictured locating Maple Tree House and knocking on the front door, although I'd ruled that out. Beyond that, I hadn't really thought.

But now that I'm here, everything is suddenly scarily real. There's a drive in me to find my birth mum that wasn't there before. Did I really imagine that just visiting Appley Green would satisfy my curiosity and I'd be able to return to Manchester content simply to have seen the place where I was born?

But alongside the desire to discover where I came from is a deep, gnawing guilt. I can't help feeling that in contemplating searching for my birth mum, I'm betraying the woman who, to all intents and purposes, *was* my mum. How would she have felt if she'd known I was thinking of following my curiosity to its natural end?

Driving through Appley Green itself is the weirdest feeling. My head feels as if it's floating away from my body and there's a buzzing in my ears as if I might be about to faint. I stare at the faces of the women walking along the high street, looking especially at the middle-aged women, going about their normal business on an ordinary Sunday morning in Appley Green.

Any one of these women could be my birth mother!

I want to tell Toby. But something is stopping me.

I think I'm worried that, if I tell anyone, it will all become overwhelmingly real and then there'll be no going back. I'll have to go with it and search for the truth.

But that's where my biggest fear of all lies.

Because what if I search for the truth and it's not the fairy tale I want? What if my birth mother had me adopted simply because she didn't want me?

What if I turn up on her doorstep and she rejects me all over again?

'Daisy?' Toby sounds tense. 'Earth to Daisy.'

I swing round. 'Sorry, what?'

'You need to direct me. I spotted a sign for a Michelin-starred manor house hotel back there if that's any help?' He looks at me hopefully and my heart sinks.

'Try next left.' I point at a looming sign announcing 'Glamping' in bold letters.

Toby looks at the sign and chuckles. 'You and your little jokes.' He shakes his head at me as if he's the patient adult and I'm the naughty, wayward child. 'So?' He glances over expectantly, as if at any moment I'm going to shout, 'Hah! Had you fooled! No, of *course* we're not going glamping for a week. Not when there's a posh manor house hotel with a couple of Michelin stars and an award-winning spa back there!'

This is awful.

What was I *thinking*, booking something that really is just one step up from a Boy-Scouts-round-the-campfire-back-to-nature sort of trip? I suppose I was carried away with how romantic the photos looked.

'Toby, turn left, please. This is the surprise.'

He looks startled, and having been about to drive straight past the turn-off, brakes suddenly and turns off. Then he drives slowly along the narrow road, looking from left to right as if he can't quite believe where he is.

We approach an impressive-looking chalet-type building on the left. It looks spacious and very handsome and there's a sign saying 'The Log Fire Cabin'.

Toby slows almost to a standstill, staring up at it admiringly. 'Very nice.' He nods in approval. 'So come on, Daisy, this is where we're *really* going, isn't it? A beautiful chalet overlooking a lake. Have we got butler service?'

Irritation breaks through my feelings of guilt.

Butler bloody service? I haven't exactly got money to burn! Although to be fair, Toby did offer to pay for it himself.

'No butler service but I promise I'll wait on you hand and foot on your birthday.' I force a cheery tone. 'We're going glamping, Toby!'

I perform a cheery *ta-dah* with my hands in the direction of the glamping sign up ahead.

There's silence from the birthday boy as he stares at the sign.

I take a breath and launch in. 'It looks absolutely gorgeous on the website. Honestly, I think you're going to love it. The tents – er, the *dwellings* – have got a proper loo and a kitchen and everything. Even a log-burning stove! And we can always head to the supermarket and splash out on a good bottle of champagne.'

Champagne actually gives me indigestion but anything to put a smile on Toby's face.

Toby turns the car slowly into the parking area for Clemmy's Lakeside Glamping, switches off the engine and nods at a small but perfectly formed house nearby. 'Nice architecture.'

I nod in agreement. It's in the same style as the Log Fire Cabin that we just passed but on a smaller scale. This one is called, not very imaginatively, 'Lakeside View'.

Toby looks over the expanse of grass towards the lake, at the elegant structures with their exotic air of a Bedouin tent. He nods slowly, gazing around him, and my heart lifts a little.

Perhaps it's going to be fine, after all.

Toby swings round. 'What about Wi-Fi? I must have Wi-Fi.'

I nod and he visibly relaxes. 'Thank God. I don't mind *where* I stay as long as I can keep in touch with the office.'

He sees my crestfallen face and adds hurriedly, 'Not that this isn't ... *great*!'

A tall girl in jeans and T-shirt with chestnut red hair and a curvy figure is walking towards us.

'This is my old friend, Clemmy,' I tell Toby, my heart lifting at her warm smile of welcome. 'Let's go and say hello.'

'Oh, Daisy,' she says. 'I was *so sorry* to hear about your mum.' She draws me into a big hug, squeezing me tight, and I cling on to her, my eyes suddenly wet with tears. 'Auntie Joan is devastated. But she's so looking forward to seeing you.' She smiles across at Toby. 'Both of you.'

After the introductions, Clemmy walks us over to our tent, which turns out to be even more beautiful than I imagined it would be.

Even Toby seems impressed.

'This is amazing,' he says, looking around him. 'I can't believe the level of style and comfort you've achieved here.' He wanders over to the wood-burning stove and runs a finger over the top of it, absent-mindedly checking for dust. (He blames dust mites for his highly sensitive nasal passages.)

Clemmy beams. 'I'm so glad you like it. I wanted to get the feel of a really first-rate hotel?' She looks a little anxiously at Toby when she says this, as if she senses it's him she needs to impress.

He tips his head on one side and frowns, as if to say, *I'm not sure you've quite achieved that.*

To make up for his lack of fulsome praise, I start going totally overboard, praising the floral-patterned quilt on the bed, which tones so beautifully with the drapes – because they *are* drapes, not just ordinary curtains. Generous swathes of lilac fabric sweep to the floor in the bedroom, which has walls of soft grey and lots of squishy cushions providing splashes of summery fuchsia pink and pale green. I can see similarly lush drapes in the living room area, although there the colour scheme is a more neutral mix of cream and mushroom, the roomy sofa providing a colour pop of deep turquoise.

The same area contains two chairs and the little table with its pretty jug of flowers, just like in the picture on the website.

Clemmy shows us how the log burner works and says there's a plentiful supply of logs and a wheelbarrow in the shed by the Log Fire Cabin. Then she gives us the run-down on the little kitchen area and the toilet and shower cubicle.

No bath for Toby, obviously. But the shower looks perfectly functional!

Clemmy has left a big basket of goodies for us on the little counter top in the kitchen – and I breathe a sigh of relief to see chocolates and a bottle of champagne sticking out of the top of it.

'I've got some basic foodstuffs at the house if you don't want to go food shopping now,' says Clemmy. 'Nothing more exotic than baked beans, though, I'm afraid.'

'I've brought some homemade moussaka,' I tell her. 'And I think I spotted a little microwave?'

She smiles. 'You did indeed. That'll be lovely. And it's such a lovely night for eating *al fresco*.'

'*Al fresco*?' Toby swings round.

'Outside?' I explain helpfully.

He frowns. 'I know what *al fresco* means. I'm just not sure it's a good idea. Bugs are absolutely rife near water. I'm not sure I fancy ingesting midges with my moussaka.' He shoots me a worried glance. 'You did pack the insect repellent, didn't you?'

I assure him I did, and Clemmy says, 'They can be a bit pesky, the midges, but usually only when it's been raining. And we've had the most glorious dry spell lately.'

'We can always eat in,' I say cheerfully, to allay Toby's worries of being eaten alive.

'Or we can go out for dinner.' Toby's eyes light up. 'There looks to be a rather fine eating establishment just along there, by the lake.'

'Yes, the Starlight Hotel,' says Clemmy. 'It's fabulous in every way. Very elegant. But – um – rather expensive?'

We glance over and Toby nods approvingly. 'Excellent.'

Clemmy smiles. 'I can phone and make a booking for you if you like?'

'No, it's fine. I'll sort it,' says Toby.

'Okay, I'll leave you to settle in then. Give me a knock in the morning if you'd like breakfast,' says Clemmy. 'I live in the converted barn over there.' She points to the chalet-style building we spotted earlier. She laughs. 'Well, it was more of a big shed, really, but Jed, who owns the Log Fire Cabin, is an architect and he did an amazing conversion job on it for us. Jed is my fiancé's brother.'

I smile. 'How lovely. When's the wedding?'

'October. There's still so much to organise, but we'll get there.' A dark shadow passes over her face. But next second she's back into professional mode. 'Jed's fiancée, Poppy, has her own catering company, and she bakes fresh bread and pastries every morning, which I can highly recommend.' Clemmy pats her rounded tummy ruefully. 'Way too moreish. Come over any time after eight if you'd like to sample them.'

As soon as she's gone, Toby picks up the jug of flowers from the table, dumps it on the bedside table and puts his laptop on the table instead. 'Just need to check in. Won't be a mo.'

My heart sinks but I smile and say, 'Okay. I'll go and freshen up while you're busy. I really hope you like it here. It's such a gorgeous lakeside setting, isn't it?'

But he's already peering anxiously at the screen and doesn't appear to have heard me. So I go off to investigate the tiny bathroom, hoping Toby won't be too long. I hope he manages to get us a table for dinner at the Starlight Hotel. It sounds utterly gorgeous. Possibly even more romantic than eating *al fresco*! And definitely no bugs.

My stomach is already rumbling like mad at the thought of Poppy's freshly baked breakfast pastries ...

*

'Let's just walk along to the hotel, Toby. It's a lovely evening.'

I finally managed to prise Toby away from his laptop in order to get ready. While he was in the bathroom, I took the magazine with my prize-winning story in it out of my case and, with a little lurch of excitement, slid it onto Toby's bedside table. Hopefully he'll finally have time to read it this week!

Toby frowns. 'I thought you were hungry.'

'I am. But Clemmy said the hotel was only a ten-minute walk away, and I thought it might be nice to take a stroll along there by the lake. You know, get to know our surroundings a bit?'

'Okay. Let's go.' He pockets his work phone and I know there's no point objecting. The office comes before everything else for Toby – even relationships. That's just the way he is, and I've always had a theory that there's no point trying to change the person you're going out with. Sure, some of your own good habits will likely rub off on each other. But essentially, they're not likely to undergo a great transformation, so you either accept them, warts and all, or you move on.

There's no doubt that Toby and I are very different in some ways. But every time I imagine us going our separate ways, I think of just how much I would lose. Toby and his family have basically taken me in and provided the love and comfort I missed so badly when Mum died. I couldn't leave Toby. And what about my friendship with Rosalind? How could we still meet up for coffee and a chat if I was no longer going out with her son?

I swallow hard. Toby and I get along fine together. Every relationship needs to be worked on. And this week, we'll have the chance to do just that ...

I tuck my hand in his arm and we start walking down the road to the hotel.

'So, what do you think of glamping?' I ask. 'I know it's not what you were expecting, but I think our tent is incredible.'

He smiles at me. 'It's certainly different. And I'm looking forward to finding out how springy that mattress is.'

'Ooh, yes, me too.' I give him a wicked grin and snuggle closer, laying my head briefly against his shoulder.

He nods. 'Of course, I prefer a pocket-sprung, memory-foam hybrid mattress. As you know. But hell, I'm willing to try something different!' He gives me a jolly wink.

This is promising, I think to myself. Toby actually seems quite relaxed now and he hasn't checked his phone once since we left our tent. Admittedly, we're only five minutes down the road, but even so ...

Approaching the hotel entrance, I spot a 'workmen' sign just to the left, with a cordon in a ring around whatever they've been working on. Toby takes my hand and guides me firmly around the obstruction.

Then he suddenly stops and takes hold of my other hand as well. 'Thank you, Daisy, for my birthday treat. I know I've been preoccupied with work today, but I promise I'll make it up to you while we're here.'

I smile shyly up at him. 'You will?'

He nods and I stand on tiptoe to kiss him. His mouth tastes of fresh minty toothpaste and it's lovely.

I slide my hands up around Toby's neck as the kiss deepens and my head spins deliciously. *This* is what a romantic break should be like.

This, right here ... kissing under the stars ... just us and no one else to ruin the moment ...

'You're blocking the way.'

I jump at the sound of a deep voice behind me.

Toby, too, is startled and springs back, colliding with the workmen's barrier.

A tall, well-built man, wearing a backpack and hiking gear, strides past us and mounts the hotel steps, his long legs making easy work of them.

'Hey, hang on, mate,' protests Toby, and the man turns at the top of the steps.

'Yes?' he snarls, glowering at me for some reason and not Toby.

I swallow, staring up at his dark shock of hair and rough, unshaven face.

'An "excuse me" would have been nice,' I point out testily.

But he just gives a snort of contempt and disappears into the hotel.

'Ah, shit. Fucking *shit*,' says Toby. And when I turn, he's extracting one foot from some syrupy, just-laid cement.

'Oh, God, your shoe!' I wail, staring at the gunge that's

welded to it and feeling Toby's pain. Toby prides himself on his quality shoes. 'Don't worry, I've got some wipes in my handbag.'

Luckily, Toby always keeps a stash of baby wipes in the car in case of messy emergencies.

We manage to get him cleaned up fairly satisfactorily, but it's put a definite dampener on the evening. This particular pair of shoes was handmade in Italy; Toby's pride and joy. It would be like if someone threw my best handbag into the back of a bin lorry. It would never be the same after that. I totally get where poor Toby is coming from.

So basically, that rude stranger who pushed past us on the stairs has managed to ruin Toby's night. Which obviously means *I'm* not exactly leaping about with joy, either. Still, it can only get better from here ...

Chapter 8

We haven't booked and the restaurant is full.

All the waiter can suggest is that we have a drink in the bar and there will be a table for us at nine o'clock. Toby's face falls and I decide not to point out that Clemmy offered to book us a table but he said he would sort it. Work, of course, got in the way ...

Toby looks at his watch. 'That's nearly a two-hour wait. Is there anywhere else around here we can eat?'

I shake my head. 'The nearest village, Appley Green, is ten miles away and I didn't see a restaurant when we drove through earlier.'

'Bloody countryside,' mutters Toby, glaring down at his shoe, as if a rural cowpat was to blame, not wet cement. 'At least in the city, everything's just a phone call away.'

He sighs, looking thoroughly exhausted, and I take his hand and say softly, 'Why don't we just go back and microwave the moussaka I brought?'

He grimaces. 'Don't fancy it.'

'Okay, well, we could get some basic stuff from Clemmy's store cupboard, like she suggested?'

He frowns. 'Beans on toast?'

I nod. 'Beans, anyway. I'm not sure there's a toaster.'

He flicks his eyes to the ceiling. 'Great.'

Toby likes to sit down to a proper dinner – at least two courses – every night. So I can understand why a tin of beans isn't exactly floating his boat. Especially when this is supposed to be his birthday week surprise!

He sees my face and shakes his head. 'It's not your fault. I've just had a piss-awful day, that's all. And I was looking forward to a nice meal.' He shrugs. 'But hey, that's life.'

He goes off to find the men's toilets and I sink down onto a stylish burnt-orange sofa by the hotel's reception desk.

What a nightmare!

It's obvious Toby isn't a huge fan of glamping or the countryside in general. We've spent all our time since we got together in the city. How was I to know Toby would be so ill at ease in the country?

Now that I think about it, the warnings were there for me to see. On the odd occasion I've suggested going for a hike and a meal in a country pub, Toby has always thought of an alternative. The showing of a foreign film he's wanted to see for a while. Or a visit to a museum. Actually, most of the time, our evenings are spent with him catching up on work while I cook dinner. Two courses at least. Obviously.

Apparently, I've failed utterly with the glamping ...

Tears spring up from nowhere. I feel so defeated.

A woman bustles into reception from somewhere within the hotel. She's wearing a smart black suit that skims her generous curves and her blonde hair is scraped back in a severe bun. She glances at me over her dark-framed spectacles and I quickly blink to despatch the tears.

'Can I help you, Madam?' she asks.

I struggle up from my slouched position and force a smile. 'I'm fine, thanks.'

She gives me a thin smile, then approaches the girl behind the reception desk and they have a murmured conversation about a hotel guest needing special pillows. I notice she's wearing a badge with 'Manager' on it.

On her way past me, she stops and murmurs, 'Are you sure there's nothing you need?'

I heave a sigh. 'A table in the restaurant? So my boyfriend can have the birthday he deserves?' I shrug and smile, as if to say: *It's no big deal.*

'Are we full?'

I nod. 'But really, it's fine. It's our fault for not booking a table.' I must look really downhearted because her face relaxes into a sympathetic smile, her head tipped to one side.

'Is it a special birthday?'

I tell her it's his thirtieth and she thinks for a second.

'Let me see what I can do.' She bustles off, her patent leather court shoes squeaking slightly on the plush carpet.

She returns less than a minute later. 'Table for two at eight suit you?'

My heart lifts. 'Yes, that's brilliant. Thank you so much. Toby will be delighted.'

She nods and smiles. 'Good. Well, enjoy!' And then she's gone.

Anxious to deliver the good news to Toby – *no baked beans for us tonight!* – I wander over to the men's toilets and lurk outside for a minute. What's he doing in there?

After another minute, I'm getting impatient. Perhaps I could just go in.

These are obviously posh loos so there'll just be cubicles in there. No urinal thingy.

Slowly, I push open the door a crack. Hesitantly, I call out Toby's name.

I hear a grunt so I push the door wider. Sure enough, cubicles only. And *very* posh, with hand cream and everything. Just one cubicle is engaged.

I walk in and call out, 'You'll never guess? I've managed to get us a table for eight o'clock. Isn't that great? *And* ...' I move close to the door and murmur, 'I've packed the wellies and the apron. If you're a *very* good boy, I'll put them on later ...'

The first time I cooked Toby a meal, he arrived early and surprised me in the garden picking herbs for the tomato sauce. I'd just emerged from the shower and was wearing little more than wellies and a large apron. Toby clearly admired my quirky 'outfit' because after we laughed about it, we ended up in bed together, tomato sauce temporarily forgotten ...

The toilet flushes and I stand back, expecting Toby to emerge all smiles at the memory of our first night together.

My mouth sags open.

It's not Toby. It's a complete stranger.

Well, not quite a stranger. It's the hulking, surly, obnoxious man from earlier. The one who barged in on our kiss and accused us of blocking his way.

'Sorry,' I mumble, edging backwards. 'I thought you were my boyfriend.'

He crosses to the sink and starts washing his hands vigorously, looking back and studying me with a faint smile on his face. 'Shame. I was looking forward to dinner at eight. And now you're telling me I'm not invited?'

He looks rakishly handsome when he smiles but his sarcastic tone rankles.

'I doubt they'd even let you *in* the restaurant looking like that,' I retort, and he laughs.

'Touché.' He turns and rubs his wet hands on his jeans. 'I'm actually just meeting an old friend for a drink in the bar so hopefully I'll pass inspection.' He leans back against the washbasin and folds his arms. 'You enjoy your meal. And I'll get back to my campfire. I know my place.'

He studies me with another lazy smile, and a flush of heat surges up into my face.

Unable to think of a witty retort, I make a hasty escape.

As the door closes, he calls out, 'Apron and wellies. Not an image to forget in a hurry.'

Heat like a blast from a furnace creeps up my neck and engulfs me.

I waft my top to cool down and go in search of Toby, hoping he'll think I'm simply flushed with happiness at the thought of food at long last ...

Chapter 9

Next morning, when I wake up and peer outside, a thin drizzle is falling.

But it's still very warm and the forecast is for it to brighten up later. Feeling optimistic, I take the little table and chairs outside.

Toby is still asleep, so I make a cup of coffee and sit facing the lake, feeling the faint patter of rain on my bare arms. The scent of recently mown grass tickles my nose as I stare out over the flat grey water, thinking of yesterday.

It was so strange driving through Appley Green.

The feelings aroused in me made me realise how eager I am now to find out the truth of my birth. I've been suppressing the desire to search because I didn't want to upset Mum. I'm not sure I can leave here without at least finding Maple Tree House ...

Yesterday wasn't the greatest start to our holiday – although when we eventually sat down to dinner, the food was excellent, as expected. But hopefully things will get better now that we've settled in. Toby very much enjoyed the apron and the wellies after we got back, although I must admit my clash with that rude man in the men's toilets rather distracted me from getting wholeheartedly into the spirit of things. I just kept thinking of his sarcastic comments and cringing all over again.

Toby enjoyed himself, though. And hopefully he'll be in a much more relaxed mood today after the stress of yesterday.

I glance around at the other tents on the site, wondering if the rude stranger is occupying one of them. But maybe he lives locally and isn't here on holiday at all. I know for a fact that the nearest tent to us is occupied by a young couple from Scotland. When we arrived back from the restaurant last night, they seemed to be having an argument. The man came out, swigging from a can, and a woman's voice followed him, yelling, 'And don't think you can come back in here and shag me senseless and everything'll be all right. Because it *won't*, Dane Cuthbertson!'

As we passed, Dane shook his head at Toby and muttered, 'Women.' Then he called back, 'You don't half talk a load of bollocks, Chantelle. You know fine well that once you've necked a few more gins, you'll be absolutely gasping for it.'

'*What* was that?' She poked her blonde head out of the tent. Dressed only in a thigh-length pink T-shirt with Mickey Mouse on the front, she clapped eyes on us and stepped back, horrified.

Toby went red and grabbed for my hand.

Back in our tent, we could already hear Chantelle shrieking and laughing raucously. Dane was obviously correct, although his prediction that it would take another few gins to get Chantelle in the mood was clearly off beam.

I grinned at Toby. 'Quite the femme fatale next door there. Wish I had a figure like Chantelle's.'

Toby frowned. 'I didn't really notice.'

I smile at the memory.

There's no sign of life from Chantelle and Dane so far this morning. They're obviously enjoying a lie-in after their passionate reunion.

After a while, as Toby's still out for the count, I take a quick shower and head over to Clemmy's house, tempted by the thought of Poppy's breakfast pastries.

Clemmy greets me at the door with a smile, wearing shorts and a T-shirt, her thick hair, the colour of gleaming conkers, falling loosely over her shoulders.

'Hi. Come in, Daisy. Did you have a nice meal at the hotel?'

'We did. Thanks to the lovely manager managing to squeeze us in.'

'Brilliant.'

I follow her through to the living room. 'I ... er ... think I might have met another of your guests at the hotel last night.'

'Really?' She frowns. 'Not Chantelle and Dane?'

I shake my head. 'A tall man ... big shoulders ... with dark reddish hair and lots of stubble?'

'He sounds delicious, whoever he is. But the only other occupants at the moment are you and Toby. We only started up the business in April, although we've got plans for more tents next year.' She smiles broadly.

'Oh. I wonder who he was then.' I shrug as if I haven't given him another thought since last night. Which I haven't. Not really. Then I turn to look at a painting in order to hide my inconvenient blushes. 'I just assumed he must be camping here.'

'*Glamping*, please!' Clemmy sounds like she's really offended.

But when I turn, she's smiling mischievously.

A baby wails in the background. I look at Clemmy quizzically and she laughs. 'Not mine. Poppy's the new mother. Come through and meet them.'

I follow her through a neat hallway into a large kitchen-diner at the back of the house. The girl called Poppy – who Clemmy said lives next door at the Log Fire Cabin with her fiancé, Jed – is standing by the window, shushing a baby in a sling.

'Poppy and little Keira. This is Daisy, an old friend of mine from school. She's staying in Harem Three with her boyfriend, Toby. She's here to sample your pastries.' Clemmy pats a wicker basket that's sitting on the island in the centre of the kitchen. It's brimming with fresh pastries, each one wrapped in a twist of cellophane.

'Harem Three?' I laugh.

'Oops, sorry.' Clemmy laughs. 'Not very professional of me. I keep forgetting you're actually a client, not just an old friend. I call them Harem One, Two and Three because they remind me of those Arabian tents in the desert?'

I nod. 'I know exactly what you mean.'

'But probably best not to advertise them by that name.' Poppy grins. 'That would be a rather more – um, *exotic* – kind of a holiday.'

We all laugh and Poppy says, 'Good to meet you, Daisy.'

'Likewise.' I smile at her then lean over to admire the baby. 'She is just *gorgeous*.'

'She is, isn't she?' Poppy laughs. 'I suppose I might be a little bit biased.'

'No, she literally is perfect,' says Clemmy.

Poppy grins again. 'Except at three in the morning when she's screaming her head off.' She pats the wicker basket. 'Daisy, there's apple and cinnamon pastries this morning, and chocolate and almond. Or can we tempt you with some croissants and some of Clemmy's homemade strawberry jam?'

'Lethal combination,' groans Clemmy. 'Which is why I'm no nearer getting into my wedding dress than I was when I started my so-called diet in January.' She pinches a few inches ruefully.

'You look fine as you are, Clem,' retorts Poppy, and little Keira gives a cute snuffle, as if she's in firm agreement.

'You do. You've got a great tan,' I tell her, admiring her shapely legs in the shorts. I start picking out pastries and croissants for Clemmy to put in a bag for me.

'I'm so excited for the wedding in October,' says Poppy, kissing Keira's head gently, and grinning broadly. 'I'm going to be a bridesmaid.'

Clemmy twists her lips, looking rather less enthusiastic. 'She's only this excited because our wedding is a sort of dry run for when she and Jed get married in December!'

Poppy laughs. 'Very true.'

A phone on the table beeps and Clemmy glances at the message. A frown creases her pretty face as she reads it, then she stares pensively out of the window.

'Are you okay?' asks Poppy.

Clemmy turns and gives her head a little shake. 'Shouldn't be looking. That's Ryan's phone.' She smiles brightly. 'I'm fine.'

'I do that with Toby's phone sometimes,' I say.

'Sorry?' Clemmy's mind is clearly still elsewhere.

I shrug. 'Sometimes I find myself reading a message on Toby's phone without meaning to. It's just instinctive.'

She smiles and nods but she still seems distracted. I wonder what was in that text message?

'Congratulations on the upcoming nuptials, by the way,

Poppy,' I say. 'You've got a lot going on. How do you manage to run a catering company *and* look after a new-born *and* plan a wedding, all at once?'

'A magical assistant called Roxy,' says a male voice. 'She arrived at Christmas and stayed.'

'Thank goodness,' breathes Poppy. 'I couldn't do even half of this without Roxy. She and her boyfriend, Alex, are sunning themselves in Greece this week.'

'Hello, you.' Clemmy turns to the man, a beaming smile on her face. 'Daisy, this is Ryan.'

Ryan and I greet each other and he steals a pastry from the basket, unwrapping it immediately. 'Chocolate and almond,' he murmurs, holding it up. 'This right here is four mouthfuls of absolute perfection.'

'Why, thank you, Ryan.' Poppy laughs. 'But I know you're only buttering me up so I'll say *have another one*!'

'Don't mind if I do.' Ryan grins. 'Right, I'm going to love you and leave you.' He picks up his mobile phone, reads the message and quickly pockets it. 'Got a ten o'clock meeting.'

I recall Clemmy mentioning last night that Ryan is a solicitor at a big London firm.

'I thought I'd do steak tonight,' she says. 'What time will you be back?'

Ryan turns away to put the discarded cellophane in the bin. 'Erm, late, actually. Probably after nine. You'd be best just having yours and I'll grab a snack when I get in.'

Clemmy nods, looking a little crestfallen. 'Oh. Okay.'

'I'll call you when I'm on the way back,' says Ryan, kissing his fiancée on the lips. 'Bye everyone. Be good, Keira.' He smiles down at the baby and offers a finger for her to curl her hand around. He shakes his head, marvelling. 'So tiny.'

'That'll be you and Clemmy soon,' says Poppy.

Ryan gives a comical look of dread and walks out, raising his hand as he goes.

'I don't think it will be,' murmurs Clemmy. 'Not if he keeps on being late home like this. We barely see each other these days and, when we do, we're so knackered there's no energy at all for sex.'

Poppy grins. 'It's called a steady relationship. Jed and I barely have the energy for a quick peck on the cheek, never mind full sex. Sleep just seems *way* more seductive when you've got a baby.'

'Yes, but at least you've Keira as an excuse for your lack of love life.'

Right on cue, Keira starts to wail.

Poppy shrugs. 'Ryan's got loads on at work. You said so yourself. Things will calm down.'

I grin. 'My other half, Toby, never *stops* working. I have to wear a lime green lizard suit and leap up and down shouting "Fire!" to attract *his* attention.'

Clemmy and Poppy look at me and burst out laughing.

Even little Keira stops crying.

The doorbell rings and Clemmy grins at me. 'That'll be Gloria and Ruby, our relatives from Newcastle. Gloria's engaged to Ryan and Jed's Uncle Bob, and Ruby's Gloria's daughter. They arrived yesterday to meet baby Keira. They're staying at Poppy and Jed's house next door.'

Clemmy and Poppy both go to the door so I wander into the hall with them.

A red-haired woman in her late forties, who I presume is Gloria, stands on the doorstep, her glasses perched on her head, with a young girl of about eighteen, who must be her daughter, Ruby.

'Hi, Mum and I are going for a walk round the lake,' says Ruby. 'Anyone want to come? Oh, hi,' she adds, spotting me.

Clemmy does the introductions and we decline the offer of a walk, so Gloria and Ruby turn to go.

'*What* is that weird man *doing*?' hisses Ruby suddenly, and we all look over.

I frown, recognising the man in question. Toby has emerged from the tent, wearing just his boxers, and is running around on the grass in small circles, flapping his arms vigorously over his head.

'Is he all right, do you think?' asks Gloria worriedly.

'I think he's doing some kind of tribal *dance*,' says Ruby in awe.

'It's Toby,' says Clemmy, following me over the grass to find out what's going on.

'Toby? Are you all right?' Alarmed, I run up to him, fearing for one hair-raising moment that work has finally pushed him over the edge.

'It's a bloody bee. I can't get rid of it,' he shrieks. 'It was in the tent and now it's following me around, the little bastard!' He flaps at the air, jumping from side to side in agitation.

'It's probably more frightened of you than you are of it,' says Ruby calmly. 'If you keep still, it'll get bored and fly away.'

'If I stay still, it'll bloody sting me!' yells Toby, continuing his tribal dance. 'Any more bright ideas? Ouch, you bloody bastard! The fucking thing just stung me!' Yelping in pain and indignation, he holds out his arm, staring at it in horror.

'We just need to get the sting out,' I say, grasping his other arm to try and calm him down.

'Here, I know what to do,' says Ruby. 'I did a first aid course.' She grabs the arm that's been stung and uses her nail to carefully flick away the sting. Toby is leaning so far back as she performs this delicate operation that he almost overbalances.

'Honey,' says Gloria. 'That's what you need. Smear it with honey and put a bandage on it, and it'll be right as rain in no time.'

Clemmy rushes off to hunt for both and returns to tend to Toby's arm.

'I feel a bit faint,' he says, frowning at me and holding out his bandaged arm as if it's a foreign object that doesn't belong to him. 'I think I'd better have a lie-down.'

'Good idea, Toby. Let's go. Thanks for your help, everyone,' I add, leading him swiftly away.

'No problem,' calls Ruby. 'Hope you're feeling better soon, Toby.'

Clemmy catches me up and slips a bag under my arm. 'Pastries,' she says and I give her a grateful smile.

'Actually, I think I'm going to be sick,' says Toby suddenly, charging the rest of the way back to the tent and making for the bathroom.

He emerges a little while later looking white as a sheet, then he crawls into bed and lies flat on his back, staring up at the ceiling and looking thoroughly traumatised by the whole experience.

I sit down on the bed beside him. 'Ruby got the sting out. You'll be absolutely fine.'

He just grunts and I feel terrible because he clearly regards it as my fault for bringing him to this awful, insect-ridden place ...

*

An hour or so later, Toby emerges from the bedroom to find me sitting outside, enjoying the sun.

'Anything to eat?' he asks.

Smiling, I hold up the bag. 'Pastries. Sit down and I'll get breakfast. Are you feeling better?'

He nods grudgingly. 'A bit.'

A fly buzzes around his ear and he slaps the side of his face, missing it, then grabs a newspaper and starts hacking violently at the air.

'Bloody flies. I wouldn't mind the countryside so much if it wasn't full of bloody great beasts crapping all over the place and attracting all these *fucking* insects.'

He storms off, back into the tent.

Chapter 10

'Do you know what?' says Toby, appearing again a little while later. 'I think I'll join you for one of those delicious-looking croissants.'

'Oh, great.' I beam up at him. Perhaps he's starting to relax a bit. They do say it takes a few days before you're entirely in holiday mode.

'This is nice,' he says, sitting stiffly on the edge of his seat, the newspaper to hand ready to swat anything that dares zoom by. He's holding his bandaged arm out at an awkward angle.

'Isn't it?' I say cheerfully, feeling on edge myself just looking at him. 'And the forecast is for a glorious sunny day, so perhaps we could go for a walk around the lake? And then ...' I swallow hard. 'And then maybe this afternoon we could go and explore Appley Green?' I roll my tongue round the words, my heart rate quickening.

Toby nods. 'Sounds good.' He peers at the jam on his croissant and carefully picks something out of it, smearing it on the side of his plate with a faintly disgusted look. 'Although I think I'll have to pass on this afternoon.'

'Oh. Why?'

He shrugs. 'The broadband signal is rubbish here, so I'm

thinking I'll have to go to the office if I want to get any work done.'

'The office? But that's back in Manchester!'

He smiles. 'That's where I'm based. But the company has offices all over the country – including Guildford.'

'Ah. Of course.' I nod slowly. 'But you're on holiday?'

'I know.' He pastes on a frown, as if the thought of dragging himself away from an insect-ridden location is going to be absolute murder. 'But what can I do? The few texts that have got through this morning have all been really urgent. I can't let the team down. But we can definitely go for that walk this morning first.'

'Right.' I nod, my heart sinking. So the reason he joined me for croissants was so he could feel less guilty about leaving me today. 'It's just ...'

He frowns. 'What?'

I sigh. 'It's probably time I told you.'

He looks at me warily. 'You haven't gone and booked another surprise, have you?' He looks genuinely fearful, so I rush to reassure him.

'No, no. Nothing like that. It's just ... well, the thing is, you know how I was adopted? Well, Appley Green is the place where I was born.' I swallow hard. 'And I think I might have found a clue that could lead me to my birth parents.'

'Right.' He nods. Then his mobile shrills out and he snatches it up with a triumphant smile. 'Hallelujah! We have a signal!' Answering it, he gets up from the table and starts wandering over the grass, in the direction of the lake, as he talks.

I slump back in my seat, a lump in my throat. I'd expected more of a reaction than that. But Toby seems more interested in work than the fact that my life could be about to change forever.

I watch him, deep in discussion with Callum from the office, feeling suddenly quite tearful at the nonchalant way he received my potentially life-changing news.

Ten minutes later, he walks back over the grass towards me, his face alive with enthusiasm. 'I think we might have cracked it. But it'll mean me working all day today.'

'Really?' I can't help the disappointment showing in my face.

He pulls the chair across to sit beside me. 'After today, I promise I'm all yours.' He pats my knee and gives me a wistful smile as if he hates the thought of leaving me. But I can tell he can't wait to get in his car and head for Guildford and proper civilisation.

'Don't worry. I can amuse myself today. Clemmy invited me over for a coffee, actually. You get yourself away and save the world!'

I can't help the snippiness in my voice.

But my ironic barb sails right over his head.

He leaps up with a smile, having clearly forgotten all about my desire to seek out my birth parents. 'But remember, tomorrow, you're all mine,' he says, wagging his finger at me.

'Is that a threat?' I mumble.

But he's far too excited about leaving to notice my fed-up expression.

He holds up both thumbs and disappears into the tent, returning almost immediately with his briefcase and car keys.

'See you later! Be good!'

Our attention is caught by next door's tent flap opening. Chantelle's blonde head appears, her hair all wild, no doubt after a night of passion. She gives Toby a coy little wave as he passes, and he trips over his own feet and almost goes sprawling.

'Toby?' I call, catching him up. There's no point spoiling the holiday by being huffy. 'Phone me to let me know when you're coming back and I'll have dinner ready.' Then I murmur in his ear, 'You seem to be a big hit with Chantelle. I bet she wishes I'd disappear so she could have you all to herself. I think you're definitely in there!'

Toby, who's looking a bit flushed from almost falling head first, gives a bark of laughter. '*Ha! What?* No. Definitely not my type.'

'I know.' I giggle. 'I was only having you on.'

'Right, well, I'm off.' He glances back at Chantelle and shakes his head in disgust. She seems to be doing some keep-fit exercises, thrusting her arms back and forward vigorously.

'*I must, I must, I must improve my bust*,' I chant.

Toby frowns. 'Why? Your bust is fine as it is.'

'No, it's just something Mum used to say when she was doing that exercise.' I smile sadly at the memory.

'Ah. Well, anyway, *she* looks bloody *ridiculous*.'

'Methinks thou doth protest too much.'

'What?'

'Nothing. I'll see you later.'

I kiss him and wander back towards our tent. Seconds later, the car roars off, splitting the silence and giving the cows in a nearby field the fright of their lives.

*

I finish my breakfast, including the croissant with delicious strawberry jam that Toby discarded because of a possible bug infestation.

It tastes perfectly fine to me. A few strawberry seeds, that's all.

The earlier clouds have vanished, leaving a beautiful clear blue sky, so after I've cleared up, I head off for a walk myself, round the lakeside track, passing the hotel where we had dinner. The manager is outside, clearing a couple of glasses that were left on a wall the night before.

'Lovely meal last night!' I call, and she comes over.

'Glad to hear it. Off for a walk?'

'Yes. You're very lucky having all this on your doorstep.'

She smiles. 'I suppose I am. Not that I get much leisure time. Owning a hotel is rather more than a full-time job, especially when you're also the manager.'

'Oh wow, you actually own this place? How amazing.'

She nods. 'I'm wedded to the job but I can't imagine doing anything else.'

'You must really love it.'

She shrugs. 'Yes, I suppose I do. It keeps me busy at any rate. I'm Sylvia, by the way.' She gives me one of her quick smiles. 'Anyway, must get on. Enjoy your day.'

Walking on, I wonder what it's like to have a passion for your work, like Sylvia clearly does. I feel the very opposite of passion for my job, something that used to bother Mum. She wanted me to be doing something I enjoyed instead of writing about plumbing all the time. Maybe she really did have an instinct that I could succeed as a writer if I put my mind to it.

The familiar feeling of panic bubbles in my chest.

I miss her so much ...

Taking a deep breath, I force myself to think of something else. The book I'm writing. After my walk, I'll go back to the tent and I'll finally finish the last chapter. I've been procrastinating for far too long. It might be rubbish but that doesn't matter. I just need to finish it!

I've always wanted to be a writer – for as long as I can remember. English/Creative writing was my favourite lesson at school and, at home, I read voraciously, often reading after 'lights out' with a torch under the duvet.

When I left school, I went to college in Edinburgh and trained to be a journalist. I had ambitions to be a roving reporter, travelling the globe, filing copy from far-flung capital cities. But it didn't quite work out that way.

Emerging keen and optimistic at the end of my course, I tried for a few reporting jobs but was always pipped to the post by candidates who already had experience. It was all very dispiriting. I had a brief stint as a reporter for a local newspaper that subsequently shut down. So then I started applying for anything and everything and eventually landed a job designing page layouts and writing supposedly eye-grabbing headings on trade magazine *Plunge Happy Monthly*.

I'd hoped it might be a good starting point and that, eventually, it would lead to something at least a little more glamorous. But so far, apart from starting to write articles for the same magazine, it hasn't worked out like that.

In between trying to come up with riveting headings for stories that would frankly send an insomniac to sleep, I started thinking about the book I would write and dreaming up characters.

My main protagonist was a girl called Hattie Walker, who was good-hearted and funny; the sort of person you'd want as a friend. Hattie was a little accident-prone and if there was a scrape to be landed in, she would somehow manage it – with amusing consequences. If it made me laugh, I stored it up, writing it down on a scrap of paper and shoving it in my bag to weave into my tale later. There was a darker side to the story, too. Hattie's sister had run away from home and Hattie was trying to find her.

Letting my imagination go wild like this kept me sane while I was writing copy about sprockets and open-end wrenches.

I walk on briskly, pulling my cardigan tightly around me, thinking about the ending to my book. It's too hot for the cardigan, really, but I'm so used to wearing it now, it's like an old friend and I feel bare without it. It belonged to Mum.

I remember when she bought it. She said it was a 'waterfall cardigan' and she joked that she was well up with the latest trends.

A few nights after she died, I was at home and Rachel was out with Adam, and all the grief that I'd been holding back, determined to stay strong for Mum, came pouring out. I sobbed as if I'd never be able to stop then I went to bed but couldn't stop shivering. Spotting Mum's cardigan on top of the box of her belongings I'd brought home from the hospital, I pulled it on, snuggling it tightly around me.

Soothed by the scent of Mum's perfume still lingering there, I finally drifted off to sleep.

I've worn the cardigan every day since.

It's been washed many times and is starting to look a little faded and shapeless but I won't be parted from it. Toby hates it. He once sneaked it into a bag destined for the charity shop but, luckily, I rescued it in time. I think he was quite shocked by my reaction and he won't be trying that again!

Deep in thought, I find myself walking for longer than I intended round the lake. It's such a lovely spot. Only very occasionally does a car drive past along the narrow tarmac road, but I stick mostly to the grass verge nonetheless. Up ahead is the woodland area that's our view from the glamping site, on the opposite bank of the lake. The band of trees hugs the shoreline and eventually peters out into an open grassy area beyond. I'd like to walk right around the lake some time, if there's a path through the trees that will allow me to make that complete circle.

As I approach the wooded area, I spy what seems to be a path disappearing into the cool shade of the trees. It looks very inviting in the heat of the midday sun.

But I decide to explore the woods another day. Right now, I'm hungry so I'll have to get back. I should have brought a packed lunch with me. If Toby had been here, he would have thought of that. He's so much more organised than me.

Back at the tent, I make some lunch and take it outside, along with my laptop. Then, with Mum's voice in my ear urging me on and Sylvia as my example of a successful, motivated woman, I finally start tapping away at the last chapter of my book.

I think of Toby, working away in Guildford. I packed my laptop thinking that I might get a little writing done if I happened to have a spare few minutes. My mouth twists into a rueful smile. I should have known it wouldn't be long before Toby was hankering to get back to his own laptop!

But I'm not as disappointed as I thought I'd be. Inspiration for my book is flowing freely. I felt terminally stuck before but now the words are tumbling out, one after the other. It's almost as if the book is writing itself. I can hardly believe it when, halfway through the afternoon, I finally write the very last sentence.

With a happy sigh, I sit back and stare at the words on the page. I made it! I actually did it! I've written a whole book. It's taken a long time but that doesn't matter. Whether it's good or not almost doesn't matter either. It's such a big achievement in itself.

Mum would have been over the moon. She'd have bought a bottle of prosecco to celebrate and made me read the last chapter out loud to her, and she'd have sighed happily over the ending and perhaps even welled up a little.

My throat hurts thinking about how much Mum loved me and cheered me on. Her dying has left a gaping hole in my life that I struggle every day to fill, never quite succeeding.

Of course I have Toby now and his family.

But it's not the same. It never could be.

Family is so precious. It's only when it's gone that you realise just how much you depended on that unconditional love and took it for granted. Mum would have done anything for me. And I would have done anything for her. That's just the way we were ...

Tears are seriously threatening now. I jump up and run into the tent, looking for something to occupy my mind, hating Toby for not being here when I need him. Just a friendly face would be nice ...

'Daisy?'

Clemmy!

I rush outside and her face creases with worry when she sees me.

'Are you all right?'

I must look terrible ... desperate. She puts her arm round me, leads me gently back into the tent and makes me sit down on the sofa.

'Where's Toby? Has something happened?' she asks, and the genuine concern on her face threatens to destabilise me altogether. 'Or is it just ... *things*?'

We exchange a look of understanding. And then I find myself pouring everything out to Clemmy. About Mum dying and feeling all alone in the world. And about finding the pink handbag and thinking maybe it was time to go searching for my birth parents. But not feeling quite brave enough ...

Clemmy listens without interruption, squeezing my hand every now and again to help me through the more difficult bits of my story.

When I fall silent, she opens her eyes wide and shakes her head. 'Oh, Daisy. Poor you. What you've been through. I just can't imagine.' She pauses. 'Your mum was such a wonderful person. Auntie Joan loved her to bits.'

I nod, quickly dashing away tears and smiling. 'I know she did.' Then I frown. 'I'm just so torn between wanting to look for my birth parents, but feeling that if I start searching for them, I'll be betraying Mum.'

Clemmy shakes her head. 'I understand, but you mustn't think like that. Your mum was such a lovely person; she'd have wanted you to be happy, wouldn't she?'

I nod. 'It still doesn't sit right, though. I realise I've been pushing thoughts of searching from my mind for ages, simply because I didn't want to hurt her or make her feel second best. And even though she's gone now, I still can't shake the feeling of guilt I get when I think of going in search of my birth mother.'

Clemmy frowns. 'Would you like to find Maple Tree House? I could drive you there.'

My heart lurches. 'Really?'

She nods. 'I came over to see if you needed a lift to the supermarket. That's where I'm heading now. We could combine it with a trip to Acomb Drive in Appley Green?'

I long to say yes. But my instinct is to hesitate.

My feelings on the subject are so complex, they're hard to pin down. I'm excited but I'm also very apprehensive. I have a burning curiosity to know who my real parents are but, at the same time, I wish I hadn't been adopted because then life would be simple.

Over-riding all these feelings is gut-curdling fear.

The fear of what I will find if I knock on the door of Maple Tree House. The fear of rejection.

'We don't have to go today,' says Clemmy.

'I do need to go shopping.'

She shrugs. 'Well, let's go to the supermarket and you can decide if you want to go to Appley Green afterwards. Okay?'

I swallow hard. 'Okay. Thanks.'

She smiles. 'No problem. It'll be nice to have your company.'

Ten minutes later, I'm sitting in the passenger seat of Clemmy's little run-around, staring at the lake as we drive by but not really seeing it, because all I can think about is Maple Tree House. I just need to say the word and we'll be there. It's so real now, it scares me to death. And yet at the same time, I can't help the hopeful imaginings crowding into my head.

'Are you okay?' Clemmy peers across at me, startling me from the fantasy I've been having pretty much every day since I found the pink bag. It's the dream where I finally locate the woman who gave birth to me and we're reunited in a burst of joyous relief, made all the sweeter when she confides that giving me up for adoption is the biggest regret of her life.

I force a grin. 'Oh, you know.' And Clemmy nods.

I'm so torn.

I desperately want to find the owner of the handbag. She might be able to answer all my questions. Who wouldn't want to find their biological mother after thirty-two years of not even knowing her name?

But at the same time, I'm terrified.

I know for a fact that real life doesn't work out like it does in dreams or in the movies. The perfect scenario can only ever be a fantasy. Because perfection doesn't exist. And how would I cope if the very worst turned out to be true – that she'd died before I had a chance to meet her or (almost worse) she were to take one look at me and reject me on the spot? Could I get over something like that, especially after all the hundreds of times I've imagined a happy ending?

'It's ... complicated,' I whisper. And then because Clemmy is looking at me with such empathy, tears well up. It's so ironic. If I'm honest, the only reason I'm in this quandary at all is because I've lost Mum. But the silly thing is that if Mum were still here, supporting me, I know I'd have the courage to knock on that door ...

We're driving into Appley Green now. It's on the way to the supermarket. We pass a pretty church and Clemmy slows down. 'This is the turn-off for Acomb Drive.' She points at a road up ahead on our right. 'Shall I?' She checks her mirror for traffic and slows to a stop, indicating at the turn-off.

My heart is hammering so fast, I feel sick.

I just can't do it.

Chapter 11

I shake my head and Clemmy switches off the indicator. A car behind us blares its horn and she drives on, staring crossly in the rear-view mirror. '*All right*, mate. I'm going.'

She pulls into a bus stop a little way ahead and switches off the engine.

'You could have gone anywhere for your holiday with Toby. Why did you choose here?' she asks softly.

I smile ruefully. 'Because I wanted to find the owner of the bag.'

She shrugs. 'Well, there you are.'

'I know but I'm scared. Sometimes I think it would be best to forget the biology bit and just remember *Mum* as my real mum – because she *was*, when you think about it. And she was the best mum I could have ever had.'

Clemmy nods, her eyes suspiciously bright. 'Of course she was. And she always *will* be your mum. But ... I don't know ... if there's even a small part of you that needs to discover the truth about your birth, I honestly don't think you'll be able to rest until you've got to the bottom of the mystery.'

'Have you seen Maple Tree House?'

She nods. 'It's quite grand. Georgian style, I think, with lovely gardens.'

I'm silent, absorbing this fresh information.

'Is there a name on the envelope?' asks Clemmy.

'No. That's why all this is so hit-and-miss.'

She nods. 'I guess it all happened such a long time ago.'

'Thirty-two years. What are the chances she'll still be living in the house she lived in when she was a girl?'

'So you're assuming it was a girl who accidentally got pregnant and didn't have the means to support her child? I mean, you?'

'Yes, but only because it's so often the case. Plus, of course, the bag definitely looks as if it belonged to someone young. There's a pink cartoon pony appliquéd onto the front.'

Clemmy frowns thoughtfully. 'Someone *very* young, then.' She looks at me warily. 'I could just drive you past the house. We wouldn't have to stop.'

I nod and try to swallow but my throat is so dry it's almost impossible.

Clemmy smiles reassuringly and looks back along the road before turning the car around and setting off in the opposite direction. A little way along, she takes the turn-off and we drive into what looks like a private lane that hasn't been resurfaced for a while. As we bump over potholes, I scan the houses, my heart thudding against my ribcage.

My birth mum might be behind any one of these doors.

My nausea ramps up to the point where I think I might actually be sick.

'Take some deep breaths,' says Clemmy.

So I do and the panic subsides a little. I tell myself she probably doesn't even live here any more. It was thirty-two years ago, after all ...

There's a small turning circle at the end of the cul-de-sac and we head for this while peering at the house names. From how Clemmy described it – a rather grand Georgian detached house – I'm guessing it's the one straight ahead of us, and as we approach, the plaque by the front door confirms this. Set a little back from the road in an acre or so of gardens, Maple Tree House is built of honey-coloured stone with a red tiled roof.

Clemmy pulls the car wheels half onto the pavement a few yards away from the front door and we both stare at the house.

There's a car in the drive, so there's probably someone at home.

'What do you think?' asks Clemmy. 'I'll come to the door with you if you like.'

I shake my head. 'I can't. I just can't. I'm not ready yet. I need more time.'

At that moment the front door opens and a woman of about fifty appears, dark hair swinging around her shoulders. She's dressed in jeans and a stylish tan leather jacket with matching ankle boots.

I stare at her, my heart in my mouth. And a single thought flashes through my head: *I look just like her!*

But next second, a bolt of panic rips through me and I slither down in my seat so I can't be spotted. It's ridiculous, really, because she wouldn't know me anyway, even if she did catch sight of me ...

Clemmy looks at me from on high as I crouch down as low as I can get, almost sitting on the floor.

'What's she doing?' I murmur, trying desperately to peer out without making myself visible.

Clemmy glances across. 'She's getting into her Mini Clubman. Brand new.'

'Don't look!' I hiss.

'Don't worry. She's not looking this way. And anyway, she doesn't know me from Adam.'

Me neither, I think to myself sadly.

The impression I got from that brief glimpse of her is of a successful woman in her prime. A woman who's happy with life.

A woman who won't necessarily welcome an intrusion from a long-lost daughter who reminds her of a sad past she might very likely want left buried.

'Can we go now?' I swallow on the painful lump in my throat. After all the build-up, the anticlimax of not actually speaking to this woman feels devastating.

But I just can't do it ...

*

We drive over to the supermarket, which is a huge out-of-town store a couple of miles the other side of Appley Green.

I'm silent on the journey, watching the scenery, lost in thought.

After my heart-stopping experience earlier outside Maple Tree House – totally freezing at the idea of meeting my birth mother at last – I'm determined to just forget about it and focus instead on the holiday.

Perhaps the time isn't right to look for her after all.

I'm dimly aware that I'm just making excuses, because the thought of introducing myself makes me so anxious I can barely breathe.

But whatever. I'm determined to put it behind me for now. This mini break is supposed to be Toby's birthday treat, not a hunt for my long-lost family! I'll cook a lavish meal for Toby when he returns this evening.

The supermarket stocks pretty much everything – including Toby's favourite, mussels in white wine, which I immediately drop into my trolley. Then I pick up some prime cuts of steak, recommended by Clemmy, and lots of lovely fresh vegetables, with a chocolate roulade for dessert. If Toby has to work, I can always try to ensure he has a lovely relaxing evening.

And if he doesn't approve of the yummy-looking roulade, that means there'll be more for me!

'Are you excited for October?' I ask Clemmy on the drive back.

We've stopped at some traffic lights and she turns and gives me a wistful smile. 'Yes. Yes, of course I am.' She shrugs as the car moves off. 'I'm marrying the man of my dreams. Why wouldn't I be excited?'

I glance at her profile. She doesn't look like a woman planning what's meant to be the best day of her life. But maybe it's just the stress ...

'More importantly, are *you* all right?' she asks, not taking her eyes off the road.

I swallow. 'Yes, yes, I'm fine. Everything's peachy. Absolutely hunky-dory in fact.' We exchange an ironic smile but, to my huge relief, she doesn't pursue the subject of what happened back there outside Maple Tree House.

I'm not sure I'd be able to answer her, even if she asked me.

Back at the tent, I turn my thoughts determinedly from Maple Tree House and settle down to read over the last chapter of my book again.

It's good, I realise. Perhaps the time is right to think about sending it off to a publisher?

I'm not really expecting to hear from Toby until early evening, when he's on his way back. But to my surprise, he returns just after five, bearing a big bunch of flowers.

'For me? Thank you.' I kiss him. He smells of the Guildford office. 'Now I just need something to put them in. Have you seen any big jugs anywhere?'

Toby snorts. 'Try next door.'

'Toby!' I laugh, glancing over at the next-door tent.

'They're not in, are they?' He glares across.

'No, they went out earlier. Chantelle was in skyscraper heels and a little sequinned dress, so I don't think they were planning a hike in the countryside.'

Toby looks disgruntled for a moment. 'Very nice. They're probably off out for a lovely meal. Back to civilisation.' He grins as if it's a joke but I know it's not.

He disappears into the tent and I follow him in.

'*We* could go for a wander?' I suggest. 'Just down to the lake and along a bit, if you like? It's getting cooler now.'

'Okay. I'll just get changed.'

'Great.'

I put the flowers in a bucket, deciding that I'll ask Clemmy when I see her if she has a vase I can borrow. Then we wander down to the lake and have a really lovely walk. Toby's had a productive day and he seems much more relaxed about the whole crisis-at-work thing. It's early evening and the air is very still with the odd midge flying about. But even this doesn't seem to bother Toby tonight.

When we get back, I decide to barbecue the steak, so Toby

sets it up while I make a salad, prepare the steaks and simmer the mussels in white wine on the little hob.

The meal turns out to be lovely and I'm hoping for a romantic end to the evening. But unfortunately, we left the tent flap open a little and we return later to find we've been invaded by some unwelcome visitors. They're mostly midges as far as I can see, although Toby seems to think we have an army of rampant mosquitoes invading our temporary homestead, which is a whole other level of nasty apparently.

The upshot is we're up half the night trying to eliminate every single one. Toby swears he won't be able to sleep if there's even one insect left flying around. This really tests my patience. And frankly, after the third time he's shaken me awake because he's heard another buzzing in his ear, I want to yell at him to pull the duvet over his head and go to sleep, which is what I'm trying hard to do.

But I know that unless I help him whack the poor things into next week, I'll not get any peace. So, at four in the morning, we're rushing around our lovely tent, armed with a rolled-up copy of the *Financial Times* each, with Toby shouting, 'It's there! On that wall! Get it, Daisy! Damn, you missed it ... over there!'

But the crowning glory happens just before dawn.

I awake to find Toby standing in the middle of the room, rolling up a magazine, a feverishly determined look in his eyes.

'Right. I'm going to *get* that bastard!'

A big bluebottle is flying around manically, buzzing with alarm at Toby thrashing his rolled-up magazine in the air as if he's practising sword-fencing.

Leaping onto the bed in pursuit of the fly, which has landed on the wall behind us, Toby almost crashes on top of me. I roll out of the way and he reaches up and splats the bluebottle onto the wall.

'Ha! Gotcha!' He subsides back onto the bed with a triumphant smile.

It's only then that I realise what he's been using as a fly swat. It's the magazine with my story in it. I'd left it open at the right page so he'd read it – and over the title, there's a giant blood spatter, courtesy of Mr Bluebottle.

'That's my story you've ruined,' I point out testily.

He looks down. 'Oh, shit. Sorry. Shall I chuck it out?'

'No!' I glare at him, horrified he should even think of it.

He shrugs, as if to say, *What have I done now*?

With a loud exhalation, I turn my back on him and pull the duvet over me, not even wanting to *look* at him.

After Toby's efforts, we're now in a bug-free zone.

As for me, I'm fervently wishing it were a *Toby*-free zone.

Would sleep deprivation count as a mitigating circumstance if I accidentally committed a murder?

Chapter 12

What seems like five minutes after I finally fall asleep, an unusual sound wakes me up with a start.

'What the ...?' I struggle to a sitting position, reaching for my mobile, as Toby sleeps on beside me. With a sigh, I realise that the reason it feels as if I've only been asleep five minutes is because it's actually true.

The rooster crows again and I want to cry and throw things because I'm so exhausted after my night of insect warfare. Toby's gentle snoring just adds insult to injury and, even though blissful silence descends after about twenty minutes of almost constant crowing, I still can't get back to sleep. Mainly because I'm now thinking about Maple Tree House and wishing fervently that I'd had the courage to get out of the car when we were there yesterday ...

It's stuffy in the tent but the minute I decide to get dressed, make some coffee and go and sit outside, I hear the patter of rain. Before long, it's coming down heavily, the noise astonishingly loud against the canvas. Amazingly, Toby sleeps through the brief thunderstorm, only waking when I finally get up to boil the kettle soon after eight.

'Coffee?' I ask as he peers outside at the rain-drenched morning.

'Great. Then I'll have a shower and, to be honest, the weather's so revolting, I might as well get some work done.'

'Today?' I stare at him, annoyed. 'But I thought you promised you were all mine today.'

'No. *You* said that.' He grins and I can tell he's feeling cheerful because the weather is on his side. 'But honestly, what can we do in the countryside when it's raining like this? Absolutely bugger all.'

Sighing, I'm about to say that we could always do something else like go to the cinema, which hardly needs a fine day. Whether it's because I'm sleep-deprived or because I'm getting fed up pandering to Toby, I'm not sure, but I suddenly realise I don't especially *want* to be with Toby today.

I only wish I'd brought my car because then I'd be free to go wherever I liked.

'Actually, I think it's a good idea,' I say to Toby and he looks at me in astonishment.

'Really? You don't mind?'

I shake my head. 'You go and do something useful. I'll be fine here, working on my book. I might pop in and see Clemmy later when it stops raining.'

'*If* it stops. Because it looks to me as if it's set for the day,' says Toby cheerfully, heading for the shower. He's obviously cock-a-hoop now that I've handed him a get-out-of-jail-free card.

After he's driven off, I make the bed, propping up all the pillows to make myself a cosy nest, and flop back against them with my laptop, a coffee and one of yesterday's pastries within easy reach on the bedside table. I want to edit what I wrote yesterday.

By lunchtime, the rain clouds have passed over and the sun

has come out. And I'm feeling really groggy by this time from lack of sleep. If I stay here, I'm just going to drift off and waste the day. So I decide now would be a good time to venture on that walk through the woods I discovered the day before. Some fresh air will perk me up.

Packing a sandwich, an apple, some crisps and a large bottle of water into my backpack, along with my pink waterproof jacket, just in case, I set off, zipping up the tent and walking along the lakeside road.

The wet tarmac is sizzling in the heat from the late morning sun. Everything is drying really quickly after the downpour. It must be twenty-five degrees today, at least. I walk past the hotel where there are already holidaymakers in the garden, sipping iced drinks. I spy Sylvia through the window, talking to one of her staff in the restaurant. Thinking of how hard she must work to make the hotel a success makes me feel glad that, for once, I've stepped off the treadmill and am able to let my mind roam free. Did Sylvia always want to own a hotel? What would I do if I could be anything I liked? Anything at all?

The answer to this question is easy and always has been.

I'd be a writer. How amazing would it be to earn a living doing something I really love? I'm aware of how difficult it would be to get published. But there's something about today that feels inspiring. Maybe it's the blue sky after the rain, or the sense of endless possibilities I'm feeling with hours ahead of me to do what I like.

Is my book good enough to start submitting to literary agents or even directly to publishers? Mum thought so but she was obviously biased.

I've never shown the book to anyone but her. Not even

Toby has read it. He hasn't really shown any curiosity about it, but then I suppose he's always so busy with his own work. And of course it wouldn't exactly be to his taste. When Toby reads, it's usually big historical tomes about the Napoleonic Wars or something equally riveting. In any case, I'd be scared he'd think it was rubbish and then I'd have to face the fact that I've been living in dreamland all this time, thinking I might have some talent.

Growing warmer with the exercise, I take off my cardigan and tie it around my waist, so my limbs are bare in the pink camisole top and shorts. Leaving the road, I cross the grass to the edge of the lake. Removing my shoes and socks, I find a flattish rock to sit on and slide my feet into the cold water. It's so clear I can see the green tendrils of some aquatic fern winding round my ankle.

I take out my apple and munch on it, staring out across the lake, trying to think about the heroine in my book, but unable to stop thoughts of Maple Tree House slipping into my head and taking over.

There's nothing I can do today without access to a car. But maybe I could persuade Toby to drive along there later, when he gets back. It's the least he can do, really, considering he promised to spend time with me and I've barely seen him!

A huge yawn escapes. I'm exhausted after getting so little sleep last night during our intense bug massacre. I could just do with curling up on this grassy bank and falling fast asleep. But the sun is beating down and I'd be burned to a frazzle.

I stare longingly at the woods on the opposite bank. They look shady and invitingly cool.

Drying my feet on the grass, I decide to walk barefoot by the lake instead of heading back to the road. It takes longer but I'm enjoying just being out on my own, doing what I like, instead of having to worry about whether Toby is enjoying himself.

An hour later, after a slow meander around the lake, stopping every now and then for a swig of water, I'm finally nearing the woods. I take a last look at the hotel on the opposite bank and I pick out our tent along to the right. Then I take the path into the woods.

I quickly realise that there isn't just one way through. The main path branches off at intervals in different directions, and when I arrive at an ancient horse chestnut tree that seems to be sitting at a fork in the way, I decide to take the least worn path. Toby would think I was silly for doing this. He would say we really ought to stick to the tried and trusted route; that we could land ourselves in danger if we deviate from the path.

But today, the thought of Toby's caution in all things just really irritates me.

To hell with him and his longing to be back in civilisation! I want to make the most of this glorious countryside. So, I'll take the road least travelled and see where it leads me ...

It's cool in the forest and the scents are earthy and intoxicating. The sudden rustles as I walk by tell me I'm definitely not the only creature exploring this woody wonderland today. The trees are magnificent – some of them are so enormous they could have been there for a century. The thought of this makes me feel a little dizzy, as I stare up into the branches of a towering, gnarly oak tree – spying slivers of blue sky above – thinking of the long-dead person who must have planted it.

Every so often, a shaft of sunlight pierces the leafy canopy overhead, spilling dappled sunshine onto the rich earth and twigs beneath my feet.

After an hour or so of walking, I find myself in a little clearing among the trees where the sun filters through, and I decide it would be the perfect place to stop and eat my sandwich.

I sit down on the soft bracken, leaning back against the sturdy trunk of an oak tree, and munch my ham sandwich, lazily waving away the odd flying bug that would have driven Toby crazy if he'd been here.

I smile to myself. There's no way Toby would have sat down. The bugs would have ruined any attempt to relax, and he wouldn't have wanted to get all manner of nasty earthy stuff on his expensive jeans. A fleeting feeling of dismay comes over me when I think of the future if Toby and I stay together.

Will I be sentenced to a lifetime of swatting bugs?

I glance around the clearing, enjoying the peace. If I stay with Toby, it won't be the sort of relationship I dreamed of finding when I was younger. But aren't all those romantic notions of blissful true love and happy-ever-after just something you read about in novels? They're hardly the basis for a life-long relationship ...

I finish my sandwich and take a long swallow of water. Then, feeling the post-lunch dip in energy more than usual because I was up all night with my rolled-up newspaper, I decide I'll have just five minutes lying on the lovely soft green bracken, with my cardigan as a pillow.

Lying down, I close my eyes. It's surprisingly comfortable and I feel like a character in Shakespeare's *A Midsummer Night's Dream*, pausing a while in their nocturnal wanderings to rest under a shady tree.

The sound of birdsong and the breeze rustling gently through the leaves is the perfect soundtrack for relaxation and, within seconds, I find myself drifting off to sleep ...

*

The next thing I'm aware of is opening my eyes and not being able to see a thing.

Panicking, I stare into the pitch darkness.

And then the same old flashback starts playing in my head ...

It's dark and I'm in a spooky place – no houses, just snowy hedges on either side. And I'm running. I'm clinging tight to something I'm terrified I'm going to lose. The scariest thing of all, though, is the hoarse gasping noise that's so loud in my ears. It's as if someone is right behind, trying to catch me – but when I glance back, there's nothing there. Panic grips me. I need to go back but something is stopping me. Then the thing I'm holding slips from my hands and I start to howl ...

An owl hoots close by, jerking me from the dark place in my head.

Sitting up, I hear rustling noises beneath me and I stare into the black void, my heart banging against my ribs. A second later, my eyes start to adjust and, through the grey gloom, I see the ghostly outline of branches reaching out towards me.

And then I remember.

Eating my ham sandwich sitting under the oak tree and thinking I'd lie down and have just forty winks ...

I must have been asleep for hours!

Scrambling to my feet, I dig in my pocket for my phone so

I can switch on the light and find my way out of the forest. But it's out of charge. Horror leaps in my chest at the thought of being trapped in the woods all night. What will Toby think? I've no idea how late it is. Will he be back yet? Will he come looking for me? But he won't have a clue where to find me.

My heart is racing but I tell myself to keep calm. The best thing is probably to try and head back the way I came. But the path, which was fairly faint in daylight, is now almost invisible, so all I've got is my instinct and a rough idea of the direction I came from.

It's just a forest. There aren't any monsters. It's going to be fine.

Something digs me in the back and I scream. Spinning around, I realise it's just a branch and relief makes me laugh out loud at my own ridiculousness.

For goodness' sake, get a grip, girl! It's just a forest. There aren't any monsters.

I shake my head, chuckling at my idiocy. The trouble with having an active imagination is you can end up making a melodrama out of nothing! What on earth did I imagine was going to happen? That I'd be attacked by a mad axe murderer, who lives in the forest and hangs around just waiting for the next knackered explorer to fall asleep under a tree?

I stumble away, trying desperately to find the path, but panic is building inside me. I keep blundering into trees, sharp twigs scratching my face, and getting my feet tangled in what must be fallen branches.

Minutes later, I realise I've lost all sense of direction. I'm staggering around with no idea where I'm going. In fact, I have the horrible feeling I'm probably walking in circles, getting precisely nowhere.

And everything looks so sinister and ghostly ...

Next second, a dark hulking shape rears out of the gloom, and my heart leaps into my mouth. I freeze in horror as The Thing walks towards me.

It's going to get me! I'm going to die a grisly death, right here in this bloody wood! Why didn't I go to Maple Tree House while I had the chance? Now it's too late and I'll never meet my birth mother!

I walk slowly backwards until I can feel the solid trunk of the oak tree at my back. Then I move behind it, hoping The Thing hasn't spotted me.

If I stay here and keep very still, I might just make it out of here alive ...

A torch shines in my face and a gruff voice barks, '*You?* What the hell are you doing roaming the woods at *this* time of night?'

Chapter 13

'I ... er ... I fell asleep.' The voice is vaguely familiar and, if he'd just put that torch down, I might be able to see his face ...

He laughs as if he can't believe it. 'Who are you? Bear Grylls? There are better places to catch up on some shut-eye.'

I swallow hard.

Oh, God. It's him. Last time we met I accidentally revealed Toby's penchant for sex in unusual footwear. But hopefully, he won't remember ...

He shines the torch on my feet. 'No wellies today, I see.'

'No, but I'm wearing my apron under here, if you'd like to take a look!' I shoot back, as my cheeks heat up like a sauna. I'm hoping to flatten him with my quick-fire riposte.

But it backfires spectacularly when he runs his eyes over me, smiles lazily and remarks, 'That's the most exciting offer I've had in a long time.'

Unaccountably stuck for words, I feel heartily glad to be under cover of darkness. Then the torch travels upwards, revealing my flushed face in all its glory.

'I presume you got lost,' he says brusquely.

I grit my teeth. I'm probably more lost than those people in that TV programme, *Lost*, but I'm not about to admit that to him. I'm not sure why but he makes me feel uncomfortable. It's as if I become magically transparent whenever he's there and he can see right into my head.

'I know *exactly* where I am, thank you very much. I was just – er – having a rest before I headed back.'

'Ah, right. Well, in that case, I'll leave you to it.' He turns away and panic sets in immediately.

'Stop!' I try to swallow but my tongue appears to be stuck to the roof of my mouth. 'I mean, could you wait a moment, please?'

He swings round and I'm flooded in light again.

'If you could just turn that torch off!' I snap.

He shakes his head. 'I wouldn't advise it.'

I shield my eyes with the back of my hand. 'Just turn it off! Please?'

'Okay.' He snaps off the torch and we're plunged into darkness so thick, I can no longer see my hand in front of me, never mind find the path to get me home. I guess he's proven his point, which is so bloody infuriating.

But whether I like it or not, I'm totally at this man's mercy if I want to get out of these woods and back to the glamping site.

I heave a sigh and say politely, 'I'd be grateful if you could point me in the right direction for the glamping site, please? And a spare torch would be useful.'

He switches the light back on but trains it on the ground. 'I can do better than that. I can give you a lift.' He motions with the torch for me to follow him.

'No, it's fine. I'll walk.'

'All right. I'll come with you. I'm not going to be responsible for you coming to grief because you're too proud to accept help.'

'I'm *not* too proud.'

'Well, take the lift, then.'

I take a deep breath in. The thought of walking all the way back to the campsite, trying to keep up with this obnoxious man's giant stride, is not an attractive thought.

'Fine. Where's your car?'

'You can trust me. I'm not a serial killer.'

'I expect that's what they all say. Serial killers, I mean.'

'You've got a point.'

'Why are you lurking in the woods at night?'

His mouth twists with amusement. 'I'm not lurking. I'm camping out here for a few days.'

'Really?' *That explains the week-old stubble.*

'Yes, if you'd walked just a few hundred yards further before you decided to have a kip, you'd have stumbled across my ridge tent. Come and take a look if you don't believe me.'

I give him a deadpan look. 'Actually, it's your driving I'm more worried about.'

He fishes in his pocket. 'You take the wheel, then,' he says and lobs something at me that I actually manage to catch.

I give a snort of surprise to find his car keys in my hand. 'No, you're all right. I'll risk it.' I throw them back at him with a little more force than I intend.

He catches them easily and holds out his other hand. 'Jake Steele.'

'Daisy Cooper.' For a second, I feel my hand captured firmly in his and a funny little tingle shivers its way along my arm.

'Come on, then.' He lets go of my hand. 'My car is parked by the lake just beyond the woods.'

'So we're taking a path right through the woods to the other side?'

'Yes, we're tracking the shores of the lake, which is just over there through those trees.' He points to our left, although all I can see is more ghostly shapes.

Toby would say I was putting myself in grave danger, being alone at night in the woods with a strange man. But there's something about Jake Steele that makes me trust him to carry me out of danger.

'Almost there,' he says, probably guessing my thought processes. 'The woods aren't actually that big once you get to know them.'

'Have you been here a while already, then?'

'A few days. Sometimes I come here to work. I like the peace and quiet and the thought that no one will disturb me.'

I make a guilty face. 'Sorry.'

'It's fine.'

'What do you do?'

'I'm a writer.'

'Wow. Really? With a publisher and everything?'

'Yes, the whole works. I'm contracted to write a book a year.' He sounds less than pleased about this.

'What are you writing about at the moment?' I ask curiously, wondering why he sounds so down. If *I* had a contract with a publisher, I'd be dancing a jig every day of my life!

'I'm not. Writer's block.'

'Oh.'

There's a heavy silence and when I glance at his profile his jaw is set and he's staring broodingly into the distance. He might even have forgotten I'm here.

'Maybe ... maybe being out here in the woods will help?' I venture.

He grunts. 'Nothing can help me right now,' he says, and I blanch at the roughness of his tone.

We walk on in silence, crunching over twigs and bracken, and I wonder what could have happened to stifle Jake Steele's creativity. Is there something more than writer's block plaguing him?

He shines the torch to our left. 'My temporary home.'

Sure enough, the light reveals a green ridge tent in the centre of a small clearing. There's evidence of a campfire that's now just smouldering and a folding chair sits beside a small table.

'The car is this way.'

I follow him through the clearing and out into the woods on the other side. Just a hundred yards further on, the trees thin out and the lakeside road comes into view. There's a car parked on the verge. Jake's presumably.

He shines the torch across the lake. 'See where we are?'

'Oh, yes. I've walked right through the woods and come out the other side!' I laugh. 'I'm amazed. I had an awful feeling I might be just walking round and round and getting totally lost.'

'You probably were,' he says bluntly.

'Yes. Well, thanks for rescuing me.'

'A pleasure.'

We get into his car and he starts the engine. 'Did you manage to contact your ... boyfriend? Or should that be husband?'

'Boyfriend. Toby. And no, I couldn't get a signal.'

He grimaces. 'Let's hope Toby hasn't called the police to report you missing.'

I groan. 'God, I hope not.' I fumble for my phone as we drive along the lakeside before remembering it's dead.

'Want to use mine?' Jake hands me his phone.

Toby picks up on the first ring.

'Hi, love, I'm so sorry I couldn't contact you. I fell asleep in the woods and my phone ran out of charge but I'm on my way back now. You must have been really worried.'

'Daisy?' There's the sound of voices and music in the background. He shouts above the noise. 'Daisy? Did you get my message?'

'No, I told you. My phone went flat. Where are you, Toby?' I ask, puzzled.

'In the bar of the Crown Hotel in Guildford. I've booked a room and I'm just going to stay over tonight and come back tomorrow. Is that okay?'

I swallow and glance at Jake.

'Yes, that's fine. Um ... see you soon.' I disconnect the call.

Jake frowns. 'Isn't he there?'

I paste on a smile. 'Yes, yes. He was just ... over at the owners' house getting some pastries for breakfast.'

'Was he worried about you?'

'No, no. I – um – told him I might be late back, so ...' I shrug as if I'm not concerned in the slightest about Toby's lack of concern.

Jake nods slowly. 'He'll be glad you're back, though.'

'He will.' My cheeks are starting to ache with all the forced smiling.

We pull in outside Clemmy's house and Jake turns the car around. It's a narrow road but he executes the manoeuvre with ease. I can't help but think that it would have been a twenty-six-point turn if I'd been behind the wheel.

He leaves the engine running. 'Right, well, enjoy the rest of your holiday, Daisy.' He sits back, looking at me with an expression I can't quite fathom in the dim light.

'I will. And thank you again for rescuing me. God knows what I'd have done if you hadn't. Stayed there till it got light, I suppose.'

'Hey, it was no problem.'

'I hope your writer's block goes away soon. That must be awful, especially if your publisher is expecting you to deliver a book soon.'

'It's not the best situation,' he murmurs.

'When's the deadline?'

'I need to get the first draft written by November.'

I nod. 'I suppose your work doesn't end there, though. It's a long process, publishing a book. You'll have more drafts to do, then all the edits and the final proofread. And then there's all the marketing and promotion to be planned.'

I'm aware I'm stalling, keeping Jake Steele talking. But I've never met a real live writer before. That's probably why I have this sudden urge to stay in the car and carry on talking to him.

He looks surprised. 'You seem to know a fair bit about how publishing a book works.'

I smile ruefully. 'I'm a frustrated writer myself. Well, not a *writer*. A writer is someone who's been published and I haven't even dared show anyone my manuscript yet.' I swallow. 'Except my mum.'

'Did she like it?'

'She loved it. But she's my mum.'

'Why haven't you shown it to anyone else?'

'I'm scared it's not good enough and they'll think I've got ideas above my station.'

'Isn't it worth taking that risk, though? If you don't put it out there, you'll never know how good it is.'

I sigh. 'You're right, of course. But it's ... I don't know. I've wanted it for so long. To be a published writer. I suppose I'm worried that if I start trying to make it a reality, I might be rejected and then all my lovely dreams of making it as an author will go up in smoke.' I give a mirthless laugh. 'And then I'll have nothing to dream about.'

'It took me seven long years of trying and failing and getting more knock-backs than anyone should ever have to deal with. The secret is to keep going.'

'And now you're a success.'

He shrugs. 'Well, my books sell. And that's all I ever dreamed of.'

'Me, too,' I say softly.

'If you go by my experience, being a published writer is ten per cent talent and ninety per cent persistence. So you need to keep going, Daisy Cooper. And show that manuscript to someone.'

'I will.'

'You'd better go in. Toby will be wondering what's keeping you,' he says.

'Yes, of course.' I'm taking up too much of Jake's time. He's here because he wants to be alone to get his writing inspiration back – not to have me bending his ear for ages about being a writer! But when I get out of the car, it's with a feeling of reluctance. I'd love to talk to him some more ...

As I get out, Jake glances across at the campsite and frowns. 'There don't seem to be any lights on in any of the tents. Are you sure Toby's there?'

'Oh, yes. He, er, said on the phone he was really tired and

he was going to bed,' I bluster, wondering why on earth I'm lying about Toby being there, when he's miles away, tucked up in a comfy Guildford hotel for the night! I suppose I don't want Jake thinking my romantic glamping holiday is already teetering on the brink of disaster ...

He nods. 'Well, if you need any advice on the route to getting published, you know where I am. Not that I'm anything of an expert. But it helps to hear of other people's journeys.'

'Thank you.' I duck down and smile at him. Our eyes meet and that funny little shiver runs through me again.

'And if you get lost in the woods again, just scream and I'll know it's you.'

His handsome face breaks into a smile, which makes me feel a little breathless for some reason. Then he reaches across and pulls open the glove compartment. Drawing out a book, he hands it to me.

'Have you read it? Every writer should,' he says.

'*On Writing*. Stephen King. No, I haven't.'

'Borrow it. You'll learn a lot. I certainly did. And it's a great read.'

I smooth my hand over the cover and smile at him, touched that he should trust one of his favourite books to me. 'Thank you. I'll ... bring it back.' I shut the door and give an awkward little wave.

He raises a hand and drives off.

*

As soon as I get inside, I grab my phone, flump down on the sofa and search on-line for 'Jake Steele, author'.

A photo of him appears – making my heart miss a beat with surprise – and after studying it for a moment, I click on the books he's written. There are three of them, all thrillers, and although they're not my usual taste in books, I can't resist ordering a paperback of the first in the series.

Later, I lie in bed, thinking about Jake in his ridge tent.

He's so tall and broad, there definitely wouldn't be an awful lot of room in there for anyone else. But I suppose that's the whole point of his wild *solo* camping experience.

I don't know why, but I get the feeling he's here to escape from something. Or *someone*? Why else would you choose to sleep out in the forest with only woodland creatures for company?

I think about Toby, wondering how he's getting on in his hotel room. I picture him lying on a massive bed, head propped against a dozen pillows, enjoying the luxury of Egyptian cotton bed linen. Padding across the thickly carpeted floor to run himself a bath and soaking there for ages, before calling room service to deliver a haute cuisine dinner.

It seems funny to think of Toby languishing in such luxury, while Jake, in his ridge tent, has all the creature comforts of a night in the jungle.

Where would I rather be right now?

The thought of squeezing into the ridge tent with Jake rushes into my head. It would be an intimate experience, no doubt about it. Would there even be room for more than one sleeping bag ...?

But that's far too disturbing an image and makes me feel oddly restless, so I get out of bed to make some tea. Which is when I find there's no milk left.

Damn! I glance at my watch and peer out of the tent in

the direction of Clemmy and Ryan's house. It's after ten but the place is flooded with light, and Clemmy did say I could call in any time if I needed anything.

So I slip on some jeans and a top, slide my feet into flip-flops and walk over the grass to the house.

Ringing the bell, I feel slightly guilty. But then Clemmy comes to the door and all reservations fly right out of my mind. Her eyes are red and puffy. She's obviously been crying.

'Clemmy? What's wrong?'

She dashes the tears away and pastes on a smile. 'Oh, I'm just all on my own tonight and being ridiculous. It's nothing really. What can I do for you, Daisy?'

'I just need some milk if you have any?' I really don't want to disturb her if she's feeling down.

'Yes, of course. Come in.'

'Are you sure?'

She nods and I can see she's trying to hold in the tears. 'Where's Toby?'

'He's staying in Guildford tonight.'

'Fancy a hot chocolate? I could do with some company.'

'Definitely.' I step over the threshold and follow Clemmy into her big, cosy kitchen.

'Sit down,' she says, and I slide onto a chrome stool at the pale wood breakfast bar, watching as Clemmy takes milk from the fridge.

'So ... how are the wedding plans?' I ask hesitantly. Looking at Clemmy's swollen eyes, I immediately wish I hadn't asked.

She sighs. 'Fine. Everything's organised. The venue, the ceremony, the flowers, the cars, the rings.'

I nod. 'Great. So now all you have to do is look forward

to being the blushing bride and making Ryan cry when he first glimpses you walking down the aisle!'

She smiles and nods.

'You're going to look beautiful. Will you wear your hair up or loose?'

She seems about to answer. Then as I watch in alarm, the façade slips and her face crumples.

'I haven't even thought about it, Daisy.' A single tear rolls down her face. 'To be honest, I'm not even sure there's going to *be* a wedding.'

'Clemmy, what's happened?'

I jump off the stool and go over to her, but she turns her back on me and concentrates on pouring milk into a pan and setting it on the hob. After several failed attempts at lighting the gas, she cries out in anguish and thumps the side of the cooker. Gently, I move her aside so I can help.

'Is it Ryan?' I ask, and her shoulders start to shake.

I abandon the milk and lead her back to the breakfast bar, where she slumps on a stool, resting her head in her hands, her gleaming red hair tumbling forwards.

'Maybe I'm just being silly but I don't think I am,' she mumbles. 'Ryan and I – we had the perfect relationship. But everything's changed.'

She looks up at me. Mascara is mixed with her tears.

'How have things changed?' I ask gently.

She throws up her hands. 'We used to tell each other everything. I mean, of course the relationship wasn't perfect. No relationship is. But we seemed so utterly right for each other and I always knew that he felt the same. He used to tell me he couldn't believe his luck having me in his life and that I made him feel whole.' She laughs sadly. 'I know it sounds corny but it was one hundred per cent genuine. And I knew it because I felt exactly the same.'

I squeeze her hand. 'It does sound perfect.'

She dashes away her tears. 'It was. And then it wasn't.'

I fish in my pocket and manage to find a clean paper hanky. She takes it and blows her nose loudly, and we exchange a little smile at the trumpeting sound.

'So what happened?' I ask.

'He's just ... *distant*. That's the only way I can describe it. And he's working late so often. Tonight, he's staying over in London and he never used to do that. However late his meeting went on, he always came home afterwards. I used to suggest he book into a hotel instead of having to make the journey back here after an exhausting day, but he was always adamant. A day wasn't right, he used to say, if he didn't start it and end it by my side.'

A lump rises to my throat. 'Aw Clemmy, that's so romantic!'

I can't imagine Toby saying something like that to me. Well, actually, I can. But it would be: *A day isn't right if I can't start it and end it with a phone call to the office!*

Clemmy sniffs and gives me a watery smile. 'I know. Isn't it? But these days, it's as if all the enchantment has gone out of the relationship. For him at least. I feel exactly the same as I ever did about him. Ryan will always be the only man for me.'

'Maybe he's just stressed about the wedding? It *is* one of the biggest stresses, after divorce and bereavement. Or so they say.'

She nods. 'Maybe. I hope so. Because the alternative is that he's got cold feet and doesn't know how to tell me he doesn't want to get married.'

I shake my head. 'I think you're jumping to massive conclusions there. Honestly, I do. I mean, he's never said anything to that effect, has he?'

She shakes her head.

'Well, there you are, then. And he's given you no other cause for concern, other than that he's maybe been a bit preoccupied and has to work late?'

She sighs. 'I know. And until yesterday, I kept telling myself not to be so silly. Of course he wants to be with me. But now ...'

'What happened yesterday?' I ask in alarm.

She stares down at her hands. 'There was a message on his phone. You were here when I looked at it, actually. He was upstairs and his phone was lying on the table, and I know I shouldn't but sometimes it's impossible *not* to look at a message that pings through for someone else ...'

'What did it say?'

She looks up, her face ashen. 'Of course it might be totally innocent. But it said: *Can you get away tonight and meet me later?*'

I stare at her, my mind reeling with possibilities.

'That could mean anything,' I say at last. 'It doesn't mean Ryan's up to anything ... with anyone. Was there a name?'

'No, nothing.'

'Well, it might be a mate suggesting the pub, or a relative wanting to – um – give you a wedding present?'

'But surely if it was family or a friend, the name would have come up.' She's right, of course.

'Why not just tell him the truth, Clem? That you saw the message by accident and you were wondering who he was meeting? There's probably a perfectly innocent explanation.'

She nods and attempts a smile. 'You're right. I'm probably over-dramatising it and reading something into the words that isn't even there!'

'Precisely,' I say, forcing myself to sound certain.

Because how awful would it be if Clemmy's instincts about Ryan are correct?

Chapter 14

Next day, I poke my head out of the tent to the perfect summer's morning. The sun is shining in a clear, forget-me-not blue sky and it's obvious the forecasters have got it right.

It's going to be a blisteringly hot day.

Toby phones and says he'll be back around seven p.m., and I find myself feeling quite pleased at the prospect of another day on my own. I plan to settle down and read the Stephen King book Jake let me borrow.

It's such an absorbing and entertaining read, and I'm learning so much and picking up so many tips, that it's midday before I realise it.

Inspired by what I've been reading, I decide to take another look at my manuscript. I've thought of a new twist that I think will raise the story to a whole new level and I'm eager to start writing.

Clemmy pops her head in around two o'clock and our chat turns to the fruitless trip to Maple Tree House the day before yesterday.

'I can't stop thinking about it,' Clemmy says, sitting cross-legged on the grass outside the tent, and reaching for the glass of chilled lemonade I've brought out. 'I keep wondering if I should have tried harder to persuade you to speak to that woman when you had the chance.' Her rosy cheeks are glowing and she looks genuinely anguished.

I sit down beside her, so we're both staring out over the lake, and take a sip of my own drink. 'I doubt you could have convinced me. I felt too frozen with fear.'

'How do you feel now?'

I shrug. 'My head is all over the place, to be honest.'

Clemmy gives a rueful smile. 'I'm too impulsive. If I was in your situation, I'd probably have gone straight up to her and introduced myself and made a total hash of the whole thing, so I really admire your restraint. But ...' She shrugs helplessly. 'I just can't imagine how you must be feeling, knowing she *might* be the owner of the pink handbag. And she *might* be your birth mother. And yet not actually knowing.'

'The not knowing is killing me,' I admit softly.

'I could drive you back there if you want,' she offers. 'I've got some time later on, if ...' She gazes at me expectantly.

I think of pulling up in Clemmy's car outside that house again – and instantly, an entire flock of birds are flapping in my chest, making me feel panicky and breathless.

I shake my head. 'Thanks, Clemmy. But not today. Can I take a rain check on that offer, though?'

'Of course. Any time. Just say the word. I take it Toby is working again?'

I nod, trying to look cheerful about it. 'Crisis at work. He didn't want to go but I think he felt obliged to. The pressures ...'

Clemmy nods understandingly, while I stand there wondering why on earth I'm always trying to make people see Toby in a better light. It was a complete lie about him not wanting to go to work today.

A rogue thought slips into my head. Does Toby deserve me sticking up for him? Aren't I always thinking of what will make him happy? Whereas he knows how much becoming a published author would mean to me and yet he hasn't even bothered to ask me how the book is going while he's off *working* when we're supposed to be on holiday. It's fairly clear that, despite me doing well in the short story competition, he thinks my writing is just a little hobby and that I wouldn't have a hope in hell of succeeding.

How would I cope if we ended up going our separate ways? There'd be no more evenings eating Chinese take-out, followed by a cuddle on the sofa watching *The West Wing*. No more lovely, cosy Sunday lunches round at his old family home. No more meeting Rosalind in town, laughing and chatting over coffee about everything under the sun. Just like I used to do with Mum.

Our parting would leave a gaping hole in my life, that's for sure. A big lump rises in my throat at the very thought.

I'd miss Rosalind so much ... and Toby, of course.

'I need to get back,' says Clemmy, standing up. 'Poppy wants to chat about the stall for the summer fayre on Saturday.'

'Sounds good. Where's it being held?'

'In a big field next to the Starlight Hotel. You'll still be here on Saturday. You and Toby should both come along.'

I smile ruefully. 'I can't speak for Toby. I have a feeling he might be working. But I'll definitely be there.'

'Great!' She peers at my book. 'What's that you're reading?'

I show her the cover and, to my annoyance, find myself blushing. 'It's a book about writing. It's a brilliant read.' I'm about to tell her about Jake but something stops me.

To cover up my sudden awkwardness, I busy myself taking our empty glasses back into the tent. Clemmy calls that she'll probably see me later and goes off, back to Lakeside View.

I sit on the bed, smoothing the cover of Jake's book, thinking about its owner. It's a well-thumbed copy, obviously much-loved. Perhaps I should return it to Jake now before he has a chance to start missing it.

Men can be very particular about their possessions.

Toby, for instance, is a bit funny about the *Financial Times*. Woe betide anyone who removes his copy from his bedside table to the magazine rack. I'm obviously talking about me here. I did that once and I think he thought I'd thrown it out. His face went so pale, I honestly thought he was about to keel over with shock.

This makes me think about the magazine I placed on his bedside table when we arrived. As far as I'm aware, he still hasn't read my story. He's said nothing about it if he has ...

It's just after four and Toby won't be back for at least another couple of hours. Just time to go for a walk around the lake and into the forest ...

There's a buzz in my veins as I set off. I think it's the thought of being able to talk books again with Jake that's putting a spring in my step, because I really enjoyed that last night.

Toby glazes over almost immediately if I start talking about books. They're just not his thing. And I can understand that. I get a bit glazed myself when he gives me his regular résumé of the week's peaks and troughs in the stock market, when we're reading in bed on a Sunday morning.

It never used to bother me that Toby didn't take much

interest in my writing. I told myself he probably played it down because he wanted to protect me from getting hurt by the rejections that would surely follow if I actually submitted the manuscript.

But now it's starting to bug me.

I'm not sure I'm prepared to give Toby the benefit of the doubt any more. I should face facts. He doesn't ask about my writing because he's simply not interested. But he should be, shouldn't he? If you love someone, surely you want to know everything about them ...

Pushing these uneasy thoughts about Toby from my mind, I walk on, my cardigan slung over my shoulder.

Finding Jake's camp again turns out to be easier than I thought it would be. It seems a much shorter distance this time – but that's probably because I'm not absolutely exhausted today, it's not late and pitch black, and I also know now that I shouldn't deviate from the main path.

I'm feeling unusually hot and sweaty by the time I get there, so I lurk behind a tree and whip my can of antiperspirant out of my backpack. Pulling out the neck of my T-shirt, I give a good long refreshing spray, the cold sensation making me gasp. Then I tackle the slightly awkward task of aiming the nozzle under each arm beneath the T-shirt.

'Daisy?'

I freeze at the sound of Jake's voice behind me.

Not wanting to be caught looking dodgy, with my hand plunged down my top, I let go of the can and trap it with my elbow before it has a chance to clatter to the ground. Then I spin round.

He's looking at me with a faintly puzzled expression, presumably wondering what on earth I was up to, fumbling with myself behind a tree.

'Jake. Hi!' I paste on a beaming smile. 'You just caught me studying the – erm – flora and fauna.'

He looks surprised.

'Yes, there's so much to discover in a forest, don't you think?' I bluster on. 'The trunk of this tree, for instance. It's just so incredibly ... erm ...'

'Brown?' he says, looking bemused.

'Yes! Brown. The colours in nature.' I shake my head. 'Amazing. I've brought your book back,' I add hurriedly, just in case he thinks I'm a stalker.

'That was quick! But thanks. I've just put water on to boil. Would you like some tea?' he offers.

'Yes – I couldn't put it down! And I'd love some, thanks.'

Following him across the clearing to his camp, I swiftly rescue the antiperspirant can and pop it back into my bag.

'Have a seat.' He indicates the solitary camp stool.

'No, it's fine. I'll just sit down here,' I say, lowering myself onto a grassy patch and admiring the campfire.

'Watch the snakes, though,' says Jake. 'Nothing worse than feeling one slithering up your trouser leg.'

'Snakes?' I stiffen and bring my knees up. 'Where?'

He grins. 'Sorry, couldn't resist it. No snakes as far as I can see. I think you're safe.'

My shoulders slump and I breathe again.

'And even if there is the odd snake or rat, the fire will no doubt ward them off,' he adds.

I shoot him a highly sceptical look. 'It's a lovely fire.'

'Made the manly way, without matches.' He twists his lips in a wry grin.

'Really? Did you forget matches?'

'I just grabbed the tent and a few things nearby and left.' A dark shadow crosses his face. 'Sometimes you just need to get away.'

I nod, studying his profile as he stares away into the trees, looking lost in some private torment.

I clear my throat and he snaps back to the present. 'Which is why I'm experimenting with a different sort of tea today.' He shrugs at my bemused expression. 'I forgot to bring teabags.'

'Ah. So what ...?'

'Ants,' he says with a perfectly serious expression. 'You've got to be prepared to eat all manner of things when you're out in the wild.'

I stare at him in horror, then I realise his mouth is snaking up slightly at the corner. I shake my head. 'Good try.'

'You're right, of course. No insects were harmed in the making of this beverage. It's nettle tea.' He reaches for the solitary tin cup, pours in some steaming liquid from the pan and offers it to me.

I take the cup and peer doubtfully into its murky depths. 'It's meant to be good for you, isn't it? Nettle tea.'

'I believe so. Never tried it myself.'

I laugh. 'Oh, charming, so I'm your guinea pig!'

He shrugs. 'Well, if you're not brave enough ...'

My hackles automatically rise. I take a determined sip and almost burn my tongue off, although I try not to let it show. The 'tea' has a strong, earthy flavour, like spinach. I make an involuntary revolted face and Jake laughs loudly. It's a lovely rich sound, echoing through the trees, and it seems to reverberate deliciously through my whole body.

'Not as good as English breakfast, then?' he asks.

I shake my head, mesmerised by the way his smile transforms his face.

Dark shadows underscore his eyes and the hint of weariness is still there, but this is the first time I've seen Jake's face relax into a genuine and full-on smile.

I'm burning with curiosity to know what's eating away at him. What has happened to make him want to escape civilisation in such a rush and take refuge in the woods? What sadness is he running from?

'How did you make the fire without matches?' I ask. 'Did you call Bear Grylls?'

'Just some useless information I've retained from somewhere.' He shrugs. 'I used the friction method with a couple of sticks.'

I nod. 'So ... are you escaping from life? No, hang on, you're here to get first-hand experience of survival in the wild for your next book!' I say, hoping he doesn't think I'm fishing. Which of course I am.

He shakes his head. 'The book I'm writing just now is set in Manhattan. Not much need for survival techniques there.'

'When will it be published?'

'Not till next summer.'

'But your next book's coming out soon?'

He nods. 'October.'

'Ooh, exciting!'

We lapse into silence, staring into the fire. He's lost in thought again, somewhere distant that etches pain on his face. I'm just starting to wonder if he's even remembered I'm still here, when he turns.

'You were right with your first guess,' he says.

I frown. 'Escaping from life?'

He nods. 'I suppose I'm in mourning.' He frowns, thinking about this. 'Funny, I never thought of it like that. I just knew I needed to get away from everything.'

'I'm so sorry,' I whisper. 'Was it ... someone close?'

He gives a jagged sigh. 'Yes.' I can tell by the tension in his jaw that he's having to force himself to hold it together. 'Laura. She was ... well, she was very special.'

The way he says the name, Laura, drawing out the syllables, squeezes my heart.

'She was an actor. An incredibly talented stage actor, in fact. Well known for her Shakespearean work. But she ... she died.'

'That's awful,' I whisper. 'How?'

Jake is staring into the fire, his face suddenly gaunt and grey. 'She drove too fast round a bend and ploughed into a tree.' There's a tense silence as I absorb the shock of this. Then, wearily, he adds, 'I blame myself.'

I gulp. 'Why? Were you there?'

He doesn't answer for a moment and I begin to wonder if he's even heard my question. Then he turns, as if he's just registered my question.

'No, Laura was alone in the car. But we'd just had a row and she drove off at speed in a bit of a state.' He shrugs. 'I keep thinking that if we hadn't had words, she might still be here.'

I frown, trying to understand. 'But you can't blame yourself just because you had an argument.'

'Yes, I can.'

'What ... what did you argue about?'

He shakes his head. 'Nothing, really. That's the sad thing.

A well-known journalist wrote some really scathing things about my latest book in his newspaper column and, as a result, it totally bombed. I'd just had the abysmal sales figures through so I was in a foul mood, and Laura started saying that I shouldn't just blame the bad review for the slump in sales. She said if I'd made more of an effort with the publicity side of being an author and worked at growing my fan base, maybe it would be a different story. She was right, of course, but I was in no mood to hear the truth.' He shrugs. 'I've always hated the whole thing of having to be active on social media and give interviews. Laura used to keep my website up-to-date, mainly because she was so much better than me at that sort of thing.'

'You still shouldn't blame yourself for ... what happened to Laura.'

'Maybe not. But I just can't stand the fact that the last time I saw her we argued.' He gives a heavy sigh. 'Sorry. I'm not great company at the moment. That's why I came here. I bloody deserve myself.' He spits these last words out angrily.

'I'm really sorry,' I whisper, feeling his pain. It's clear he loved Laura very much. How awful to be left with such great regrets ...

He forces a smile. 'Thanks. Yeah, it hasn't been the best of years. And if the next book doesn't sell more than a handful of copies, I can kiss my writing career goodbye.'

'Surely not.' I gaze at him in horror. 'Your next book will be a success, I'm certain of it.' But the words sound hollow and rather naive.

'I like your confidence. But when your book has been trashed by a well-respected reviewer, absolutely nothing is certain.' He glowers into the flames. 'I'd love to get my hands on that journalist. I doubt he'd even read the bloody book!'

We're both silent for a while.

Then he turns with a wry smile. 'Sorry. I suppose it's the grief talking. As you can tell, journalists aren't exactly my favourite people in the world. I'd lock them all up and throw away the key ... if it were up to me.'

I swallow. 'No, of course. I mean, yes, I don't blame you ... for – erm – thinking that.'

He frowns. 'What is it *you* do, anyway?'

'What do I do?' Confused, I stare at him.

'For a living? You said you write in your spare time, which suggests you've got another job?'

'Ah, yes.' Feeling a flush creeping into my cheeks, I swallow hard. 'I'm – well, it's funny you should ask.'

I'm a journalist.

I'm one of those bloody pariahs that you hate so much.

'Well, it's not funny at all, actually, because the fact is, I'm – erm ...'

Oh God, I can't tell him I'm a journalist! Not after the conversation we've just had about his book bombing!

I take a deep breath. 'Actually I'm – um – I'm a financial analyst!'

'Really?' He looks surprised, as if this was the very last thing he was expecting to come out of my mouth.

He's not the only one ...

My whole body is hot with shame.

What the hell made me say that?

As Jake gets up to throw the rest of the nettle tea away, I surreptitiously pull out the neck of my T-shirt and blow a waft of cooling air down it.

'So what do you analyse?' he asks, sitting back down and

looking fascinated.

My stomach drops. 'Oh – erm – this and that, you know. The Footsie? The stock market? The Dow James? That sort of thing.'

He grins. 'You mean the Dow *Jones*? Or is that some sort of private joke among you analysts?'

My face must now be the colour of cooked beetroot.

'Haha! Yes! We analysts never stop larking around. Honestly, it's just one big laugh-fest where I work.' I shake my head fondly. 'The Dow James. Hilarious!'

'I always imagine it to be quite labour-intensive, the work of a financial analyst,' he says. 'The guys I know never even seem to have the time to take holidays.'

I nod with confidence, thinking of Toby. 'That's very true. We almost didn't make it here.' I give a casual shrug. 'Big meetings with investors, high-level negotiations ... sort of thing.'

He nods sagely and I congratulate myself. I almost sound as if I know what I'm talking about!

'Toby must be very patient,' says Jake.

'Yes, I suppose he is, considering the workload his boss expects him to undertake.'

Jake looks surprised. 'Toby's an analyst as well?'

I stare at him. I'm such a rubbish liar, it totally slipped my mind we were supposed to be talking about me.

'Oh. Yes.' I nod enthusiastically. 'Toby's an analyst. He's a much better one than me. That's – er – that's how we met, in fact.'

'Working for the same company?'

I nod, frantically searching my brain for a speedy exit before I do a Houdini and tie myself in complete knots.

Jake's mouth curls up at the corner. 'You're not a financial analyst, are you?'

I shake my head. 'No, I'm not.'

His brow furrows a little. 'So why ...?'

I shrug, feeling really stupid for telling such a big fat lie. I feel like a naughty child.

'I write for a trade publication. I didn't want you to think I was one of those journalists you hate.'

'Ah.' He nods. 'What's it called, this trade publication?'

I cringe like I do when anyone asks this question. 'What would you like it to be called?'

He laughs. 'That bad?'

I nod. '*Plunge Happy Monthly*.'

'Oh! That sounds ... fantastic.' He's trying hard not to smile.

'Go on. You can laugh. I'm used to it.'

His lips twitch. 'Never. And, for the record, I could never hate you.'

His eyes meet mine and linger there, and a funny little shiver runs all the way up my spine. *What's happening to me?*

Then I remember his grief over Laura and the moment passes.

I search for a safe topic. 'I've just finished writing the first draft of a book!'

'That's great.' Jake looks impressed.

'It's taken me five years, though, and there were times I thought I'd never finish it.'

He nods. 'That often happens with the first one. What's the book about?'

Flushing, I give him a brief summary of the plot.

'Sounds good. What pushed you to finish it in the end?'

I swallow hard. 'Well, I ... I lost my mum earlier this year. She always believed in me. I suppose I'm doing it for her.'

His face is full of compassion. 'I feel for you. I've gone through a similar thing. Losing someone is the pits.'

I nod sadly. And then for some reason I start telling him about how she was actually my adoptive mum, and that part of the reason for being down here this week was to find out more about my actual birth mother.

'Something stopped me knocking on the door of Maple Tree House,' I add sadly, after describing how Clemmy took me there in the car. 'I just couldn't do it.' I shrug. 'I'm thinking it might be best to just remember the loveliest mum I could ever possibly have had. And leave it at that.'

He nods slowly. 'Maybe. I suppose you never know what you're going to find.'

I sigh. 'That's the thing.'

'You might want to try again.'

I swallow hard. 'Can't today. Toby's away with the car.'

He looks puzzled. 'All day?'

I nod with a sheepish smile. 'He's working from the Guildford office. Toby finds the countryside ... *challenging*.'

'Ah.' Jake nods thoughtfully.

I shrug. 'But never mind. It's given me a chance to talk books with you!'

It seems so natural talking to Jake, even though part of me can't quite believe I'm telling all this to a relative stranger. Jake is easy to talk to, though. Maybe it's because we have a love of writing in common.

He listens attentively as I talk about Mum and how I found the handbag after she died. And the envelope with the scribbled address on it.

It feels so good to talk about it; to describe Mum's best qualities to someone who seems genuinely interested, knowing that he's seeing the person who meant the whole world to me through my eyes ...

'Does the heroine in your story find her lost sister in the end?' Jake asks, when we get back onto the subject of writing.

'Hattie? Yes, she does. Her sister, Jenny, has been living in a squat, too ashamed to go home but secretly longing for her family to come looking for her.'

He nods thoughtfully. 'I suppose Hattie could have given up on finding her sister when it seemed impossible. No one would have blamed her.'

'True, but that wouldn't be a great story, would it? I wanted to write about a feisty, resourceful heroine who's scared of what she'll find but is nonetheless determined to do whatever it takes to uncover the truth about her beloved sister.'

'I'd like to read it,' says Jake.

'Really?' I shake my head, feeling pleased but shy all at once. 'You don't mean that.'

He frowns. 'What makes you say that?'

'Well, you're a successful writer. You must have loads of aspiring Stephen Kings asking you to give them your opinion of their work.'

He grins. 'One or two, I suppose. But seriously, you've sold me the story with your description of your battling heroine and the high stakes she's faced with. I'm intrigued.'

I can't help the delighted smile tugging at the corners of my mouth.

A real writer wants to read what I've written!

It's quite a terrifying thought, to be honest, but maybe it's time I left the safety of my writing cave and started putting the results of my efforts out there.

There's always going to be the risk of rejection. Even J.K. Rowling must have at one stage felt she'd never make it as a writer. I heard that her first manuscript was turned down by no less than twelve different publishers before Bloomsbury spotted something they liked ... And what was it Stephen King said in the book? When he started writing, the nail on his wall eventually couldn't support the weight of rejection slips impaled upon it. So he replaced the nail with a spike and carried on writing ...

'So will you?' Jake is smiling. 'Let me read your book?'

Shyly, I nod.

'You clearly know what makes a great story. The kind that draws in the reader and has them rooting for the main character right from the start. But one thing does puzzle me.'

'What's that?' I stare at him, my heart sinking.

Oh God, here we go!

Jake has detected a flaw in my writing even before he's read a single word!

'No, it's just that you've given your heroine, Hattie, an epic journey with a hugely satisfying ending. And yet in your own life, you're thinking of giving up on your search at the first hurdle.' He shrugs and his unspoken question hangs in the air between us.

A quiver of nausea snakes through me. He's right, of course.

He looks genuinely interested in my answer but he's taken the wind out of my sails. My mouth opens but I'm at a loss as to how to answer him.

'You can tell me to shut up if you like,' he murmurs softly, seeing my expression. 'I know you're more than capable of doing that.' He twists his lips in gentle amusement. 'It's just that you seem to me to be every bit as feisty and resourceful as Hattie. Don't you deserve the same chance you've given her to find what you're looking for?'

'But Hattie's just a character in a book,' I blurt out. 'It's pure make-believe. A fantasy. In real life, there's absolutely no guarantee of a happy ending.'

'True.' He shrugs. 'But you never know ...'

I stare at him, tears pricking at my eyelids.

You never know ...

Chapter 15

I can't believe I'm doing this.

That disgusting nettle tea must have held some kind of devilish magic potion. Because how else can I explain the fact that after deciding I was going to stop the search for my real mum even before it started – and instead, just feel thankful for the wonderful one I already had – I'm now in Jake's passenger seat, my stomach in knots, watching the scenery in a daze on a return visit to Maple Tree House?

'Okay?' murmurs Jake.

I turn and smile at him. 'No.'

He chuckles. 'I think that's to be expected.'

'I think I might be sick.'

'Deep breaths.'

I do what he suggests and, actually, I do feel calmer.

But then we turn into the cul-de-sac and Maple Tree House comes into view, and my heart starts banging so loudly, it feels as if it's about to break out of my chest altogether in a desperate bid for freedom.

Only Jake's calm and reassuring presence is keeping me from flipping the door lock and hurling myself from this moving vehicle!

We draw up outside Maple Tree House and Jake turns

off the engine. Then we sit in silence for a while, looking over at the house with its perfectly manicured garden and the spotlessly clean, white Mini Clubman parked on the driveway.

I take a deep breath to calm my nerves. Then another and another.

'Right. I'm going.'

Jake nods. 'Good luck. I'll be waiting here.'

A wave of gratitude washes over me and I smile at him. 'Thank you for this.'

'Hey, no problem. If your birth mother really does live here, this is her lucky day.'

I groan. 'Let's hope she thinks so.'

I get out of the car and walk through the garden gate on legs that feel like they might give way at any moment. *How am I even going to introduce myself with my tongue welded with fear to the roof of my mouth?*

I ring the bell and stand there, holding the pink handbag behind my back, waiting for someone to answer the door. And at the same time, desperately hoping no one comes.

Through the bevelled pane of glass, a figure appears, walking towards the door. The shape is definitely female. There's a whining noise in my ears and I feel a little faint.

What shall I say? What shall I say?

Hi there, I really hope you don't mind me coming here but is this your handbag by any chance? And if it is, do you think I might be your long-lost daughter?

Oh God, no, I can't say that. The woman might think I'm a deranged bunny-boiler-stalker-type person.

Breathe, breathe.

The door opens and the woman Clemmy and I saw the

other day is standing there. She glares at me and looks pointedly at her watch.

'Hi there,' I begin, aiming for warm and friendly, and definitely not strange weirdo. 'I really want to apologise for just turning up—'

'Late?' she snaps. 'Yes, you most certainly are!' She brandishes her watch at me. 'I honestly don't know why I persist in using this agency – it would probably be less hassle to do my cleaning myself! Still, now that you're here, you might as well get on with it.' Her frown deepens. 'Where's your uniform? I thought at least you cleaning minions could be relied upon to dress appropriately. Jeans and a flimsy top are hardly suitable. Still, I suppose beggars can't be choosers.'

I stare at her in dismay.

She thinks I'm the cleaner!

I shake my head. 'I'm afraid you've got it wrong. I'm not here to clean. I—'

'What do you mean you're not here to clean?' she barks. 'You have to. Do you know who I am?'

I wince.

'I'm Arabella of Arabella Exclusive Designs.'

When I look slightly bemused, she shrieks, 'The women's clothing emporium on the high street?' From her glare, she might as well have added, *you blithering idiot!* I feel a brief pang of sympathy for any cleaner sent to Maple Tree House.

'The thing is, I'm holding a very important event tonight – a meeting of top VIPs in the world of high-end couture – but I can't *possibly* have people round with the place looking like *this*!'

She pulls the door open further to let me observe the chaos within.

But all I can see is a neat and tidy hallway, with not a single speck intruding on the smooth perfection of the mushroom-coloured carpet.

'I'm really sorry but I'm not from the cleaning agency,' I tell her firmly. 'Perhaps you should give them a ring?'

She sighs and folds her arms, looking thoroughly disgruntled.

I try to imagine things from her point of view. There's nothing worse than having people round for dinner when you feel your house is a tip. Even when it isn't.

Children's voices beyond the gate float over and we both glance across. A group of kids in high spirits are kicking a ball along the street. There's a thud and a cheer as the ball whacks against Arabella's fence.

'That had better not land in my garden,' she calls in an imperious tone, 'because you *won't* be getting it back.'

I can well believe it. And so can the kids, clearly.

There's an instant silence beyond the fence.

Arabella shakes her head. 'Little brats. I mean, I don't *mind* children but I definitely couldn't eat a whole one!' She laughs at her own joke – a series of strange high-pitched snorts – and there's an immediate response from one of the 'little brats' beyond the fence. His impression of her laugh is really rather good. I have to fight to look solemn.

'This is a lovely house. Have you lived here long?' I ask, my heart beating fast.

'Oh, most of my life. I grew up here, and then when Mummy and Daddy wanted to downsize, I was doing well enough to buy it from them.' She leans closer, taps the side of her nose and murmurs, 'Cash,' in a confidential manner.

'Gosh,' I respond obligingly, since it's clear she expects me to be impressed. 'So ... did you have to bargain with your brothers and sisters to get the house?'

She shoots me a sharp look. 'I don't *have* any siblings. Thank God. What is it they say? You can pick your friends but you can't choose your family? No, I was far too deliciously spoilt as a kid to have *ever* wanted to share Mummy and Daddy with some pesky brothers and sisters.'

My heart sinks. It must be Arabella, then. She's the only daughter of Maple Tree House. But could she really be my mother?

My feelings about this are mixed, to say the least.

There's no denying we *look* alike. We both have straight dark hair and hazel eyes, and there's something about the mouth that seems familiar, although I could be imagining that.

If she's the owner of the handbag Mum kept all these years, she could well be my birth mother.

So why am I feeling this sinking sense of anticlimax? And keeping the handbag clutched firmly behind my back, the pink plastic making my hands sweaty?

I suppose that what I feared all along is actually coming to pass. I was worried that, after all my imaginings, I was bound to be disappointed by the reality.

But whatever my feelings about Arabella, I need to know one way or another if she's my real mum. And this is my one opportunity to find out.

Arabella's mobile starts ringing. She answers it and is immediately into an intense conversation about artichokes, presumably with her caterers for tonight. Forgetting all about me, she closes the door without even bothering to find out why I'd rung her bell in the first place.

I stand there for a few seconds longer, feeling strangely numb. Then I turn and walk quickly back to the car.

Jake leans across to open the passenger door and I slip inside gratefully.

'Bad?' he asks, seeing my face.

I blow out a long breath and shake my head. 'I wish I hadn't come here.'

'Is it her? Is she the owner of the bag?'

I shrug helplessly. 'I don't know. She shut the door in my face before I could figure out a way to ask. But she's an only child and she was definitely living here in her teens, so I guess it must be her.'

'You can always go back,' he says at last. 'If you want to.'

I nod. 'I just need to work out how I feel, having met her.'

'Let's go, then.'

We drive back in silence. Toby won't be back for a few hours yet and, to be truthful, I'm glad. It will give me some time alone to think about this weird day. And Arabella.

But when Jake pulls up at the glamping site, I see to my surprise that Toby's car is there.

'He's back,' says Jake, looking over at me with a strangely tense expression. I suppose he guesses I'd have liked to be alone for a bit to think.

'Yes!' I try to look pleased.

'So ... do you think you'll be going on any more woodland walks any time soon?' asks Jake. He's switched off the engine, which surprises me because I assumed he'd drive straight off once he'd dropped me off.

'I ... yes, probably.' Suddenly I'm covered in confusion. Is he inviting me to pop by again? 'I mean, obviously it depends on what Toby's doing ...'

'Of course.' He shifts in his seat and starts the engine. 'Right, well, if you need any more support in your quest, just let me know. I'm happy to be the getaway driver.'

We smile ruefully at each other, and it hits me that, actually, given the choice, I'd rather go back to the woods with Jake now, than go in and see Toby. It might be pretty basic at Jake's camp – and that's a bit of an understatement – but I can relax there and just be myself.

I feel as if Jake has found out more in the past few days about the real me – all my dearest hopes and dreams – than Toby has in the entire three months we've been together.

I feel a twinge of guilt. It's not Toby's fault if his work puts such pressure on him and limits our time together.

It's been lovely talking to Jake about everything – especially the writing – and just knowing he was waiting for me in the car definitely helped give me the strength I needed to knock on Arabella's door. But he's obviously still grieving over his lovely Laura. That much was clear from our conversation earlier.

Laura's death has totally devastated Jake. He's not likely to be looking for a replacement any time soon.

Also, I need to get back to Toby.

Chapter 16

A sigh escapes me as I get out of the car. 'Thank you for today.'

Jake raises a hand in response. 'I meant it about wanting to read your book.'

I smile as I lean back in. 'Okay. But you'd better be kind.' Then I shake my head. 'Actually, no. I don't mean that. I want to know the truth about my writing. Be as horrible as you like.'

He gives me a full-on smile and my stomach flips over. 'Okay. I'll be really mean and nasty. I promise.'

I pull a funny nervous face and, with a wave, he drives off.

I watch the car until it disappears behind the trees, then I straighten up, paste on a smile and walk over to our tent, aware that my heart feels strangely heavy.

Toby pops his head out of the door before I get there. 'I've brought dinner,' he says, beaming.

'Have you? How lovely and thoughtful of you,' I say, taken completely by surprise. Toby flushes a little and shrugs it off.

As I'm stepping inside, there's a big crash from the next tent. It sounds like someone's dropped a pile of plates from a height. I exchange a horrified glance with Toby, just as the man, Dane, charges out of the tent, turning the air blue with a string of expletives. We pop our heads out just in time to see Dane striding over to his car, with Chantelle running after him, begging him to stop.

Dane totally ignores her, gets into his car and drives off with a screech of his wheels on the tarmac. Poor Chantelle stares after the car, then turns and walks slowly back to the tent. Luckily she hasn't spotted us spying on them.

'Oh dear, she's crying.' My heart goes out to her. Dane seems a bit of a bully. 'I'm going over there to make sure she's all right.' I pause at the entrance. 'Do you think I should invite her over for dinner?'

'Really? Are you having a laugh, Daisy? They're probably the sort of couple who exist purely on burgers and chips.' He pulls open the fridge door and brandishes a packet. 'I doubt the lovely Chantelle will be a huge fan of *beef kofta with Mediterranean vegetables*.'

'Toby!' I gasp. 'Don't be such a snob.'

He shrugs, looking a bit red in the face. 'Invite her if you want. I don't care.'

I stare at him, puzzled. 'She'll probably say no.'

'Fine. Whatever.' Avoiding my gaze, he walks through to the bathroom and flicks the lock.

Poor Chantelle is distraught and already halfway down a bottle of red by the time I go over. Apparently Dane has left for good. She seems pleased at the invitation, though, and takes me up on it straight away.

I wait while she changes and she emerges in a short floral dress and a pair of vertiginous heels that aren't hugely suitable for stumbling across the grass to the next tent. I glance at her outfit warily, knowing it's bound to irritate Toby. He'll turn his nose up at that low-cut neckline for a start! I just hope he's polite to her.

I've never seen this intolerant side to Toby's character before and I can't say I like it.

'Oh, what's happened to your arm?' Chantelle asks as soon as we walk in.

'Bee sting,' says Toby.

Chantelle looks horrified. 'Oh, poor you! I hate bees! And wasps. And flies. And moths. And spiders.' She gives an exaggerated shiver of disgust.

'They are pretty disgusting,' Toby agrees. 'Especially the way they invade our space. I mean, what other living thing *does* that?'

She nods as I usher her into a seat. 'Precisely. Even *bears* keep their distance normally. And you'd never see a squirrel just wandering in and getting into bed with you. But insects – they get *everywhere*!'

'Can I get you a drink, Chantelle?' I offer. 'Wine?'

'Yes, it's their total lack of *boundaries* that disturbs me,' says Toby. 'You're right about squirrels. They'd never dream of invading your house but bloody flies just barge in and take over the place.'

I pour Chantelle some wine and leave them to it while I go through to the kitchen to make dinner.

When I return and we sit down to eat, they're discussing the countryside as if it's an alien land to be avoided at all costs. But I'm happy that at least they seem to have found some common ground. The only thing I find a little disconcerting is the extent to which Toby is appreciating Chantelle's low-cut dress. The more wine he drinks, the more he's talking to her cleavage instead of her actual face, which seems quite disrespectful to me.

'Toby, will you *stop* staring at her *boobs*?' I hiss, when she goes to the loo.

He shoots me a bemused look. 'But I'm not.'

I sigh. 'You might not be aware of it, but you've just basically conducted an entire conversation about the evils of cows *with her breasts*. It's embarrassing, Toby. And she's definitely noticed.'

He's looking at me as if I'm a chicken fillet short of an E-cup. 'Honestly, Daisy, I don't know what you're talking about. I happen to think she's got ridiculously large mammaries. Not my thing at all.' He frowns. 'I think you spend far too much time in your imagination. But then, I suppose that's part of trying to be a writer. Making up stuff.'

'I'm not *making up stuff*,' I whisper angrily. 'I saw you with my own eyes. My *real* eyes, not my *made-up ones*!'

Out of nowhere, I'm on the verge of tears. I lurch from the table on the pretence of fetching something from the kitchen.

Toby being in denial about the boob-gazing doesn't particularly bother me. It's quite amusing, really. But his remark about how I'm '*trying* to be a writer' really hurts. It shows, in a nutshell, exactly how seriously Toby views my dearest ambition in life. He still hasn't bothered to read my story, despite nearly destroying the magazine using it as a fly swat.

I think of Jake, wondering what he's doing right now. Boiling water on his campfire to make more nettle tea maybe? I smile at the thought. I doubt that will be happening again after the last lot. Instead, I picture Jake lying on the grass, staring up at the stars in the night sky and dreaming up ideas for his next book.

A pang of real longing hits and the thought runs through my head: *I want to be there, lying on the grass beside him.*

I stand stock still for a moment. Then I wander into the bedroom and subside onto the springy mattress. I've been telling myself that it's our meeting of minds that's the real draw for me with Jake. But perhaps it's more than that. A whole lot more ...

'Daisy?' calls Toby. 'Can you grab the cream from the fridge? I'm ready to serve up.'

'Okay.'

Toby pops his head in. 'Are you okay?'

'Fine.' I stand up, pasting on a smile.

He sighs. 'Look, Dais, I'm really sorry we haven't spent much time together since we've been here.' He pushes me gently back down on the bed, takes my face in his hands and kisses me ever so softly. 'And I'm sorry you thought I was distracted by the boob show. But you must admit they're hard to ignore.'

'You're right there,' I concede, his sheepishly apologetic expression thawing my heart a little.

'Look, how about we get rid of Chantelle after dessert and have an early night?'

There's such a hopeful light in his eyes, I find myself nodding. 'That would be lovely.'

I've been feeling really irritated by Toby's attitude so far this holiday – but on reflection it's not really fair of me to criticise him. Not when I've been spending time in the woods with another man!

It's been an emotional few days and my head is all over the place.

My encounter with Arabella was so dispiriting, I've started

to have second thoughts about finding my birth mum. If it turned out to be her – and I can't see any other possibility just now – I'm not sure Arabella would actually want to know me. Not after her caustic remarks about children. She seems a fairly self-centred sort of person and, if I'm honest, I didn't warm to her at all. I desperately wanted to, but I just didn't.

Perhaps if I got to know her properly, I'd feel differently.

And if she found out I was her long-lost daughter, who knows what a difference that might make to her life? She might have buried the sadness of her baby being adopted deep inside her and grown a hard shell as a result – and that buried grief might well have made her into the rather cold, brittle sort of person she is today.

But this is all just speculation; the product of my imagination. Maybe Toby is right and I live in my head far too much. The truth is, I know nothing about Arabella and, the sad thing is, I'm not even sure I want to now.

After we've eaten dessert and Chantelle has had two more glasses of wine and is almost falling asleep in her chair, Toby murmurs to me that maybe he should walk her back over to her tent.

I flash him a grateful look. By the looks of her, she wouldn't make it over there by herself. And while he's making sure she gets back safely, I'll carry the plates into the kitchen, leave the dishes for the morning and be in bed waiting when Toby returns. It's a long time since he's suggested an early night. Hopefully a romantic night will help revive our flagging relationship ...

Clearing away, I hear Toby shout, 'Careful,' and Chantelle giggling hysterically as he apparently tries to heave her to her feet. I smile to myself, glad he's escorting her back and I don't have to. I run hot water onto the dishes in the sink then I quickly shower, slip into the silky shorts and vest top Toby likes to see me in, then dive into bed. After a second, I leap out again and apply a slick of lip gloss, pouting seductively at myself in the mirror. Back in bed, I wait for Toby to return.

He arrives back twenty minutes later.

'Is she okay?' I ask, worried she's been sick or something and poor Toby has had to clear it up.

He groans, nipping through to the bathroom. 'You don't want to know,' he calls.

I laugh. 'What happened?'

'Oh, she kept falling over and then when we finally got back to her tent, she dropped the key to the padlock and we ended up crawling around on the grass trying to find it.'

'But you managed it in the end?'

'Sorry?'

'You did it.'

'Did what?'

I frown. 'Opened the tent for her?'

There's a brief silence. 'Oh, that. Yes. Yes, of course.'

'So she's fine now? All tucked up in bed?'

He appears at the door. 'Well, I just helped her into the tent and onto the bed. I didn't exactly tuck her in.' He looks a bit flushed at the very thought.

I laugh softly and hold my hand out to him. 'As long as she's back safely. Are you coming to bed?'

'Yes. I'm just applying insect repellent. I'm bloody determined those bastard insects aren't going to get me tonight.'

He returns and slides into bed naked, and I turn towards him with a smile, recalling the early days of our relationship when the sex was really quite good.

He feels a little sticky but I wrap my arms around him anyway, my hands tangled in his chest hair.

'Thank God for an early night,' he murmurs. 'I'm positively knackered.'

Two seconds later, he's snoring gently ...

Chapter 17

Unable to sleep after my night of passion that never was, I lie there formulating a plan.

I'm going to book a night in the local boutique hotel so that Toby has at least one night of luxury. Because he's working so hard, he really does deserve it. Maybe then, after we've had a lovely dinner in the restaurant, we'll both be feeling relaxed enough to let our hair down and enjoy a properly romantic night together.

Romance and sex have never been the biggest features of our relationship, but I'm beginning to think that maybe they should at least be higher up the list than liking the same breakfast cereal and me getting on really well with his mum!

I finally drop off in the early hours. Next morning, when I wake up around eight, I'm surprised to find that Toby's still in bed beside me. I smile as I watch him sleep. Bless him, he certainly deserves a lie-in after all his early mornings. He'll probably still want to go into the office, but that doesn't mean I can't spoil him with a nice breakfast before he sets off.

Quietly, so as not to disturb the sleeping beauty, I climb out of bed, slip into my dressing gown and wellies, pull a comb through my hair and go across to Clemmy's to collect some breakfast pastries.

She opens the door and seems taken aback to see me.

'Morning, Clemmy! I just wondered if Poppy had delivered her pastries yet?'

'Er ... yes.' She blinks a few times then colour rushes into her cheeks. 'Yes, come on in.' She stands back and I follow her through, wondering what's going on. Clemmy is the sort of person who wears her heart on her sleeve and simply can't hide what she's feeling, and she's definitely behaving a little weirdly this morning. I wonder if it's Ryan again?

'Are you all right?' she asks me as she hands over my bag of goodies.

'Yes, I'm fine,' I say, surprised. Then I realise she's probably thinking of our abortive trip to Maple Tree House. I frown. 'Actually, it's not exactly great news.' I need to tell her about going back there with Jake and meeting Arabella ...

She groans, cocking her head to one side. 'Oh, poor you. Do you want to stay and talk about it?'

'I'd love to but I really need to get back. I want to treat Toby to breakfast in bed before he leaves for work.'

She looks bemused for a second. Then she nods. 'Right. Excellent. Well, I won't keep you chatting, then.'

'Thank you!' I call as I scuttle across the grass, pulling my dressing gown around me. When I turn to wave, she's staring after me, a far-away look on her face.

Very odd.

I'll catch up with Clemmy later. For now, I need to get breakfast for Toby, wave him off to work then go and see about booking the best room available at the Starlight Hotel. Perhaps I'll ask them if they'll put a bottle of champagne in the room. Toby would love that.

As it turns out, Toby's planning to work from the campsite today.

I make coffee and we eat breakfast in bed, abandoning the pastries when Toby smiles and asks me if I'm feeling frisky. We finally have the sort of morning I was looking forward to when I booked the glamping holiday in the first place. This new, more relaxed Toby is quite a surprise but I'm definitely not complaining.

'You should go out for one of your walks,' he says as we lie entwined in bed later. Toby is trying to motivate himself to get up and do some work but, weirdly, he doesn't seem as stressed when his mobile rings as he usually is.

'I'm just going to leave it,' he said, yawning and stretching, when it went off a few minutes ago. 'If it's urgent, they'll phone back.'

'I could always stay here and make you coffee while you work,' I suggest now with a flirty smile. 'I could read in the sun. It's such a gorgeous day.'

He frowns. 'I'll just get distracted if you're here.'

I smile mischievously. 'Is that such a bad thing?'

He laughs. 'No. Well, actually, yes, it is – if I'm planning to get any work done, that is.'

'Okay. I see your point. I'll make myself scarce, no problem.'

'Now I feel terrible.'

'No, honestly, it's fine. I'd rather be out and about on such a lovely day. It's just a shame you can't come with me.'

He makes a sad face. 'I know. There's nothing I'd love more than to come for a walk in the countryside with you. But the boss will kill me if I don't deliver this report by tomorrow.'

I play along, nodding in sympathy, even though we both

know Toby just told a big fat lie. (I'm quickly realising that on Toby's list of things he loves doing, a walk in the countryside is probably on roughly the same level as having root canal work done.)

I'm not too disappointed. I want to go to the hotel to book a room for tomorrow night anyway. So at ten-thirty, I leave Toby propped up on the bed, surrounded by papers, and set off for the hotel.

To my surprise, I find Clemmy is in reception, talking to the manager, Sylvia.

Clemmy catches my eye and gives me the same sort of wary look she gave me when I arrived at her door first thing this morning. Then she makes a big show of being delighted to see me, even giving me a hug, which puzzles me even more. She seems to have forgotten that Sylvia is standing there waiting to carry on their conversation.

'Hi, Sylvia. Busy as usual?' I say with a smile.

'That's the catering trade for you.' She smiles ruefully. 'I never seem to stop.'

'It's the summer fayre on Saturday,' Clemmy reminds me, 'and Sylvia has very kindly offered to provide a refreshment stall next to Poppy's cake display.'

'Will you and Toby be at the fayre?' asks Sylvia.

'Yes, we're planning to be. If he doesn't have to work.'

'So what are you doing here, Daisy?' asks Clemmy. 'Booking dinner in the restaurant?'

'Er, yes, I thought I might.'

This is awkward!

I don't really want to confess to Clemmy that Toby's not at all keen on the current living arrangements so I've decided to treat him to a *properly* luxurious stay here in the hotel!

I smile at Sylvia. 'If I could have a word?'

'Of course. I'll be over at the desk.' She bustles off.

'Right, better get back. I've got a dress fitting at twelve,' says Clemmy, frowning.

'Aren't you looking forward to it?' I ask, surprised.

She shrugs. 'Poppy was going to come with me but Keira has a cold and she's taking her to the doctor's. And Gloria and Ruby are going out for the day with Ryan's Uncle Bob.'

'*I* could come to the dress fitting with you. If you like,' I offer.

Clemmy's eyes widen. 'You would? Oh, that would be fab!' She gives a rueful grin. 'It's just I'm sure I've put on weight again, which means the dress will have to be taken out. I could do with your company to cheer me up.'

I nod. 'I'd love to come with you.'

'Why don't I drive you over to see Auntie Joan? She's been having trouble getting hold of you, I suppose because of the stupid mobile signal. But she's dying to see you. And she might be able to tell you more about your adoption – if your mum told her about it.'

'Oh no, I couldn't ask you to do that.' I start distractedly playing with a button on my cardigan, the thought of having a big emotional chat about Mum immediately stirring panic within.

'Why not? I'd like to. I know how I'd feel in your situation. I'd be desperate to find out the truth.'

My heart is beating in my throat, adrenalin rushing through my veins at the thought of speaking to Joan. Clemmy's right. She could have the answers I need about my adoption. Maybe – just maybe – she'll be able to shed some light on the mysterious handbag.

In a flash, my decision to forget about the search is overturned.

I smile at Clemmy. 'Okay. Thank you.'

'Great.' She looks really pleased. 'And I can update you on the wedding shenanigans.' She groans, shaking her head. 'The relatives are driving me up the wall over the table plan.'

Her fed-up expression makes me laugh.

'See you later, then.'

I watch her go, then I catch up with Sylvia who's now chatting to the receptionist about covers for this evening.

'I was hoping to book a room for Friday night? It's a surprise for Toby. He's not enjoying the glamping very much, so I thought I'd treat him to a night here. The rooms look gorgeous on your website.'

She frowns. 'Oh dear, I think we're fully booked. Wait a moment, please.'

After an exchange with the receptionist, she comes over and murmurs, 'We *are* fully booked but there's a room on the top floor that we keep in reserve. It's smallish but it has a four-poster bed, a free-standing bath and a balcony overlooking the lake?'

'It sounds gorgeous,' I gasp. 'But are you sure you can fit us in?'

'Oh, yes. Don't worry about that.'

'It sounds marvellous. As long as we're not putting you out?'

Sylvia smiles. 'Not in the least. All you have to do is have a splendid time with your Toby.'

'Well, thank you.' My spirits rise, thinking I might still be able to make this a memorable birthday for Toby. 'I really appreciate it.'

'Well, all relationships need a little help at times. Not that I'm any sort of an expert, I'm afraid.'

There's a wistful look in her eyes and I find myself wondering if there's ever been a *Mr* Sylvia. Would you ever have *time* for a relationship if you were running a hotel like this single-handedly?

It makes me think about how much I'd love to settle down and have a family of my own. If I'm honest, being welcomed into Toby's large family was a bit of an eye-opener for me. I never expected to feel such a lovely sense of warmth and cosy familiarity ever again – not after Mum died. But they accepted me almost immediately as one of their own. Toby might think it's all a bit full-on and chaotic – being part of a big family – but to me, it seems like bliss.

'You can check in any time after three on Friday,' says Sylvia. 'It'll be all ready for you. And for your dinner reservation, I'll make sure you get the table in the window that overlooks the lake. Very romantic on a clear night with the moon shining on the water.' She smiles a little wistfully.

'Lovely. Thank you so much.'

The receptionist comes over with a question for her and I say goodbye and head out.

There's a poster on the wall by the entrance, advertising wedding packages, and as I walk out into the brilliant sunshine, I have a sudden vision of a church and wedding bells. I'm emerging arm in arm with Toby to the flutter of confetti, and his mum is rushing over with tears in her eyes to draw me into a hug, officially welcoming me into the family.

I hate the thought of a wedding day without Mum. But Rosalind will be there to soothe away my fears ...

Having booked the room for Friday night, I feel a burst of

optimism about my love life. I decide against going over to see Jake later. I'll be out with Clemmy this afternoon anyway. I'll send him the manuscript but it's probably not a good idea to spend any more time with him ...

Not wanting to examine *why* it wouldn't be a good idea, I focus instead on Toby. Thanks to Sylvia, there's no reason why we can't have a wonderful night on Friday.

I'll make sure Toby has the best birthday ever.

*

'God, I knew it!' Clemmy breathes in desperately as the assistant tries to ease up the zip on her glorious cream satin and lace wedding dress. 'It's not going to fit.'

'It's totally gorgeous, though, and it's hardly a drastic alteration,' I point out. Personally, I think Clemmy suits her curves, and if that's what I think, then I'm certain her fiancé has no complaints.

The assistant shakes her head. 'I wouldn't worry. A slight alteration at this stage is quite normal.'

'Except it's usually brides losing weight with excitement, not putting it on with double chocolate muffins. I blame Poppy.' Clemmy tries to laugh it off but I can see the stress in her face. She looks exhausted, as if she hasn't slept properly for days. I have a feeling the little bit of extra weight is the least of her worries.

'You look absolutely stunning in that dress,' I tell her as we leave the shop, and she gives me a wistful smile. 'Let me buy you a coffee. Where's a good place?'

She points at a coffee shop over the road.

Endeavouring to cheer her up, I say, 'Seriously, Ryan is going to think every one of his birthdays – plus a good few Christmases – have all come at once, seeing you walking down the aisle towards him.'

'I love him so much, it hurts, Daisy,' she murmurs, turning slightly puffy eyes towards me as we cross the road. 'But the thing is, there's always been this little voice in my head telling me he's too good for me.'

'What? But that's rubbish.'

She shakes her head. 'I don't mean that I'm a minger or anything. I'm actually quite happy in my own skin. It's just Ryan is so gorgeous in every single way and I can't help wondering sometimes why the hell he's bothering with boring old me when he could have anyone he wanted.' She forces a laugh as if to say she knows she's being pathetic.

'Whoa! Hold on there.' I shake my head at her. 'First, you're definitely *not* boring, Clemmy. You're funny, you're beautiful and you've got the kindest heart of anyone I've ever known.'

Her eyes fill with sheepish tears but I rush on. 'And second, it's because you *love* Ryan so much that you think he's gorgeous in every way, isn't it? So if Ryan is in love with you – and he's asked you to marry him so it's a pretty fair bet that he does – the chances are that *he* also thinks *you* are perfect in every way!'

She sniffs. 'But *I* asked *him*,' she says in a small voice. 'I was the one who proposed.'

I shrug. 'And Ryan said yes! Didn't he?'

She nods. 'You're right, I know. I'm just being daft.'

'Of course you are. You're about to marry the man of your dreams. How lucky are you! If I were in your position, I'd be on top of the world!'

Her expression changes suddenly. She peers at me intently. 'Would you?'

'If Toby asked me to marry him? Um – of course I would!'

I falter slightly over my answer. I've never considered how I'd feel if Toby proposed. But it would definitely be a good thing, wouldn't it?

She closes her eyes and swallows. 'Daisy, there's something I need to tell you—'

We're entering the coffee shop and our conversation is interrupted by a couple of women getting up from their table. One of them smiles at us and indicates that they're leaving if we'd like their prime spot by the window.

'Do you want to sit down, Clem, and I'll get the coffees.' I turn to Clemmy but she's staring over at the counter, a stunned look on her face.

'What is it?' I ask, far too loudly, following her eyes.

'Ryan,' she whispers.

Sure enough, he's standing at the counter, his back to us. He's chatting to a tall, slender blonde-haired girl, their heads close together. As we watch, he nudges her playfully and she looks up into his eyes and laughs. They break apart when the assistant asks what they'd like. Clemmy grabs my hand and pulls me out of the café. Every last drop of colour has drained from her face.

'Do you know who she is?' I ask, my heart beating uncomfortably fast.

She shakes her head. 'Never seen her before in my life. But Ryan clearly knows her *very* well.'

'There's probably a perfectly innocent explanation,' I tell her gently. 'You should talk to him tonight.'

'I can't.'

'Why not?'

'Because he's at a two-day conference in Paris. He's flying out there this afternoon. He'll be back on Saturday.' She turns bewildered eyes on me. 'At least, that's what he told me.'

Chapter 18

'Let's just go straight home,' I suggest.

Clemmy shakes her head. 'No, we're going to see Joan.' She grabs the piece of paper with the postcode and punches it into the satnav.

'But we don't need to go now. We could do it another day, when you're—'

Clemmy turns with a smile that's too bright. 'No time like the present.'

The tension in the car is palpable as we drive the twenty or so miles to the village where Joan lives. Clemmy is no doubt brooding about Ryan and his blonde friend. And as for me, my stomach is churning at the thought of seeing Joan.

On arrival, Clemmy parks by the village green and says she'll take a walk along the high street to look at the shops while I'm at Joan's.

'Will you be okay?' she asks as we part.

I nod. 'And you?'

She shrugs but says nothing.

'There's a nice-looking pub over there,' I say, pointing across the green. 'Let's grab a drink after?'

'A drink or three,' she says with feeling, no doubt thinking about Ryan grabbing that girl around the waist.

'Hey, stop worrying. You can talk to Ryan when he gets back from this conference. He'll set your mind at rest, I'm sure.'

She gives me a half-smile. 'Good luck at Joan's. Phone me when you're leaving.'

I nod, wishing Clemmy was coming with me for support. A message pings through on my phone and I grin when I read it.

'Surprise, surprise. Toby has decided to go into the Guildford office today after all. He says the sheep are getting on his nerves.'

Despite everything, Clemmy giggles. 'Are they bleating too loudly, then?'

I shrug. 'Presumably.'

*

The last time I saw Joan was when she came up for the funeral and stayed overnight to support me, but to be honest, I was on another planet altogether and wouldn't have known even if the Queen had popped in, concerned about my emotional welfare.

When she opens the door, her face lights up in the warmest smile of welcome – while at the same time, her eyes swim with tears. I knew this would happen. Seeing me is bound to make Joan really emotional about Mum.

'Daisy, my love. How wonderful to see you! Come in, come in.'

Joan's brown hair has vibrant strands of auburn and caramel running through it and she's wearing a kaftan-type top in deep turquoise with a jewelled neckline, over loose linen trousers. We hug in the tiny hallway of the cottage and I breathe in the floral scent I remember from last time I saw her. It brings memories of the funeral flooding back but I brush them away and force a smile.

She strokes my cardigan fondly. 'I remember this. It was your mum's favourite. She used to say it made her feel like royalty wearing it!'

'Oh, this thing?' I say brightly, looking down as if I've just noticed what I'm wearing. 'Yes, it's a great cover-all. You can wear it over jeans or if you're going out somewhere nice. It's very versatile.' I'm prattling, I know, but panic is rising inside me. Joan's sorrow is like a living, breathing thing in the room with us, and I'm not sure I can handle it.

Her smile wobbles for a second. Then she rubs my arm briskly. 'Come on, love, let's get us a cuppa. Or perhaps you'd prefer a soft drink?'

'I'm ... I'm sorry I've been so bad at being in touch,' I say, watching her pour lemonade over ice into a tall pink glass. 'I've just been – um – so busy.'

She brushes off my apologies. 'Time just seems to run away. Your mum and I always used to say we should arrange to meet up more often, but then we only ever managed once a year. Life gets in the way!'

'She loved her trips down to see you.'

'And so did I.' Her gaze is far away, remembering. 'Now, of course, I wish we *had* made the time ...' She gives her head a sad little shake. Then she rallies herself. 'But it can't be helped. So how are you, Daisy? Tell me what's been happening.'

Sitting in her cosy country-style kitchen, we swap news, Mum never far from the subject, and I start to relax a little. It's comforting being with someone who loved Mum almost as much as I did. Watching Joan refresh the teapot with more boiling water, a sharp pang of longing takes me by surprise. In an ideal world, my biological mum would turn out to be someone warm and homely like Joan or Toby's mum, Rosalind. Not the rather vapid, cold, fashion-obsessed woman that is Arabella. I mean, how could I possibly be her offspring? I've worn double denim in the past and felt totally fine about it!

At last, I pluck up the courage to broach the subject with Joan. When she brings the teapot back to the table, I just come out with it. 'Joan, did Mum ever tell you who my birth mum was?'

The teapot freezes in mid-air as she looks at me, and a strange expression flits across her face. For one wild second, I wonder if she's going to say that *she's* my biological mum. That Mum and Dad couldn't have children so she offered to be a surrogate ...

But next second, my ridiculous hopes are dashed when she says softly, 'Your mum never knew the girl's name. Even though she did actually ...' Joan trails off.

'She did actually ...?'

Joan gets up and crosses to the window, staring out over the garden.

I watch her struggling with whatever conflict is going on inside her, as my heart hammers like fury. Despite the tea, my mouth feels suddenly bone dry.

At last, Joan turns. 'Your mum met her,' she says softly. 'She was just a young girl. A teenager. She came to the house when you were about three or four and tried to take you back.'

A bolt of shock thrusts through me, leaving me temporarily speechless.

Joan pours more tea and sits down in the seat next to me,

laying her warm hand over mine. 'Your mum rang me afterwards, in complete shock.' She shakes her head, remembering.

'So how did she ... I mean, did she just try to snatch me away? The girl?'

'She didn't just try. She actually succeeded. Apparently she was quite hysterical. But your mum managed to get to you just as she was about to whisk you away in a car that was waiting.'

'There was someone with her?'

'Another girl, I think. Your mum couldn't be sure.' She shudders. 'She used to say to me, "What would I have done, Joan, if I'd been too late to rescue her? I might never have seen Daisy again."'

Something occurs to me. 'Oh my God, the nightmare!'

Joan looks puzzled as I stare at her in shock.

'I've never known if it was a nightmare or an actual memory but I've experienced it a dozen times at least. I'm in the dark, running along a lane with giant snowy hedgerows on either side, and I'm desperately afraid. And then I lose something. And even though I don't know what it is, I feel the loss of it like it's the most important thing in the world to me.' I take a big breath in and let it out slowly. 'I guess now I know it actually happened. It was a memory of that time I was snatched from Mum.'

Joan nods eagerly. 'I think you're right. The house you lived in was set back from the main road, at the end of a narrow lane with tall hedges on either side, just like you describe. It happened in January and there was snow on the ground. I remember your mum saying the snow slowed the girl down. She kept slipping in her unsuitable shoes, which was how she managed to catch up with her and wrestle you away from her.

She was home alone because your dad was working late that night.'

'Thank goodness she managed to get me back.'

Joan murmurs her agreement. 'You dropped your teddy bear in the lane and your mum never found it. She thought the girl must have taken it.'

'That's part of the memory,' I gasp. 'I just have this horrible panicky feeling that I've lost something forever. It must have been the teddy bear!'

Joan nods. 'Of course, your mum was scared stiff after that. She realised the girl must be the biological mother, who'd somehow managed to find out where you lived. She never had a moment's peace in that house after that day. Especially when you were at school or where she couldn't keep her eye on you.'

'That's why we moved.' It suddenly makes sense. 'They wanted to make sure I was safe and the girl couldn't snatch me again.'

'Yes. They called the police after it happened, of course, so presumably the girl would have received a caution at least for trying to take you. But your mum was terrified it would happen again. She wanted to move to Scotland, as far away as she could, but your dad persuaded her that Manchester was far enough and it would be easier to keep in touch with everyone here.' Joan smiles sadly. 'In the end, though, she only really kept in touch with me. I think she was worried that if people knew where you'd all gone, word might somehow get back to the biological mother and she'd track you down.'

'Did she tell you about the handbag?' I ask suddenly.

Joan frowns. 'I don't think so. The girl's handbag?'

I nod. 'I think she must have dropped it in the struggle.' I produce the envelope from my pocket to show her. 'This was in a zipped pocket inside. It's got our address scribbled on it. And I assumed the typed address on the envelope must be hers, but now I'm not sure.'

Joan stares at the envelope. 'Have you been to this Maple Tree House?'

'Yes. A woman called Arabella lives there.'

Joan looks at me. 'And do you think she could be ...?'

I heave a sigh. 'I really don't know. She might be. She's about the right age, I think. But something doesn't feel right.' Then I shrug. 'Maybe it's just wishful thinking because I can't really imagine having – someone like her for a mum.'

Joan looks sad. 'Daisy, no one is ever going to be as lovely as your *real* mum,' she says softly. 'And she *was* your real mum. Make no mistake about that. No mother could ever have loved her daughter more than that woman loved you.'

She smiles at me through her tears and I bite the inside of my mouth hard.

'You were truly the light of her life.' She squeezes my hand so tightly, it hurts. 'But maybe you need to give this other woman a chance?'

'It might not be her. Even if she owned the handbag, it doesn't necessarily mean she's my birth mum.'

Joan nods slowly, thinking. Then her eyes widen. 'I think I know who could help. I go to the local WI and one of the members, Lottie, lives in Appley Green, in Acomb Road. She's lived in the same house all her life, so she might be able to shed light on the family who lived in Maple Tree House.' She leans forward. 'Actually, Lottie has a reputation for being a bit – um – *curious*, shall we say?'

'You mean she's the village gossip?'

'Yes. But don't tell her I said that.' Joan smiles. 'If anyone would know about a baby being born years ago at Maple Tree House, it would be Lottie. Would you like me to talk to her?'

I shoot her an anxious look. 'I'm not sure.'

'I promise I'll be very subtle about it.'

'Okay, then.'

My stomach is churning at the very thought of being one step closer to the truth.

Chapter 19

I leave Joan's cottage soon after, promising to keep in regular contact and let her know if I discover anything significant. And she tells me she'll phone me after she's spoken to Lottie.

She hugs me really tightly on the doorstep and I know she's remembering Mum. I cling on to her, the familiar feelings of panic rising up more powerfully than ever, making my whole body tremble.

Clemmy is shocked when I tell her about my biological mother coming to the house and trying to snatch me back.

'But I can't understand how she could possibly have got hold of your address,' she murmurs in wonder. 'Aren't personal details meant to stay private in adoption cases?'

I shrug. 'Who knows? It obviously scared Mum to death, though, and I really hate the thought of how she must have suffered after that. She must have been terrified the girl would come back to try again.'

Clemmy murmurs her assent.

'But aside from that, I'm actually glad she came looking for me because at least I now have a clue to her identity. If she hadn't left her bag, finding her would have been impossible. Joan says she knows the village gossip who's lived along the road from Maple Tree House all her life.'

'That must be Lottie.' Clemmy grins.

'You know her?' I ask, astonished.

Clemmy nods. 'Poppy caters at her dinner parties and Lottie sometimes pops along here to talk over the menu. We have a theory it's just an excuse so she can get the gossip from Poppy over a cuppa in the Log Fire Cabin.'

'Perhaps Lottie will know, then. If there was a baby,' I murmur.

We drive a little way in silence and when I glance at Clemmy she looks far away, wrapped in thought – definitely not like an excited bride-to-be.

'Are you okay?' I murmur. 'Will you phone Ryan tonight?'

She heaves a sigh. 'He'll be in Paris until Saturday. I need to tackle him face to face about this, not over the phone, so it looks like it'll have to wait.'

'It's probably nothing, you know,' I venture, wishing I could be sure it was true.

The look she gives me – full of sad wistfulness – makes me realise she doesn't believe that for a moment.

'Come over later if you like,' I tell her when we arrive back at camp. 'Toby probably won't be back until after nine so we could talk.'

'Thanks, Daisy, but I said I'd help Poppy with preparations for her stall at the fayre on Saturday.'

She looks far away, no doubt stewing over Ryan.

It's only when I'm out of the car and walking over to the tent that I remember Clemmy was about to tell me something in the café, before we were interrupted. After her shock at seeing Ryan with that girl, it must have gone from her mind.

*

I don't know what's wrong with me today but I'm feeling really emotional.

Wandering around the tent, I feel jumpy, like I don't really know what to do with myself. It's a weird feeling. I wish I could call Toby and ask him to come back, but I can't because I know he'll be engrossed in work and won't appreciate the interruption.

In the end, I decide it must be seeing Joan again and talking about Mum that's made me feel as if my mind has been thrown into a whirling pit of unwelcome feelings.

Thinking about it, visiting Mum's oldest friend was always going to be a stumbling block on my route to recovery. Joan is the only person alive who loved Mum nearly as much as I did. Her display of grief was clearly going to have an effect on me.

Needing to shake off my mood, I decide a walk would do me good. I'll email my manuscript over to Jake then I'll go on over there. I bat away a little niggle of guilt. Jake's a friend and I enjoy talking to him. That's all ...

I've almost reached the woods when my mobile rings. It's Toby.

'Just wondered where you are,' he says.

'Oh. Well, I'm out for a walk round the lake.' There's a blaring of a horn in the background. He must be driving.

'Right. So what time do you think you'll be back?'

'I'll be an hour at least. Why?'

'No reason. I'm on my way home but you just enjoy your walk. Take your time and I'll see you when you get back. No hurry!'

I hang up, feeling slightly less shaky inside. I've been trying hard not to feel abandoned by Toby over the past few days.

But he's en route here now so everything will be fine. I'll make dinner and I'll open up to him about everything that's on my mind ...

I think about turning back now so I'm in the tent when he returns. But I really want to make sure Jake has received the manuscript. I won't be away for long.

So I walk on, thinking about Toby's call. He sounded pretty relieved to have missed the walk. Looking back, I realise I made entirely the wrong choice in deciding he'd enjoy a glamping holiday – but I'm learning fast! I guess that's half the fun of embarking on a new relationship – learning all about each other's likes and dislikes and funny little habits.

It's clear that if Toby and I stay together, I'm going to have to get used to doing the outdoorsy stuff by myself. Not that it particularly bothers me. I rather like going for walks alone. It's nice being able to just let my mind drift, instead of finding myself discussing complicated work matters – as I often end up doing when I'm with Toby – and trying my best to understand the job of a financial analyst!

When I arrive at Jake's camp, he's not there. The tent is zipped up and the fire has gone out. A huge pang of disappointment hits, I suppose because it's been a totally wasted journey. Ridiculously, I almost feel like crying.

I carry on through the woods until I come out the other side, and then I see his car parked in the lane. My tummy gives a funny little lurch. Wherever Jake's gone, he must be on foot, which means he's probably not too far away.

I'm pondering whether to turn back into the woods, in the hope that I might find him, when a deep voice behind me says, 'I've been thinking about you.'

I swing round and there he is, standing in a shaft of sunlight filtering down through the trees. He's balancing branches on his shoulder, presumably to make a new fire, and he's smiling at me in that eye-crinkling way that always catches at my heart.

'Admit it. You've come back for more nettle tea.' His lips twist and I start to laugh.

'In your dreams.'

'Perhaps nettle soup might be more to your taste?' he suggests, raising an eyebrow. 'I must have known you were coming. I made a big pan of it this morning.'

'Mmm, yes. Sounds lovely. But sadly, I've just eaten.'

We beam at each other, enjoying the moment, and I feel an excited fluttering inside.

Jake rubs his hands together. 'Right. I've got ordinary teabags. Or whisky?' he says, pointing into the woods by way of invitation.

I nod, unable to stop smiling, and we start walking side by side back to his camp.

'Thanks for the manuscript,' he says.

My heart skips a beat. 'I guess this is the point where you tell me you've broken your glasses. So you're not faced with having to tell me it's rubbish,' I joke nervously.

'I don't wear glasses.'

'Right.'

'And I'd love to read it. I said so, didn't I? You should have more confidence in yourself, Daisy.'

'It's just it's a really big thing.' I give a sheepish shrug. 'Letting someone read what you've written.'

He nods. 'I know the feeling. You shut yourself away for months creating this thing but not having any clue if it's even worth the paper it's written on.'

'Do you write by hand, then?' I ask, surprised.

He grins. 'No way.'

'Then shouldn't you have said "worth the *laptop* it's written on"?' I smile pertly.

'Yes but that's not a saying, is it, clever clogs?' He pokes me in the ribs teasingly.

'No!' I shriek and pull myself away from him, and we lock eyes, laughing.

My heart is suddenly beating really fast as we fall into step again. I sneak a glance at Jake's profile. He's staring at the ground, his jaw tense.

We walk in silence like this for a while, then Jake murmurs, 'Emerging from the writing cave into a world full of critics can be very scary.' He glances at me then he looks away. 'Has ... Toby read your book?' He kicks at a fallen branch lying in our path and it flies into the undergrowth.

His question takes me by surprise. 'Oh, erm, no. Not yet.' I feel a flush rising to my cheeks. 'He will, though. I'm sure he will ... when he's got the time.'

Jake nods thoughtfully.

'So who gets the first look at *your* manuscripts? Is it your agent?' I ask, suddenly keen to change the subject. 'From what I can gather, most people seem to have a friend they trust to give their verdict before the book goes out into the big wide world. Is that what you ...' His face closes up and I trail off.

Bugger! Talk about putting your foot in it!

'Did Laura used to read your manuscripts?' I ask softly, feeling strangely conflicted. I really need to know the answer to this. But at the same time, I wish I could take my words back to restore the smile to Jake's face.

'She did, yes. And she was brilliant. I could always rely on her to give it to me straight.' He smiles wistfully. 'There were times, of course, when I wished she would be a little less brutal in her suggestions, but that's what you need. An objective point of view from someone you really trust, who cares enough to tell you the truth.'

We walk along in silence again.

'You must miss her so much,' I murmur at last, my heart squeezing with emotion at the thought of what he's going through.

'I do.'

We lapse into a heavy silence.

'Hey, sorry,' he says a moment later, attempting a smile. 'The reason I came here was so no one would have to put up with my moods. I reckoned I could vent my anger on chopping wood and be as miserable as I wanted. And there'd be no more of those well-meaning, sympathetic faces struggling to know what to say to make things better.'

'I know exactly what you mean. After Mum died, I used to duck into shop doorways to avoid people because I couldn't bear the sad looks on their faces.' I grin. 'You can be as mean and moody as you like. Honestly. I totally understand.'

He looks at me and something leaps inside.

'You do, don't you?' he murmurs, his eyes lingering on mine, an expression in them that I can't quite fathom. 'Understand.'

We've stopped walking for some reason, and I nod, trying to swallow down the emotion that's suddenly flooding through me. Looking into Jake's eyes, I feel breathless with something akin to joy, yet I feel as if I could – at any moment – break down in tears and never be able to stop.

I also have an urge to move closer to Jake and kiss his beautiful mouth to make everything all right for him.

We're standing close already. Close enough that I can smell

his scent, a tantalising mix of musk and the body spray he probably used after his early morning dip in the lake.

Thoughts of Jake emerging from the cold water, dripping wet, roughly towelling his body dry are suddenly filling my mind, sending little electric pulses of desire through my whole body. I swallow hard and stare at his strong, tanned neck above the washed-out pale T-shirt, trying not to notice the way the garment clings to his broad chest, moulding the hard muscles beneath.

My gaze travels upwards. Jake is staring at me with an intensity that makes the breath catch in my throat, and I find that I can't drag my eyes away from his. I feel like I'm drowning in their gorgeous dark depths and my legs are suddenly those of a newly born lamb. I sway towards him and he catches me round my waist.

An image of Toby suddenly flashes into my mind, bringing me back to reality.

Get a grip, girl!

What the hell is wrong with me?

Breathing in, I take a step back and clear my throat, which seems to be seriously clogged. 'I'd better not be too long.' My voice sounds croaky. 'Toby might be phoning me and there's no signal at all in the woods here.'

Instantly, the spell is broken, which I suppose is what I intended. Jake looks away and we walk on to the camp.

The camaraderie between us seems to have vanished and, for a while, our conversation is stilted and awkward. But then he says he has something he'd like me to see.

It's getting dark quickly now. Jake flicks on his torch and leads me through the trees until we arrive at the open, grassy area by the lake where his car is parked.

Stripping off his jacket, he lays it on the ground and says,

'You can use it as a pillow.' He grins. 'Would Madam like to lie down and watch the show?'

'The show?' I laugh but do as he says, and he flicks off the torch and lies down beside me.

'Look up,' he murmurs.

When I do, I let out a gasp.

The sky is heavy with stars, glowing and twinkling all around us, enveloping us in their breathtaking magic. I get a feeling of space so vast it makes my head spin – and yet the sky seems somehow within touching distance.

For a long time, I just lie there, drinking in the beauty. Then I catch a movement high up in the heavens.

'That was a shooting star!' I cry, excitedly.

'It was,' Jake murmurs. 'You might see a few more if you're lucky.'

Despite being light years away, the stars, cushioned in the velvety sky, seem weirdly close. I almost feel as though I could reach out and draw down one of those gleaming orbs as a prize.

'Why have I never done this before?' I whisper. 'It's totally magical.'

Jake's voice at my ear seems to reverberate right through me. 'People don't often look up. And I'm guilty of that myself. We're far too busy looking where we're walking, afraid we're going to fall flat on our faces.'

I turn and we exchange a smile. His hand touches mine – whether by accident or not, I'm really not sure – and a little shiver ripples through me, running from the tips of my fingers all the way down my legs to my toes.

I turn my head and our eyes meet and I experience a strong tug of desire that completely overwhelms me. He rolls closer and then his mouth finds mine and we're kissing so deeply, my body seems to melt. For a few heady seconds, I'm swept along, helpless to resist, every single nerve leaping in response to the feeling of Jake's mouth on mine, his hard body against me.

His arms around me are powerful and strong and I give myself up to the total bliss of having what I realise I've wanted ever since I first laid eyes on Jake Steele.

A little voice of reason calls out, fighting its way through the shadowy depths of my consciousness to be heard, competing with the overwhelming feelings of ecstasy that are rushing through my entire body as Jake kisses me and I cling to him desperately, never wanting to let go.

Toby!

What the hell am I doing?

'No!' Panicking, I push myself violently away from Jake and scramble to my feet, stumbling slightly.

Jake is on his feet in a flash, reaching out to steady me. Then we stand facing each other, panting, our eyes locked in shock at what just happened between us.

'Sorry.' His voice sounds strained.

I shake my head, a maelstrom of emotions whirling inside me. 'My fault.'

He looks away, at the fire that's struggling to take a proper hold, and the tense set of his jaw says it all.

He kissed me … but I'm not Laura. And now he regrets it.

Or maybe he doesn't regret it at all and that's the problem? Because there's Toby …

I need to get back to Toby.

Swallowing hard, I push away the memory of Jake's mouth on mine.

A moment of madness.

That's all it was …

*

The guilt I'm feeling is almost too much to bear.

What just happened was an aberration, brought on by emotion. It can never happen again ...

Walking back, having refused a lift from Jake, I break into a run from time to time, so anxious am I to get back to Toby and reassure him that all is well. Not that he needs reassuring. He obviously has no idea that things just got weirdly out of hand with Jake and me.

A nagging voice in my head whispers: *Isn't it you who needs the reassurance? That your future lies with Toby?*

But I dismiss this thought immediately. Toby and I are fine. Okay, things aren't perfect. But then, no relationship is. The reason I kissed Jake back was because I'd had such an incredibly emotional day. Seeing Joan stirred up all sort of feelings I've been trying desperately hard to lock away in a box, to protect myself from breaking down entirely. My head was all over the place ...

I've realised since seeing Joan again, that I've been in denial since Mum died, pretending I was fine, holding in my emotions, often refusing to allow myself the solace of healthy tears. Rachel could see that, which is why she was so worried about me.

I think I was scared that if I started to cry I'd never be able to stop ...

Anyway, there's no doubt in my mind that today's emotional rollercoaster accounted for my moment of madness with Jake. And now I need to put it behind me and focus on Toby.

I need to forget about Jake ...

Touching my cheek, I find my face is wet with tears. But I brush them away angrily.

Tomorrow night at the hotel is going to be wonderful. There'll be champagne in the room and Toby and I will have time to really talk. It will be a whole new beginning. The start of the rest of our lives together ...

*

Toby's car is there when I finally make it back.

But walking over the grass, I'm wondering why – despite the warmth of the July day – the tent flap is closed. Maybe Toby's gone for a walk. Not that this seems likely ...

Puzzled, I reach to unzip the flap.

The first thing that strikes me is the radio, blaring rather loudly. It must be tuned into a play on Toby's favourite Radio Four – a play that's reaching quite a dramatic climax, by the sounds of things. Someone appears to be suffering from a wheezy attack that just might be fatal. They're fighting for breath, the gasps getting faster and more urgent by the second.

'Toby? I'm back!'

I walk in, expecting to see Toby propped on pillows on the bed, surrounded by papers.

But what confronts me instead is a naked bum, pumping up and down.

As the full horror filters into my shocked brain, I'm faced with the fact that Toby isn't propped on his pillows.

He's completely naked and propped up on Chantelle from next door.

Chapter 20

It's apparently Chantelle who's making the escalating squeals. She sounds like she's being pushed by a murderer ever nearer the edge of a cliff, although the view from where I'm standing, on the threshold of the bedroom, is somewhat less cinematic. They're on the bed, far too near the hard wooden headboard for comfort. A thrust too far and Toby will knock himself out. Not that either of them are aware of this. They're far too busy going at it hammer and tongs, their passion no doubt heightened by the fact that I could arrive back at any moment.

The unavoidable focal point is the spectacular pumping action of Toby's neat rear, which seems far more enthusiastic than it's ever been my privilege to witness ...

A feeling of nausea hits, and as the full horror of what I'm witnessing finally penetrates my disbelieving brain, Chantelle's cries build to a crescendo and she tumbles with one final shriek of surrender onto the rocks below.

Five seconds later, she spots me beyond Toby's shoulder and gives a horrified squeak.

When Toby turns, his face is a picture.

I've seen plenty of dramas where the heroine catches the hero naked in their bed with another woman, and I've sometimes wondered what I'd do in those circumstances.

Let fly with a stream of abuse? Start hurling things at them, such as hair-drying implements and bedroom chairs? Or stand there speechless (which is what I'm doing), wondering how he could possibly do this to me?

Time freezes as we gape at one other and my future crumbles into dust around me.

I'd like to be cool about it and say something like, 'Hey, this looks fun. Budge up, will you?'

But frankly, I'm feeling the very opposite of cool. In fact, as Toby scrambles off the bed and starts pulling on his jeans, hopping all over the floor in his haste, I can feel an angry flush spreading over my whole body. Chantelle hasn't moved, apart from to grab the duvet and clutch it around her bosomy nakedness, staring at me all the time in frozen horror.

I can't believe Toby would do this to me! After all the negative things he said about Chantelle! He must have fancied her all along ...

Tears sting my eyes at his unbelievable betrayal. I thought I knew him; I really thought I was safe with Toby. *How stupid I was to imagine he'd never ever hurt me!*

I recall his words when he phoned me earlier. 'You just enjoy your walk. No hurry!' He wasn't thinking of me. He was just making sure he had the time to get down and dirty with Chantelle, the low-life snake!

Fury is mounting inside me.

I glance at the bedroom chair but it looks a bit awkward and unwieldy.

So instead, I hurl some choice words. 'You ... *fucking bastard*! I suppose that's why you phoned me. To make sure the coast was clear for a while so you could ... do *this*.' I gesture wildly.

Toby blanches, not accustomed to hearing me swear. Then he utters the classic line, 'Daisy ... this really isn't what it looks like.'

I give a hoot of laughter. 'Right, so what is it *actually*? Chantelle wanted some advice on her finances so you thought you'd conduct the meeting *in our bed* stark naked? Do me a favour, Toby, and at least admit when you've been caught with your pants down, shagging a woman with "ridiculously large mammaries".' I do the quotation marks in the air and shrug at Chantelle. 'His words, not mine.'

This snaps Chantelle out of her trance. 'Toby? Is that true?' she asks crossly.

Toby shakes his head. He looks so painfully conflicted, I'd feel sorry for him if I wasn't currently trying to contain the urge to cut off his extremities with a blunt knife.

I go to pull my cardi around me but realise it's not there. I must have dropped it after leaving Jake's camp in such a hurry. It strikes me as horribly ironic that I raced back to Toby, determined to shower him with love – only to find him showering Chantelle with something else altogether ...

Emotion is welling inside me to dangerously unmanageable levels. If I don't leave the tent now, I'll break down completely and it will all be very messy, and I don't want to cry in front of them.

I'm determined to hold on to my pride, if nothing else.

Escaping the tent, I blunder over the grass towards Clemmy's house, tears rolling down my face, feeling totally humiliated. I just want to see a friendly face. Plus something else is starting to worry me, stabbing my gut with panic, making me feel quite sick.

It's a dread that seems surprisingly out of proportion, bearing in mind that I've just witnessed my boyfriend committing the ultimate betrayal in our bed.

What if I dropped my cardigan somewhere in the woods and I never find it?

*

Clemmy answers the door. I must be looking pretty terrible because she immediately bundles me inside, asking what's happened.

I flump down at the table and stare at her. My head is whirling with gut-wrenching images of Toby and Chantelle, and Clemmy has to gently tease the facts out of me. Saying the words – *I just found Toby shagging our next-door neighbour* – smacks me in the gut and makes me feel as if I'm going to throw up. But I take a few deep breaths to calm down and then I start telling Clemmy about the sneaky phone call Toby made to ensure I'd be away from the tent.

'Were you out for a walk?' she asks gently.

Nodding, I glance down at my lap, thinking of Jake and feeling suddenly ashamed. What will Clemmy think of me if I tell her about Jake? If I tell her that actually, while Toby and Chantelle were getting it on, I was kissing Jake in the woods?

I don't have the right to be angry at Toby. I'd be a hypocrite.

'You can stay here tonight,' says Clemmy firmly. 'You're definitely not going back over there.' She hesitates. Then she adds, 'And listen, Daisy, this might not be the right time to say this – but I'm going to say it anyway because I care about you.' She takes a deep breath. 'What if Toby isn't the right man for you anyway?'

'What do you mean?'

She shrugs. 'I know you're fond of him but maybe, after all, he's not for you.'

I immediately think of Jake and more feelings of guilt rush in.

Oh God, I *can't* be in love with Jake Steele. Not when he's still so obviously hung up on Laura ...

A cloud of despair settles over my head. I wish I could be the sort of person who inspires the kind of enduring devotion Jake so obviously feels for Laura. I thought Toby felt that way about me. I fooled myself into imagining he was the rock I could always rely on. How wrong could I be?

I think of Rosalind's reaction when she finds out Toby and I have split up, and a wave of unbearable sadness washes over me. Rosalind will be devastated. She was already joking about buying a hat ...

What will happen to our friendship?

Rosalind is Toby's mum so of course she's bound to be loyal to her son. I can't see how our friendship will be able to continue under the circumstances. So I'm not only losing my relationship, I'm losing the whole happy future I envisaged as part of Toby's family ...

Suddenly, it's all too much. Laying my head on my arms, I start to sob, and Clemmy jumps up and puts her arms around me.

I'm not even sure what I'm weeping for. Everything, I suppose.

My wrecked relationship. A glamping holiday that's ended in disaster. Being plagued by thoughts of kissing Jake and what that implies. His grief over Laura. Finding that a woman called Arabella might actually be my biological mum but secretly hoping it's not true.

It's all those things, I realise, but there's a bigger, much more powerful reason for this deluge of sorrow that I no longer have the strength to stem.

I'm crying for Mum.

For the first time since she died, I'm allowing myself to feel the raw edge of my grief, instead of automatically swerving away from it. If she were still here, she'd hug me tightly, wrapping me up in her love and telling me that Toby was never good enough for me anyway.

But she's not here and the pain of my loss is overwhelming.

There's an empty cavern inside me that I wanted Toby and his family to fill. But no one can ever replace my mum. That's the brutal truth and I can see it now. Even the search for my biological mother now seems like simply a desperate attempt to fill the frightening void in my life.

'I miss my mum so much,' I whisper and Clemmy's arms tighten around me. I've never felt so glad of another human being's touch. I feel safe enough in Clemmy's care to sob for Mum until there are no tears left.

Chapter 21

Next morning, I wake feeling exhausted as if I've had no sleep at all.

Sitting in the kitchen in a bit of a daze, I'm watching Clemmy make tea when the doorbell rings. Clemmy shoots me a glance then dries her hands and goes to answer it.

Hearing the mumbled voices in the hallway, my stomach drops.

Toby.

I really don't want to face him right now.

Hopefully, Clemmy will send him packing, because if he's come to apologise and somehow try to explain away his actions, I'm really not interested. He's hurt me too much for me to ever contemplate forgiving him.

I can tell Clemmy is trying to head him off but Toby seems adamant he needs to speak to me. Feeling like I'm making trouble for Clemmy – who's got her own problems with Ryan to handle – I swiftly get up and go to the door. I probably look as if I've had my face painted for Hallowe'en with my puffy eyes and all the mascara smudges, but I don't care. When he sees the devastating effect this has had on me, hopefully he'll feel even more guilty for betraying me ...

He looks up as I enter the hallway. 'Daisy. Are you all right?'

I exchange a glance with Clemmy. 'Erm, not great, Toby. As you can imagine.'

He glances down. 'No. Of course.'

'Where's the lovely Chantelle?' I ask, walking towards him, as Clemmy makes a discreet exit, back into the kitchen.

Looking up, he sighs. 'Look, Daisy, I don't know how the hell it happened but I never meant it to. Something – I don't know – *weird* came over me.'

'Oh, well *that's* all right then,' I snap.

He ignores this. 'She's not even my type. It was just – I don't know what it was – a moment of ...' He looks around for inspiration.

'Madness?' I supply the word, thinking of the irony. At least *my* moment of madness was over before it had barely begun and was regretted by both parties.

Toby obviously has regrets, too. But however much he might want to undo what happened, I'm not sure I could ever look at him again without visualising him with Chantelle in the most compromising position ever.

'Madness,' he repeats. 'Yes, exactly!' There's a strange light in his eyes. 'It was a sort of madness, Daisy. I'm so glad you understand because, to tell you the truth, I was dreading coming over here. I would never want to hurt you. You know that. I think you're brilliant in every way.' He holds out his arms, his face full of love and ... *happiness*?

I stare at him, remaining rooted to the spot.

Does he really think I've forgiven him already?

'Hug? Please?' He gives me the benefit of his charming smile.

I sigh. 'Look, Toby. If you've come here to tell me how much you regret what happened and to persuade me that we can put it all behind us and carry on as before, I'm afraid it's a no.' I shake my head, determined to stand my ground, whatever excuses he starts coming up with for his appalling behaviour.

His eyes widen. 'Oh, I don't regret it.'

The world stops for a moment.

I stare at him. Did he just say what I thought he said?

Perhaps he means he doesn't regret the thing with Chantelle because it's made him realise how much *I* mean to him?

He's shaking his head sadly. 'The thing is, Daisy, when you find true love, there's really no way you can resist its power. You just have to go with it. That's what I said to Chantelle.'

'You said *what* to Chantelle?' I snap, unable to believe my ears. *Is he stupid or something?*

Toby smiles serenely at the mention of his lover's name. 'Chantelle felt bad about you. She wanted us to go our separate ways. She wanted to pretend the spark between us never erupted into the raging flames of all-consuming love. But I told her you wouldn't want that.'

'I wouldn't?' I swallow, wondering if this is a joke. Perhaps a cameraman is about to jump out of the bushes and ask me if I want to be on a brand-new prime-time reality comedy show called *Gotcha!*

Toby gives an earnest shake of the head. 'No, you wouldn't. I told her you're a truly loving, understanding sort of person and that you'd be really pleased for us both. And that we actually *owed* it to you to make a real go of it together.' He shrugs in a philosophical manner. 'There's just nothing you can do when you fall in love at first sight, is there?'

His question jerks me out of my stunned state.

'Well, you could try keeping your *cock* in your pants until you've informed your *current* girlfriend of your change of heart,' I blurt out, trying to push him out of the door. 'Goodbye, Toby. I hope you and Chantelle have a wonderful life together.'

I catch sight of Chantelle peering out of our tent doorway.

Pulling Toby back in towards me, I treat him to a full-on snog, grabbing his bum in the process.

Toby goes limp with shock for a moment then he starts struggling to get away, twisting round anxiously to look at Chantelle, who's now come out of the tent and is standing with her hands on her substantial hips.

'Just letting you know what you'll be missing,' I trill with a cheerful smile. 'Have a nice life.'

Hustling him off the doorstep, I slam the door in his face.

As soon as he's gone, Clemmy comes out of hiding.

'Sorry, I really didn't mean to listen, but ...' She shakes her head in disbelief. 'What a spud.'

'A massive spud.' I nod in wholehearted agreement, then I frown. 'What's a spud?'

Clemmy smiles. 'It's Ruby's expression. Apparently in Newcastle it means a completely clueless person.'

I sigh. 'Well, Toby's that all right. Imagine coming over here and waxing lyrical about finding love with bloody Chantelle!'

'Unbelievable.'

'Bastard.'

She nods, looking suddenly nervous. 'I ... God, I wish I'd had a chance to tell you that time in the café. But then I saw Ryan with that girl and it went right out of my head.'

'Tell me what?' I ask, puzzled.

She sighs. 'That night Chantelle was in your tent. You must have all had dinner together?'

'That's right.'

'I happened to be looking out of the window when Toby was walking her back to her tent. She looked pretty drunk.'

I nod. 'She was. She'd had about a gallon of red wine.'

'Well, she staggered to the ground, dragging him with her. And they ... well, they didn't get up for quite a while after that.'

I make a face. 'Ugh. What a thought.' Inside, I'm dying a little bit more. 'He told me they had trouble getting the tent open. That's why he was such a long time. And, like a bloody fool, I believed him.'

Clemmy shrugs. 'You're not the fool. Toby is. For taking you for granted.'

'Thank you for that.' I smile wistfully and wander over to the window that overlooks the camp. The tents look beautiful from here. Little palaces of elegance and luxury. 'It's really gorgeous, you know. What you've achieved here.'

Clemmy joins me at the window. 'We were planning to expand the business, put more tents in the adjoining field. Ryan was going to start working for himself so that he could be here to help with the glamping. But now ...' She trails off sadly.

'Talk to him tomorrow when he gets back from the conference,' I tell her firmly. 'Everything will be fine, I'm sure of it.'

She nods. Then she points out of the window. 'Look!'

Toby is emerging from our tent, lugging his case, a sports bag and his laptop over the grass to his car. As we watch, he loads the boot then walks over to Chantelle's tent, emerging a moment later with two lurid pink cases and wearing a bright yellow Donald Duck neck pillow. Chantelle totters out and stands watching while he packs her belongings alongside his, taking his usual time making sure they fit in there perfectly. At one point she tries to help but he holds out his hands in a 'stop' sign, and Chantelle steps back, folding her arms a little sulkily.

'I've probably had a lucky escape,' I say gloomily.

'I didn't like to say so.'

Clemmy turns and, in spite of everything, we smile.

*

Later, I lie on the bed in the tent, staring up at the slanted pale ceiling, hugging one of the squashy cream pillows. Toby's forgotten to pack his wash bag. It's lying on the bed and I reach my foot over and kick it onto the floor.

What will he do without his special shower gel, I wonder bitterly.

For good measure, I lean over and pick up the flowers he bought me, hurling the vase onto the floor to join the wash bag. The pottery jug smashes and water goes everywhere. I stare at the mess. I'll have to buy Clemmy another jug.

Exhausted, I sink back against the pillows.

I need to move forward and forget I ever met Toby. Or his family.

I'd love to think Rosalind and I could keep in touch, but what are the chances? It would be far too messy.

Toby will probably be halfway back to Manchester by now, with the lovely Chantelle in tow. They'll no doubt be congratulating themselves on their good fortune at having found each other, and Toby will be planning to introduce her to his family, just as he did with me. Will Rosalind take to Chantelle like she warmed to me?

I swallow down the emotion that's threatening to swamp me. I need to stop thinking about things like that because it doesn't do me any good to—

Hearing the sound of rustling footsteps outside, I sit up straight and tilt my ear to the door. Oh God, Toby must have come back for his wash bag. Well, he's not getting in! I have no desire at all to listen to him prattling on about how the stars aligned in the heavens to bring him and the wondrous Chantelle together ...

He clears his throat.

'Bugger off, Toby. I mean it. You're not getting in!' I pick up his wash bag, go to the door and open the flap just a few inches. Then I launch the bag at him through the gap with as much force as I can muster, hoping the million-pound shower balm doesn't survive the shaking up. It's childish, I know, but you have to find the upside in situations like these.

'OUCH,' calls a deep voice that definitely isn't Toby's.

I freeze in horror.

What the hell is Jake doing here?

Chapter 22

Before answering him, I leap to the mirror to check my make-up isn't too disastrous.

A creature stares back at me, all bare and exposed with puffy eyes and a slightly reddened face. My make-up has apparently been completely washed away by the copious tears of earlier.

I consider pretending I'm not here, but the wash bag missile is a bit of a give-away, so reluctantly, I unzip further and peer out.

Jake is standing with the bag balanced on his upturned hand, a questioning look on his face. 'Are you okay?'

I snatch back the bag, feeling a blush spreading upwards. 'Yes, thank you. Sorry about that. I thought you were ...'

'Toby. Yes.' His eyes rake over my face. 'Did I come at a bad time?' He looks over his shoulder as if he thinks Toby might appear at any moment to claim his property.

'A bad time?' I snort, feeling flustered and as vulnerable as a new-born calf standing there in the old T-shirt I normally wear for bed. I tug at the hemline, which is halfway up my thighs. 'You could say that.'

'Had an argument?' He frowns, his eyes flicking to my bare legs for just a second.

Sighing, I open my mouth to tell him about finding Toby rolling around with Chantelle. Then I close it again. I feel hurt and humiliated, and the last thing I need right now is Jake feeling sorry for me. I can't bear him to know the truth. That I'm not attractive enough or fascinating enough to keep a boyfriend from straying to the tent next door.

So instead, I force a laugh and say airily, 'Oh, just a little tiff. Toby will be back any moment with his tail between his legs.'

'Right.' His eyes turn to flint and he looks away. Then he glances at something behind me and I groan inwardly. The smashed flower vase. I should have cleared it up.

Suddenly, I spot he has something with him.

'My cardigan! You brought my cardigan back! I didn't lose it after all!' He holds it up and I take it in my arms, hugging it in delighted relief as tears spring to my eyes.

'I knew you'd be missing it.'

His eyes catch mine and hold, and I wonder if he's remembering the moment we last saw one another, when we were kissing. A shiver runs through me. He has such a beautiful mouth ...

I dash away the tears. 'It was my mum's. I thought I'd lost it forever. Sorry.' Turning away, I fish out a paper hanky and blow my nose.

'Hey, don't apologise. I've still got Laura's reading glasses on my desk at home. They remind me how quirky and wise she was, and they make me smile.'

I nod, understanding, although his words make me feel bleak inside.

So Laura had style and wisdom, as well as the sort of magical presence that meant no man would ever stray from her ...

'Do you want to come in?' I ask doubtfully, glancing down at my T-shirt.

'No, no. Toby will be back.' He half glances round.

I shrug. 'Probably not for a while.'

He hesitates and my heart starts racing.

'Maybe for a minute, then?' He slides his hands in his jeans pockets, looking oddly vulnerable. Not like the confident, self-assured Jake I'm used to.

'Of course.' I usher him in, feeling strangely breathless at his nearness. 'Mind the vase.'

He steps sideways to avoid it and we collide. I slide a little in the spilt water and he grabs my waist to steady me.

For a long moment, time seems to stand still as I stare up into those mesmerising dark eyes. The firm touch of his hands is having a disturbing effect on me, just like last time. Little pulses of longing ripple through my entire body, making me desperately want to do what I swore I would never do again – launch myself against him and kiss him until I've no breath left and my lips are raw.

His eyes seem darker than ever, locked on mine, and I feel like I'm diving ever deeper into them ...

Then Jake draws in a ragged breath and steps back, pushing his hand through his tawny hair.

And reality hits.

I can't believe I'm feeling these things with Jake when *I just split up with Toby a few hours ago*! What sort of weird, mixed-up person does this make me?

'Sorry.' Jake's gaze moves around the tent and I realise he's avoiding my eye. 'I'd better go. Toby ...'

I swallow hard. 'Yes.'

He moves towards the tent flap and panic grips me. Is he just going to walk away?

I don't want him to go!

He turns and looks at me, and his eyes are burning with such feeling, it stops my breath for a second.

He raises his hand. 'Bye, Daisy.'

And then he's gone.

*

After Jake has gone, I lie on the bed again, staring up at the ceiling.

I can see it all so clearly now.

I never felt the raw physical attraction for Toby that I feel for Jake and now I understand why. Toby was my shelter. My port in the storm. He was never meant to be the great love of my life. But as long as he was with me, I could tell myself that I had a future; that I wouldn't be on my own.

Looked at in that light, I can see why Toby would be turning cartwheels at finding a woman like Chantelle who's probably attracted to him for all the *right* reasons.

But where does it leave me? Now that my desperate hopes of belonging to a real family again have come crashing down?

I'm alone. And I need to face up to that.

Put starkly, I'm an orphan – and no amount of lovely Rosalinds are going to fill the gap left by Mum, however much I wish they could. Even meeting my birth mum couldn't do that. I need to drag myself out of this pit of despondency and start focusing on the future. A future on my own ...

Shouts from outside break into my gloomy thoughts.

I unzip the tent and peer outside. Clemmy is sitting on a

blanket on the grass with Ruby and Gloria, and they appear to be having a picnic.

I glance at my watch. It's nearly one. Lunchtime. I've been sitting here stewing for ages. Clemmy spots me and waves me over.

I wave back and duck into the tent to pull on clean shorts and a T-shirt. Then I force a comb through my wild hair and venture out to join them. Anything beats lying here, staring at the ceiling, mulling over the disaster that is my life.

They all look up as I approach, shielding their eyes against the glare of the sun.

'How are you, Daisy?' asks Clemmy. 'We didn't want to disturb you.'

'Sit down and have some strawberries,' says Ruby, shuffling along the rug to make room for me.

I drop down beside them gratefully. 'Don't mind if I do.' I smile and choose a luscious-looking berry from the punnet Ruby is holding out.

Gloria leans over and presses my hand. 'You're better off without that waste of space, love. There's someone far nicer out there for you.' She wafts herself vigorously with a lettuce leaf. 'I can't believe how hot it is today.' Realising the lettuce is not exactly fit for purpose, she drops it on the rug with a sigh.

'Thanks, Gloria.' In spite of my resolve to be glad Toby has gone, a rogue tear springs up.

Clemmy looks anxious. 'I hope you don't mind but I told Ruby and Gloria what happened.'

I shake my head. 'Not at all.'

Ruby grins apologetically. 'I was about to charge over to your tent and get you to test my latest batch of chocolate brownies for the fayre tomorrow. But Clemmy stopped me. She said cake was probably the very last thing on your mind this morning.'

I laugh. 'Ooh, I don't know about that. Are they the brownies in question?' I point at a colourful cake tin full of goodies that's nestled on the rug.

'Yes.' Ruby beams and holds out the tin. 'Try one.'

I finish my strawberry and take a brownie. I haven't eaten anything since yesterday and I'm suddenly starving.

Ruby offers them round then takes one herself.

'Holy batshit, Robin!' she mutters suddenly, through a mouth full of cake.

'They are good,' agrees Clemmy, munching on hers.

But Ruby is staring out over the lake. 'Is that an apparition before me?'

We all swing round to look. Someone is emerging from the lake. A tall, broad-shouldered man, wearing nothing but a pair of the briefest of swimming shorts. He ploughs out of the water, sun glinting off his impressive muscles, and steps onto the bank. Then he turns his face to the sun and runs his hands slowly through his dripping hair.

'Daniel Craig, eat your heart out,' murmurs Gloria, transfixed.

My heart lurches in my chest. 'It's Jake.'

The words are out of my mouth before I can stop them. I pick up Gloria's lettuce leaf and start fanning myself furiously. Then I realise everyone is staring at me, so I stop and try to brazen it out.

'You know that man?' asks Clemmy.

I shake my head. 'Not exactly. In fact, no, not at all.'

Right at that moment, Jake looks over at us and waves.

Ruby giggles. 'Well, he seems to know you, Daisy. Unless Mum's having a secret fling with a devastatingly handsome toy boy.'

'Ruby!' Gloria's hot flush deepens. 'As if!'

'Keep your hair on, Mother.' Ruby grins. 'So come on, Daisy, you dark horse. How do you know him?'

I watch as Jake towels himself dry then starts ambling off along the lakeside, presumably heading back to camp. My face is now blazing hotter than a furnace and I can tell that my three companions are trying, with varying degrees of success, to pretend they're not fascinated.

With a sigh, I start telling them the story of how I met Jake when I was walking in the woods and we struck up a conversation. And how I've seen him several times since then.

I turn to Clemmy. 'Sorry I didn't tell you. I didn't want you to think badly of me.'

She smiles. 'But I'm sure it was perfectly innocent. He's a writer and you love writing. I can totally understand the attraction.'

I nod, wishing it were as simple as that. Because it very definitely isn't. I have such an urge right now to run after Jake. The fact that I'm still sitting on this rug is all down to sheer force of will alone ...

It's suddenly blindingly clear that I've been fooling myself. Yes, I like him because we have writing in common – but it's so, so much more than that. I have fallen hook, line and sinker for Jake, and there's nothing I can do to reverse the damage. I'll be leaving here in a day or two and then I'll never set eyes on him again.

My eyes are suddenly burning with unshed tears. This holiday has turned out to be a disaster in so many different ways.

But falling in unrequited love with Jake Steele surely tops the lot!

'You really like this Jake, don't you?' says Ruby, and my face catches fire all over again. 'I mean, really *really* like him.'

I swallow, glancing at their rapt faces, one by one.

'Actually, I do,' I confess miserably.

There's a brief silence, then Ruby says cheerfully, 'Well, hey, that's good news. It'll mean you'll get over scumbag Toby much more quickly than you otherwise would have.'

'Ruby!' protests Gloria. 'I wish you wouldn't just blurt out what comes into your head!'

I exchange an uneasy smile with Clemmy. 'It's okay, Gloria. Ruby's right. And actually, I have no right at all to call Toby a scumbag. I ... I kissed Jake.'

'Oh my God, do you love him?' asks Ruby.

I give an embarrassed laugh. 'No, of course not. Well, maybe. Oh God, I don't know ...'

'Actually,' says Gloria, reaching for a glossy magazine. 'I was just reading this quiz about the signs that you're really attracted to someone.' She rifles through the pages until she comes to it. 'Right, Daisy. Do you get butterflies in your stomach every time you think about him?'

Everyone turns and looks at me expectantly.

'No!' I protest, while flushing like a beetroot.

'That's a yes, then,' says Gloria, smiling and pretending to tick a box. 'Next question. Do you feel as if you could talk to him forever and never get bored?'

I'm about to say no again, but it's so obvious the answer has to be yes.

'Ooh, that's another yes,' says Ruby with a triumphant smile.

'Oh, stop it. Please!' I start to laugh and everyone joins in.

'When you kissed him, did Jake kiss you back?' Ruby asks.

I swallow, thinking back. I've relived the moment a thousand times. I can remember exactly how it went. We were lying on the ground, staring up at the stars, and he rolled closer and touched his mouth to mine ...

'He definitely kissed me, too,' I say firmly, and Ruby nods her approval.

'Jake could be the love of your life but you'll never know it if you don't go and talk to him,' she says. 'From what I gather, love can be anything *but* convenient. It often happens in the weirdest of circumstances. Like my mate's sister, Clara, who was in the pub celebrating her boyfriend's birthday when she walked out of the loos with her dress tucked into her knickers. A perfect stranger called Jon alerted her to this highly embarrassing fact. And they're now engaged and getting married next June.'

'And the moral of the story is?' Gloria laughs.

'Don't worry about tucking your dress in your knickers because it might just lead to true love?' says Clemmy, with a wistful smile.

'Well, anyway, you should go and see Jake,' says Ruby determinedly.

'I need to cancel the hotel room I'd booked for tonight,' I say gloomily.

'Right. So you cancel the booking *then* you go and see Jake.'

I laugh. 'You make it sound so easy.'

'But it is.'

'I've just split up with Toby. It doesn't seem right to be thinking of someone else already.' A wave of weariness rolls over me. I just want to lie down on the grass and go to sleep.

This rollercoaster of emotions I've been on since I arrived here has obviously taken its toll because I actually don't know what I think about *anything* any more ...

'You need to send Jake your book,' says Ruby. 'If he really likes you, he'll definitely want to read it!'

I smile at her a little sheepishly. 'I already have. I e-mailed it to him.'

'Ooh, nice one. And has he read it?'

'I don't know. Maybe ... maybe I should go and ask him?'

'You definitely should.'

'Okay, I will.' I feel a little spark of excitement at the thought.

'Yay!' Ruby punches the air. 'I should be an agony aunt. All my friends say so.'

'You do talk more sense than the average obnoxious teenager.' Gloria grins.

'Thanks, Mother dear.'

'You know,' says Gloria, taking my arm and squeezing it, 'if this Jake person kissed you back, it could mean he's ready to move on from this Laura person.'

Ruby nods firmly. 'I think this Mother person might actually be right for once.'

Soon after, I find myself striding along the road that leads around the lake, keeping to the grass verge when an occasional car headed for the hotel motors past. My heart is in my mouth and the butterflies in my stomach are flapping so furiously I feel quite breathless. Every so often, I question what I'm doing. Then I remember what Ruby said. I need to find out what Jake thinks about my book. I don't need any reason other than that to call in on him, do I? It's clear he likes me as a person, at the very least. We have such interesting conversations.

I'm trying to ignore the little voice in my head saying it's not just Jake's interesting conversation that's drawing me into the woods today ...

If I'm honest, the most cheering words came from Gloria. *If this Jake person kissed you back, it could mean he's ready to move on from this Laura person.*

I smile to myself, hoping she's right and thinking what a lovely family Clemmy is marrying into. I really hope I stay in touch with her this time and that it all works out for her with Ryan ...

Suddenly, I remember I need to cancel the hotel booking. I can't believe it. My mind was so focused on Jake, I actually walked right past the hotel and didn't even think about it. It's too late to double back now. I'll see Jake first and call in at the hotel on the way back. I just hope Sylvia understands.

I'm almost there now, and as I crunch over the bracken and fallen twigs, making my way to Jake's camp, I'm filled with a sense of optimism that almost borders on happiness. Talking to Clemmy, Gloria and Ruby seems to have given me the perspective I needed, and I feel ready to move forward and find out what life has in store for me.

What if Jake were to tell me he likes my book?

And that he likes me, too ...

My heart beats faster at the thought but I check myself. I mustn't hope for miracles. What will be will be. I need to just relax and go with the flow instead of allowing my fear of the future to take over, like I did with Toby.

My step is light as I walk along, breathing deeply in an effort to calm the butterflies. Another few yards and the camp will come into view and I'll see Jake again.

I should have been honest with him. I should have told

him that Toby and I have split up. I just didn't want him feeling sorry for me. But I can make up for it now. We can have the chat we should have had earlier.

Walking along, I spot the little clearing up ahead and quicken my pace. Stepping through the trees to the camp, I stop abruptly and stare around me.

This isn't Jake's clearing. There's nothing here. My heart sinks. I must have strayed from the main track somehow and wandered in entirely the wrong direction. In my defence, when you're surrounded by nothing but trees, one clearing looks very much like another. Plus my sense of direction has never been very good.

I walk on a little less confidently, but five minutes later, I see daylight up ahead and realise I'm almost through the woods and out the other side.

Feeling panic start to rise, I retrace my steps and soon I'm back at the same familiar little clearing. And that's when I spot the unmistakeable remains of Jake's campfire, which I missed in my confusion earlier.

All the breath goes out of me. Sagging against a nearby tree, my legs feel like jelly as I stare at the space where Jake's tent used to be.

I'm too late to talk to him.

Jake has packed up his things and gone ...

Chapter 23

Sinking down onto the grass, my back against the trunk of the tree, I pull up my knees and hug them to my chest. Then I stare for a long time at the remains of the campfire.

I've no idea where Jake lives. He mentioned it was about an hour's drive away but that could be anywhere.

I can't believe I'll never see him again.

Recalling I have his email address, a little surge of hope rises up. But it quickly dies when I remember the hundreds of miles separating us, once I'm back in Manchester. It's not as if I could casually email him, suggesting we meet up for a coffee ...

I think what hurts most of all is that he didn't come to say goodbye.

When I leave the campsite on Sunday, I'll be leaving my friendship with Jake behind, too. I thought we had a genuine connection. But it obviously meant far more to me than it did to Jake.

A panicky feeling flutters in my throat.

Why do I keep getting things so badly wrong?

Tears spring up but I dash them away and get to my feet.

I need to cancel that hotel booking. It's so late in the day, I'll probably be required to pay for the room anyway but that's the least of my worries.

Feeling slightly wobbly on my feet, I set off, walking in a daze back to the hotel. It's good to have something practical to focus on. After I've sorted things out at the hotel, I'll go back to the camp and ask Clemmy's advice on ordering a hire car to get me home. Then I'll pack up and leave first thing tomorrow.

I think of home and have a sudden longing to see Rachel. I'll have so much to tell her. And none of it good.

The sooner I can get away from this place, the better ...

*

I stare at the bill the receptionist has just presented me with.

I'm having a hard job processing the total in bold at the bottom of the print-out. Can it really be that much? As I haven't given twenty-four hours' notice of cancellation, I'm apparently required to pay the whole amount.

Looking back, I was so excited about treating Toby to a night of luxury, I didn't pay much attention to how much it was all going to cost. I suppose I thought that if I were a few quid short, I could always borrow from Toby and pay him back later. How foolish it all seems now, in retrospect.

'Are you sure this is right?' I ask, thinking frantically about the state of my bank balance. I doubt there's enough in there to cover it.

'Yes, I'm afraid it is. Our policy clearly states that there's no charge for cancellations we receive up to forty-eight hours before your stay. But after that, the whole amount becomes due.'

I stare at her, wondering if I should tell her about the exceptional circumstances. That my boyfriend decided to knock off the next-door neighbour.

'It's just that we're unlikely to be able to fill the room at such late notice.' She frowns. 'Sorry.'

My throat feels too choked to speak so I fumble in my bag for my debit card. And then when she tries to put the transaction through, my card is declined.

'Do you have another card?' she asks. 'We could split the amount.'

I shake my head. My only credit card is maxed out after paying for the glamping trip.

Suddenly, it's all too much. I've been an emotional wreck ever since I arrived here. *And now this …*

Tears spring to my eyes and the total on the print-out dances around in a blur. My throat aches with the effort of keeping the despair inside.

The receptionist swiftly provides a box of paper hankies and I pull out a couple and cover my face, sobbing uncontrollably. Trying to minimise the noise just makes it worse. The receptionist is staring at me in horror and I feel quite bad for her. She's trying her best to remain professional but she clearly hasn't a clue what to do with me.

Then someone says, 'Daisy. What's wrong?'

It's Sylvia. I shake my head, unable to speak, making awkward little involuntary gasping noises instead. She leads me over to a sofa in a little alcove, well away from the busy reception desk, and sits down beside me, her hands in her lap.

In between sobs, and feeling ridiculously dramatic, I blurt out my sorry tale, explaining why I'm having to cancel after Sylvia went to such great trouble to find me a special room for tonight.

She observes me with a sympathetic frown. Then she says firmly, 'We'll waive the cancellation fee.'

'Really?' If anything, that makes me feel even worse about the situation. 'But are you sure? I could pay some today then pay the balance next month?'

She shakes her head. 'I wouldn't hear of it. You'd no idea Toby was going to – um – be such a cad. You booked in all faith that things would be lovely.'

I smile sadly and nod. 'Well, if you're sure. I'll definitely be back, though. It's such a gorgeous place you have here.'

'Thank you.' Sylvia's face lights up. It's the first time I've seen her smile with her eyes and it totally transforms her. 'Running the hotel is my life,' she says simply, 'and comments like that make me think that maybe I've made the right choices.'

I nod, envying Sylvia her passion for her work, yet at the same time feeling a sadness emanating from her.

She leans forward suddenly, an intense gleam in her eye. 'Don't let Toby's betrayal stop you from forging other relationships. You deserve to find someone special.'

Her words take me by surprise and tears spring to my eyes again. 'Gosh, you're going to start me off again if you keep being nice to me.' I try to laugh it off but thoughts of Jake are making me feel hollow inside. I *had* found someone special but it wasn't meant to be ...

Sylvia stands up, snapping back to her usual professional manner. 'Right, I'd better get on. Take care, Daisy. And if there's anything I can do, just let me know.'

'I will.' I can't imagine there'd be anything – unless I found myself stranded here with nowhere to stay – but it's really nice of her to say so.

As I leave the hotel, I make a mental note to do what Sylvia says and not dwell on the bad things but move forward as best I can.

Back at the tent, I pick up my cardigan, remembering how delighted I was when Jake brought it back. I wish now that I'd told him the truth about Toby and me. Perhaps then he wouldn't have just disappeared without a word.

I'd been planning to stay for the summer fayre tomorrow to help out on Poppy's cake stall. Now, I'm tempted to just pack up and leave early tomorrow morning. Move on with my life, as Sylvia advised me to do.

I bury my face in the cardigan's softness, as though Mum's scent might still be lingering there. But all I can smell is the faint aroma of fabric conditioner and an outdoorsy, smoky scent. The garment has been washed so many times, it now has more bobbles than a shop full of woolly hats. Carefully, I fold it up. Then I open my case and lay it inside.

It's the middle of summer.

I have no need of an extra layer ...

Chapter 24

Next morning, I'm up early after a disturbed night's sleep.

I've had breakfast, showered and made a start on my packing when Clemmy calls round just before nine.

She gives me a sheepish grin. 'I hope you don't mind me calling this early but I wanted to make sure you'd be here for the fayre?'

When I make an uncertain face, she says, 'Oh, please stay. Poppy wants me to man the cake stall and it would be so much more fun if you were there to help me.'

She looks so disappointed that I'm going, I feel quite emotional. After less than a week, I feel like Clemmy and I are as good friends as we ever were. And I need all the friends I can get right now!

'Okay, I'll stay another day and leave tomorrow morning. If you help me get a hire car to drive back to Manchester.'

'Yay!' Clemmy punches the air. 'Of course I'll help. I've got the number of the local car hire firm in my phone.' She smiles expectantly. 'I also came over to ask how it went with Jake yesterday. Did you talk to him?'

When I tell her what happened, her face falls. 'Oh my God, I can't believe he just left without saying anything to you. I have to say, he's gone way down in my estimation ... unless it was an emergency?'

I shrug off her question, determined not to waste any more time thinking about the reasons for Jake's hasty departure.

We'd known each other barely a week after all. He didn't owe me anything.

Sylvia's warning flashes into my mind.

I'm not going to let any man stop me from moving forward into my future ...

*

It's a lovely day for a summer fayre. A hot sun shines in a clear blue sky but there's a cooling breeze keeping the temperature just right.

Clemmy, Poppy and I drive over in Poppy's van, the back loaded with cakes and pastries of all descriptions. We unload the trays of goodies over at the stall we've been allocated, on the far side of the field behind Sylvia's hotel, then Poppy drives the van to the car park provided for stall holders.

I'm on edge all the time, wondering if Jake will be here.

I know that, logically, it doesn't make sense because he's no longer camping out in the woods.

He won't be here. I know that.

But a tiny part of me is still hoping ...

In the short time I've known him, Jake has managed to creep into my heart and take up residence there, and there's not a thing I can do about it. Every time I see a tall man in jeans with tawny hair, my heart starts racing fit to burst out of my chest and I'm in a permanent state of excited expectation at the thought I might see him.

Sad or what?

As Clemmy and I start arranging the cakes in a mouth-watering display, a band – presumably hired for the day – is warming up nearby, playing old jazz classics, perfect for a hot summer day. There's also some fairground roundabouts and a variety of other stalls that are beginning to take shape, including a Women's Institute table selling homemade preserves and pickles.

Clemmy is expecting Ryan to arrive any moment, back from the Paris conference, and I can tell she's as distracted as I am. She wants to tackle her fiancé about the woman we saw him with in the café the other day. I really feel for her. Asking questions that could forever change your life as you know it isn't always the easiest thing to do ...

I think about Arabella, wondering if she'll be at the fayre today.

Clemmy peers over at the WI stall. 'That's Lottie over there,' she murmurs.

I swing round to look. 'The village gossip? Where?'

'With the pale lilac perm? And the winged spectacles? She'll be in her element. She's got so many people here to winkle nuggets of gossip from!'

'Maybe Joan will be here,' I say, remembering she's also a WI member. I glance around but I can't see her. She said she'd be in touch when she'd spoken to Lottie about Maple Tree House, but so far, I've heard nothing.

'Shall we go and talk to Lottie?'

'What?' I glance at her, startled. 'Now?'

'It'll be fine,' says Clemmy reassuringly. 'I know her quite well so I could talk to her myself if you like. I could say I'd heard that Arabella had had a baby when she was very young and I wondered if Lottie knew about it.'

'Really?' I gaze at Clemmy, my stomach doing somersaults at the very thought.

She shrugs. 'You need to find out who your birth mum is. And I'm sure Lottie will be only too glad to tell me if she knows anything.'

I swallow. 'Okay.'

'Great.' Clemmy beams at me. 'I'll go and talk to her now.'

'Wait!' I need to tell her not to mention me by name, but she's already walking over there. And before I can run after her, I'm stopped by Sylvia who's next in the queue for Poppy's cakes.

'You stayed on for the fayre?' she says, and I have no choice but to stop and talk to her. Especially after her kindness in waiving my bill the day before.

'Yes. I'm in no real rush to get back. I was living in Toby's flat, so I'm going to have to find somewhere else to stay.'

She nods in sympathy. 'A brand-new start.'

'Yes. That's a nice way to put it. What are you doing buying cakes from Poppy, by the way?' I smile at her. 'I would have thought your chef could turn his hand to all manner of wonderful sweet things?'

Sylvia touches my arm and murmurs confidingly, 'Poppy's chocolate muffins definitely have the edge. But don't tell Chef I said that.'

'Can I help you, Sylvia?' asks Roxy, Poppy's assistant. 'Let me guess. Chocolate muffins by any chance?'

Sylvia smiles. 'Got it in one. Half a dozen, please.'

Clemmy is racing back over, almost tripping over her own feet in her eagerness to talk to me.

She pulls me to one side. 'You're not going to believe this,' she murmurs. 'But Lottie actually remembers a baby at Maple Tree House.'

'She does?' My heart starts racing. 'But when?'

'She reckons in 1987. She says she remembers because she'd just given birth herself to her son, Joe. She didn't know the owners of Maple Tree House because they'd only recently moved in, but she recalls passing the garden with little Joe and seeing another baby in a pram. A woman came out into the garden and – Lottie being Lottie – immediately got talking to her over the hedge. She remembers jokingly saying, "Everyone seems to be having boys at the moment. Is this another one?" But the woman said no, it was a girl, and took the pram inside.'

'It was a girl?' My heart lurches.

'Yes, but here's the interesting bit. That was the one and only time Lottie clapped eyes on that baby.' She raises her eyebrows meaningfully.

'And that's because the baby was adopted,' I say slowly, my mind reeling.

Clemmy nods. 'It would certainly seem so.'

'Was the woman Lottie spoke to Arabella?'

Clemmy shakes her head. 'Arabella would have been just a teenager. Lottie says the woman was probably in her forties.'

'Arabella's mother?'

'I'd guess so.' Clemmy frowns, then says just what I'm thinking. 'I suppose another possibility is that you're Arabella's sister.'

'But that wouldn't really make sense, would it? It was a young girl who snatched me away.' I sigh, my head going round in confusing circles.

Clemmy nods thoughtfully. 'At least we now know there was a baby living at the house and it was a girl.' She smiles. 'You might have to stay on here a little longer to get to the bottom of this mystery.'

I grin at her. 'I wish I could, but I'm back at work in Manchester on Monday.'

'It's looking more likely that Arabella is your mother.'

'I wish I could be pleased.'

'Is it time you talked to Arabella? Asked her outright about the baby?'

'I think it probably is.' I hold out my hand. 'Look, I'm trembling.'

'It'll be fine,' says Clemmy reassuringly. 'She's here, actually. I just saw her.'

'Really?' I turn, surveying all the people milling around at the fayre. 'Where?'

'Clem, are there any more trays of pastries in the car?' calls Roxy. 'We're running out fast.'

Clemmy signals there are, then she touches my arm. 'Back in a sec.'

I nod vaguely and she goes off to the car. I've just spotted Arabella, over by the refreshments stall, talking to Sylvia.

They seem to be arguing, if Arabella's jerky hand gestures are anything to go by. As I watch, Sylvia rakes both hands through her hair and looks skywards, as if she's trying to hold on to her anger. It's not like her to lose her cool. I wonder what Arabella is saying to make her so annoyed?

I start walking over and neither of them even notices me approaching.

I'm within earshot just in time to hear Arabella say in her grating, high-pitched tone, 'She probably *will* find out eventually but it certainly won't be from me!'

They both clock me standing there at the exact same moment and Arabella's shocked expression is almost comical. Sylvia smoothes her hair, takes a breath and moves away, back to the stall, while Arabella's eyes narrow and she gives me a look that could kill. It's so full of venom, I almost gasp out loud. She storms past me, deliberately knocking my arm so that I stumble sideways. Then she disappears in the direction of the car park.

What the hell is her problem with me?

Perhaps she's found out who I am. The baby she gave up for adoption …

Oh God, Sylvia was standing behind us when Clemmy and I were talking about me searching for my birth mother. Could Sylvia have put two and two together and gone to tell Arabella? Sylvia doesn't strike me as a gossip. She seems a very private, discreet sort of person. But then again I hardly know her.

I walk over to the side of the field, my legs shaking, and sit down on the grass, leaning back against the fence.

Tears are pooling in my eyes but I look upwards and determinedly blink them away.

However much I might not like Arabella, seeing that look of venom on her face felt like a dagger in my gut. I've never felt so alone as I do right now. It's a real physical pain inside.

I think about Mum and what I've lost, and the lonely future I'm facing without her, and my shoulders start to shake. And then it's impossible to stop the tears flooding down my face.

After a while, I realise someone is standing over me.

Ruby.

'Is it your mum?' she asks, frowning.

I nod, wiping my face with a hanky and attempting a smile, and she drops down onto the grass beside me.

For a moment there's silence, broken only by an occasional post-weeping shudder from me.

Then Ruby says in a matter-of-fact tone, 'You're lucky, really.'

'*Lucky*?' I stare at her, feeling such a burst of fury towards her that I find myself scrambling to my feet to get away, worried I'll say something I'll regret.

'But you are,' she says, calm as a cucumber, sitting cross-legged and staring up at me. 'I mean, think of it this way: not everyone gets on with their mum. My best friend, Chloe, absolutely hates hers. I mean, she *loves* her, obviously, but she'd rather snog Simon Cowell than willingly spend any length of time with her mum. I know lots of people like that. They love their parents but they're not exactly the people they'd choose to spend their precious free time with. But it was different for you and your mum.' She shrugs. 'I can tell you had such a close bond by the way you talk about her. You were the best of friends as well as mother and daughter, right?'

I swallow and try to speak but my mouth is too dry.

'So you were lucky. *Really* lucky to have experienced the sort of bond that I think must be quite rare. You should celebrate it and make your mum proud by ...' She pauses, searching around for inspiration. 'By doing great things!' She grimaces. 'Because, let's be realistic here, that's really all you can do. And I'm not trying to say it's easy, all this grief stuff. Because I know it's not. When my gerbil died, I cried for days. *Weeks*.' She shrugs. 'Mind you, I *was* only ten years old. And I *know* we're not talking about gerbils, but it's love all the same ... isn't it?'

I gaze down at this wise-beyond-her-years eighteen-year-old, a grudging smile breaking through. 'Perhaps I'll get a gerbil, then.'

Ruby nods enthusiastically. 'Perhaps you should. Or learn to fly a plane. Or become a cordon bleu cook. Or backpack around the world with just a chimpanzee for company. And you can do it in your mum's memory and know that she'll always be in your heart, cheering you on.' She makes a face. 'Ugh, I sound like a bad romance novel.'

'No, you don't.' I drop down to join her on the grass. 'Well, admittedly that last bit was a little nauseating. But in general, you're on the right track.'

'Good.' She nods as if to say her job is done.

'I could send my book out to some publishers.'

'There you are! Brilliant! You'll be a writer!'

'As easy as that, eh?' I tease her, nudging her so that she loses her balance and rolls on her side with a dramatic shriek then collapses into giggles.

She springs to her feet. 'I need cake. What about you?'

I nod, holding out my hand. 'Cake. Definitely.' She hauls me to my feet and we wander companionably in the direction of Poppy's stall, where a large queue has formed.

A car roars by and I glance up and see it's Arabella's Mini Clubman breaking the speed limit.

'I wonder what rattled her cage?' mutters Ruby, staring after it. 'Maybe she's just had bad news.'

'I think you might be right,' I murmur.

I take a deep breath and turn my attention to the cakes. It's probably for the best.

I'd hate to have Arabella as a mother anyway ...

Chapter 25

'I can't believe it, Daisy. He's brought *her* here. Look!' Clemmy hisses in my ear as Ruby's chatting to Roxy, paying for her strawberry-topped angel cake.

Pulling Clemmy away from the queue so we can talk, I look over at where she's pointing and, sure enough, there's Ryan walking over the grass with the slim, blonde girl from the café.

Clemmy's pretty face is flushed. 'He's just driven back from London. I told him to come straight here and find me, but I didn't expect him to be bringing a bloody passenger!'

As we watch, Ryan spots us and waves. The blonde girl says something to him, raises her hand and strolls off in another direction.

'Right, I'm going to have it out with him,' says Clemmy, looking more focused and determined than I've ever seen her. 'He's never mentioned her to me and there's only one reason why he wouldn't. He knows I wouldn't like it.'

'It might be totally innocent,' I remind her.

She throws me a sceptical look and marches over the grass to meet Ryan.

I feel tense and apprehensive watching her spiky body language as she approaches her fiancé, head held high to give her confidence. Underneath the façade, I know she's as vulnerable as a new-born chick.

I'm so fond of Clemmy. I want her to have the wedding she longs for with the man she loves, but from where I'm standing, things look very far from rosy right now.

They've stopped in the middle of the field and Clemmy is throwing her arms around wildly. Ryan is standing there staring at her, with the bewildered look of a man who's just been ambushed.

Then *he* starts gesticulating, at which point Clemmy tosses her head and starts marching in my direction, Ryan following a few paces behind.

As they get nearer, I can hear their conversation, though I'm pretending to examine some silver earrings on the jewellery stall.

'I can't believe you've been keeping all this in. Why didn't you just come out and *ask* me who she was?' demands Ryan.

'Because it wasn't just *her*. It was all the late nights and sleepovers in London you've been having lately. You must admit, you never used to stay over. You always came home, no matter how late it was.'

'Yes, because I was desperate to see you, but it was starting to affect my performance at work. I'm *knackered*, Clem! Planning a wedding is *stressful*. I'm just trying to stay sane.'

Clemmy doesn't seem particularly reassured by this.

'You still haven't told me who your blonde friend is,' she hisses, looking around as if she expects her to pop up and join in the free-for-all.

Ryan doesn't answer. He just looks at her, drawing in a huge breath and expelling it slowly.

'Well? I'm waiting.'

Poor Clemmy is so worked up, she's actually trembling.

Ryan gives a frustrated growl and turns away. 'I should have known I wouldn't be able to keep it a secret.'

My heart rate picks up speed. *What the hell is Ryan about to confess?*

'Go on, then. Who is she?' demands Clemmy.

Ryan glares at her for a long moment before he answers. 'Nicole is my dance teacher.'

Clemmy falls silent.

I sneak a look at her. It's fair to say Ryan has taken the wind right out of her sails.

'So well done, Clem, you've managed to ruin the surprise with your stupid suspicions. I was going to impress you at the wedding with my moves but it turns out you don't trust me, so maybe we shouldn't even be *having* a wedding.' Ryan turns on his heel and walks off.

Clemmy stares after him. Her face is a study in shock – and starting to creep in are traces of horror at how she could ever have doubted him. She covers her eyes and murmurs, 'Shit.'

I touch her shoulder. 'Hey, at least now you can relax. Ryan's turned out to be the lovely man you always thought he was.'

She groans. 'I know. But what does that make me? A paranoid flake who's just messed up the best thing that ever happened to me!'

I frown in sympathy. 'You're not paranoid or a flake. You're just a woman in love who's terrified it's all going to go wrong. Blissful happiness always comes at a price to us contrary humans.'

'But what if he means it about there being no wedding?'

'He didn't,' I tell her firmly. 'He just said it because he was angry with you for spoiling his surprise.'

'And for not trusting him, which is far worse,' she groans. 'Oh God, no.'

She's staring in horror across the field and I follow her eyes.

'He's bringing her over,' she whispers, quickly flicking at her hair and standing tall.

Sure enough, Ryan and the girl called Nicole are walking over to us. Nicole is smiling openly but Ryan's face is tense.

'Clem, Daisy – let me introduce you to Nicole, who used to be a professional dancer.'

We shake hands and Nicole smiles at Clemmy and says, 'I've been working him hard but I think I've got him wedding-ready! When's the big day again?'

'The first Saturday in October.' Clemmy smiles awkwardly. 'I must admit, this is all a big surprise.'

Nicole grins. 'You wouldn't believe the number of men I've put through their paces in preparation for their wedding. And couples, too. But I think he'll do you proud.' She turns and nudges Ryan. 'He's quite the confident mover now.'

'Really?' Clemmy laughs. 'Well, in that case, you've definitely worked wonders.' She smiles hesitantly at Ryan and, after a moment, he smiles grudgingly back.

'Right, well, I'll leave you to it. My parents live in Appley Green and I'm here for the weekend.'

'Did you drive through?' Clemmy asks.

Nicole nods and I can see Clemmy thinking what a fool she's been.

After she's gone, Clemmy looks at Ryan with tears in her eyes. 'I'm so sorry. I don't know what I was thinking. I guess it's just wedding nerves and stupid hormones.'

Ryan draws her into his side and kisses her.

'I'll never doubt you again, I promise.'

'You'd better not because I'm here to stay.' He grins suddenly and clears his throat. 'Clementine Rogers, would you do me the honour of dancing with me?'

She laughs. 'What, now?'

He nods, smiling into her eyes.

'In front of all these people?'

'Which people?' he growls, pulling her against him and slipping his arms around her. 'All I can see is you, Clem.'

My heart gives a happy lurch as I watch them moving in time, staring into each other's eyes, Ryan holding his fiancée close to his heart. The people milling around stop what they're doing to watch, and the crowd parts to give the lovebirds more space.

Then suddenly Ryan is down on one knee, holding Clemmy's hand and smiling up at her.

Clemmy's hand covers her mouth as she stares down at him.

'We got engaged after you proposed to me. So I never got the chance to ask you if you'd marry me. But I'm asking you now.' He clears his throat. 'Clementine Rogers, will you please do me the honour of becoming my wife?'

Clemmy gives a little shriek of joy. Then she starts saying yes, over and over again, happy tears spilling from her eyes.

I swallow hard, surprised at how emotional I feel myself.

Afterwards, it's clear the happy couple are eager to get home and make up for lost time, and as it's nearing the end of the afternoon and Poppy has almost sold out, we decide to pack up and leave.

'That was well worth doing,' sighs Poppy, looking happy

but exhausted as we load the empty trays into her van. 'I've handed out loads of business cards, so hopefully that will translate into lots more business.' She beams at us. 'Brunch on me tomorrow?'

She includes me in the invitation but I have to refuse.

'I'm heading home to Manchester tomorrow and I want to make an early start to beat the traffic. If that's okay with you, Clemmy?' She's giving me a lift into Guildford to pick up my hire car.

'Absolutely. Shame you can't stay for brunch, though, Daisy.' Ryan tickles Clemmy and she shrieks and drags him into the back seat of the van with her.

I sit in the back with them, feeling a mixture of emotions. I'm so pleased for Clemmy and Ryan. After their little hiccup, all is set fair for the wedding in October and I couldn't be happier for them.

There's a hollow feeling inside, though, when I think of Jake.

I'm still waiting to hear what he thinks of my manuscript.

At first, I kept checking my emails constantly, anxiously waiting for a response, which was stupid, really. I mean, he was hardly going to read it immediately. It could be weeks before he has the time to get to it.

Anyway, I couldn't bear the disappointment of checking and finding nothing, so I've forced myself to stop looking now. At least, not every five minutes like I did at first.

'You will be able to come to the wedding, won't you, Daisy?' asks Clemmy, breaking into my gloomy thoughts.

'Oh, wow.' It's so unexpected, I'm almost speechless. 'Of course I will. I'd *love* to!'

'Brilliant! It's been so great having you around this week.'

She leans close, nudges my shoulder with hers and murmurs, 'We've bared our souls to each other, that's for sure.'

I nod happily. Who would have thought that booking a glamping site holiday would lead to a renewed friendship and a wedding invitation? At least this whole crazy week has an upside to it!

'It's amazing how a crisis or two can bring people together!' We exchange a rueful smile.

'Would you like to join us for dinner?' asks Clemmy. 'I hate to think of you spending your last night on your own.'

'What, with you two lovebirds cooing all over the place?' I laugh. 'Thank you very much but no. I'll have plenty to do packing up and then getting an early night.'

'You should come, Daisy,' Ryan says. 'I'm not sure I'm up to talking weddings all night, so I'd be *extremely* grateful for your input.'

'Hey, you.' Clemmy nudges him and he grins.

'Only joking. Working out the seating plan is quite the most fascinating thing I've ever had to do. But it would still be great if you came over, Daisy.'

I laugh at their antics. 'No, really, if you don't mind I'll just chill on my own before my long drive tomorrow.'

All the same, going into the empty tent after they've dropped me off feels a bit sad after the bustle of the day. I busy myself getting a meal of sorts together, basically eating what's left in the fridge – a small piece of quiche and half a tub of coleslaw. Then I wash up and get my case out.

Unzipping it, I find the bag with Mum's cardigan in it and stare at it sadly. It gave me such comfort wearing it, and I certainly won't be parting with it. But I'm feeling a little bit stronger now.

The cardigan stays in the bag.

I'm in the middle of packing when my mobile rings. It's Clemmy.

I answer, wondering if she's phoning to repeat her dinner invitation or to make sure I'm not feeling down all on my own.

'Daisy?' She sounds excited. 'Can you come over?'

'I'm just packing ...'

'You need to come now,' she says. 'Lottie's here. She's remembered more stuff about the occupants of Maple Tree House.'

'Really?'

'Yes. Can you come over now? I'll open a bottle of wine. I think you might need it.'

'Clemmy!' My heart starts beating frantically. 'You can't leave me dangling like this. What is it? Tell me now!'

'No. I'd rather Lottie explained. Just get your butt over here immediately,' she shrieks, having clearly been at the wine already.

My heart is pounding as I make my way over the grass to Clemmy's door.

She hustles me inside as soon as I knock and I follow her into the kitchen, where Lottie is sitting at the table, a cup of tea in front of her, munching her way through a chocolate muffin. Ryan must have taken himself off to watch TV.

Lottie looks at me over her glasses when we walk in and she waves the muffin in greeting. 'You must be Daisy.'

I nod and she says, 'Sit down. Sit down. Clementine tells me you've been on a search for your long-lost mother?'

'My birth mother, yes.'

'Well, I've remembered something that may or may not help.'

'More tea, Lottie?' calls Clemmy and, infuriatingly, I have to wait while Lottie has her cup topped up and stirs in three teaspoons of sugar.

Clemmy joins us at the table, bringing a glass of wine for me.

I take a large glug of it immediately.

'So.' Lottie leans forward, her eyes round, clearly relishing her moment in the spotlight. 'After I spoke to Clementine here at the fayre, I kept thinking about Maple Tree House. It was always such a fascinating place. The most expensive piece of property in the street. Six bedrooms, I think, if you count the rooms in the extension that was added twenty years or so ago.' She pauses to take a big slurp of tea.

'Well, anyway, I got to thinking about Fiona and Graham Watson, who owned the house, and their little daughter, Arabella. They ran a business manufacturing computer accessories and I remember thinking that poor little Arabella must hardly have seen them because they always seemed to be working. And that's when I realised something.'

She pauses dramatically and leans forward, prolonging the suspense for just a little longer.

'You realised ...?' prompts Clemmy.

Lottie sits back in her chair and folds her hands over her stomach. 'Well, I remembered that, at one stage, the Watsons had a housekeeper. They liked to think they were rather grand, you see, living in the big house, and the mother and father both worked full-time. So they employed someone to look after the house. She was quite young, as far as I can recall. Probably not even out of her teens.'

'Do you ...' I try to speak but the words get stuck in my throat.

Clemmy, sitting next to me, covers my hand with hers and leans forward. 'Do you know who she was? Can you tell us the girl's name?'

Chapter 26

Lottie draws in a big breath and lets it out slowly. Then she smiles triumphantly from me to Clemmy and back again.

'Her name, girls, was Sylvia.'

Shock clutches at my heart and I stare at Lottie in a daze.

Clemmy gives a little gasp and turns to me. 'The Sylvia who owns the Starlight Hotel?' She swings back to Lottie. 'Is it *that* Sylvia?'

Lottie nods. 'She only worked for the Watsons for a short while – probably no more than a few months. That's why I'd forgotten all about it until you asked me about Maple Tree House. I've been debating whether to tell you, but in the end, I thought you needed to know.'

She carries on talking but I'm barely aware of what she's saying. I feel as if I'm swimming underwater. It's a very weird sensation. Lottie and Clemmy are talking but the sounds aren't penetrating through to me properly.

Clemmy puts her hand on my back and turns to say something. Her face looms in front of me and I find myself trying to lip-read but being completely unable to understand what she's saying.

I scrape back my chair as the churning in my stomach gets worse. 'Sorry, can I use your loo?'

Clemmy gets up quickly and leads me to the downstairs toilet. Inside, I lock the door and stand in front of the mirror, leaning on the washbasin, staring at my reflection in the mirror until it blurs.

Could Sylvia be my biological mother? Did she leave her job as housekeeper at the Watsons' after such a short time because she found herself pregnant?

I run the tap and splash some water on my face. Then I take a few deep breaths and, thankfully, the nausea that had gripped me begins to subside.

I examine my face, looking for traces of a resemblance to Sylvia. There's something about the eyes that might be familiar, although I've no idea what colour hers are. And I think Sylvia has the same pronounced bow-shaped upper lip as me.

Still stunned, I've no idea how I feel about this sudden turn of events. Should I be ecstatic? Excited? Or worried in case it all ends badly? Is Lottie even *right* about Sylvia being the Watsons' housekeeper?

Someone knocks softly on the door. 'Are you okay in there, Daisy?'

Clemmy.

'Fine. I'll be out in a minute.' I force myself to speak, although my voice sounds strange.

'Okay.' There's a pause. 'See you in the kitchen.'

Pressing my hands to my burning cheeks, I stare at myself in the mirror one last time, wishing Mum hadn't died because then I wouldn't have had to go through all this emotional chaos.

But that's just pointless. This is the reality. I must face it.

When I enter the kitchen, Lottie has gone. Clemmy gets up from the table. 'I think we should go and see Sylvia,' she murmurs, looking at me anxiously.

'Now?' I stare at her in horror. *Is she mad?*

She shrugs. 'You're never going to be able to sleep until you know the truth,' she points out gently. 'Are you?'

I shake my head as my throat clogs with tears. Clemmy's right, of course. There's no point in putting it off. I need to know ...

It's still light when we emerge into the balmy night air, the sun a big glowing red ball on the horizon. I glance at my watch. Nine-thirty. What will Sylvia be doing now?

Silently, we get into Clemmy's car and drive along to the hotel. She parks outside and we walk into reception. My heart is in my mouth as Clemmy asks to speak to Sylvia.

'Can *I* help, Madam?' asks the receptionist with a bright smile, and I almost laugh. The question we're going to be asking has the potential to be rather more life-changing than whether or not there are any rooms available for tonight!

'No, we really need to talk to Sylvia if possible,' Clemmy says. 'It's personal.'

The receptionist frowns, thinking. 'She's in the restaurant, I think. Wait one moment.'

My heart hammers as she starts speaking on the phone. 'Sylvia? Yes, there are two ladies waiting for you in reception. They say it's a personal matter.' She nods then asks for our names. 'Clemmy and Daisy?' After a brief instruction from the other end, she says, 'Yes. Yes, of course. I'll tell them.'

She puts the phone down and says, 'I'm so sorry but Sylvia's busy right now. She won't be able to see you tonight.'

'Oh.' Clemmy looks at me with a frown. 'But it's important. Can we make an appointment to see her tomorrow morning?'

'I'm afraid not. She's going away to a conference and is leaving first thing in the morning.'

My heart is beating very fast. 'But I need to talk to her. Tonight.' There's an edge of desperation in my voice. Tears of frustration are pricking at my eyes. *I've come this far and now to be denied the chance to talk to her …*

The receptionist is apologetic but firm. 'Why not leave your number and she'll call you when she's back?'

She's in the restaurant. I need to see her now, otherwise I'll never have any peace …

Clemmy shouts after me as I walk quickly away.

As I approach the restaurant, I see Sylvia slipping out and walking briskly up the nearest staircase.

'Sylvia?' I call, and she hesitates but doesn't turn around. 'Please. I need to talk to you.'

She draws in a breath and raises her head to the ceiling. Then she straightens her jacket and turns. Her face is in semi-darkness as she looks down at me. I can't see her expression very clearly.

'I'm busy, Daisy. I can't talk now.'

She turns to go and it suddenly occurs to me that perhaps she really is just busy.

'Sylvia?' *Perhaps she has no idea why I'm here!* 'Do you know who I am?'

Slowly, she turns to face me. 'Yes. I know who you are,' she says in a voice weirdly devoid of emotion.

My stomach drops to the floor.

I stand there in a daze, watching Sylvia walk away from me up the stairs, holding herself stiffly upright.

I finally find my voice.

'Sylvia? Please! We have to talk about this.'

But she carries on climbing the stairs. So in desperation, I run after her, my heart in my mouth.

'Sylvia. For God's sake. You're my birth mother. You *have* to talk to me! You gave me up for adoption. Don't you think I at least have a right to some *answers*?'

She hesitates and I wait, holding my breath.

But when she turns to me, her face is as unyielding as stone, her eyes as cold as a day in mid-winter.

'I have nothing to say to you, Daisy. What's done is done. I can't change the past and I have no desire to.'

She turns away but I grab her arm and she flinches as if I've struck her. Her whole body is trembling, I realise.

She looks back at me, her eyes huge and haunted, and a single tear tracks its way down her cheek. But she brushes it away roughly and runs up the stairs, away from me.

'I can't believe you won't at least talk to me,' I shout, but she's gone.

I feel Clemmy's arm around me and I crumple, the tears flowing freely down my face. My heart feels as if it might break in two.

The irony of the situation pierces me like a blade.

I've finally found my birth mother – only to be rejected by her all over again ...

'Perhaps now isn't the right time?' murmurs Clemmy.

I shake my head. 'There'll clearly never *be* a right time. She's made that very plain.'

Clemmy sighs. 'You don't know that.'

'Yes, I do. It's obvious she knows why I'm here and she's just made it abundantly clear that she doesn't want to know me.' Feeling unsteady on my feet, I walk back through reception and head for the door.

I should never have come to this place. It was a stupid idea, thinking I could track down my real mother and everything would be happy-ever-after.

Actually, I never did think that. I was always worried it would end in disaster. And I was right!

Why the hell didn't I listen to my instincts and leave well alone?

Chapter 27

We drive back in fraught silence.

Clemmy asks me if I want to stay at hers but I tell her I need to be alone to think. So, reluctantly, she leaves me at the tent, making me promise to call her if I need to talk about it.

But as I go through the motions of getting ready for bed, I know I won't be calling Clemmy.

I'm done talking about it.

I just want to go home; get away from this place as soon as I can.

The week has been a complete disaster and I've never felt so emotionally drained. I've fallen into a horrible pit of desperation. It's going to take forever to haul myself back to square one, never mind start moving up towards the light.

Toby, Jake, Mum, Sylvia. I'm grieving for every one of them in different ways.

And after all the torment I've put myself through, agonising about my real mother and finally finding the courage to search for the answer, the message has come back, loud and uncompromisingly clear.

My birth mother wants nothing to do with me.

*

I wake next morning to the alarm and a drizzly, overcast day.

I want to be at the car hire company early so Clemmy is coming to pick me up at eight. After a restless night, I can't wait to be on the road and heading home.

When Clemmy opens the door, I'm standing there with my case and the first thing she says to me is, 'Are you sure you don't want to pop into the hotel before we go?'

'To see if Sylvia is there?' I frown. 'No way. She's made her feelings about me perfectly clear. And anyway, she's away at a conference. The receptionist said so.'

Clemmy nods in understanding and helps me lift the case into her boot.

We get in the car and Clemmy starts the engine. 'I'm so glad you came glamping.' She turns with a wistful smile, and suddenly I'm thinking of the good things that have happened while I've been here.

Reconnecting with Clemmy, for a start, has been brilliant. She's been such a great friend to me through this awful birth mum business. And meeting the rest of her family has been great, too. I'll never forget Ruby's brilliant words of wisdom.

I think of Jake and a pang of real heartache hits me, clouding my happy thoughts.

'I'm glad, too.' I smile. 'I can't wait to come back for your big day.'

'October.' She gives a little shriek. 'God, it's galloping nearer.'

I nod, grinning. 'It'll be here before you know it. You must be so happy now you and Ryan are back on track.'

She smiles. 'Yes. I think he knows I hate myself for doubting him.'

'I'm sure he understands.'

She looks over. 'It's a shame about Jake, though. Can't you email him and ...' She trails off.

'And what?' I ask gloomily. 'Ask if he fancies meeting up for a coffee if ever he's round my way? Which is probably never since we live hundreds of miles apart!'

Clemmy sighs, puts the car into gear and moves off. 'If it's meant to be, it'll happen.'

I shake my head. 'It's not meant to be. If it was, he wouldn't have gone off like that without any warning and – *oh my God*!' I've just clapped sight of someone in the wing mirror.

'What?'

I swing round and my eyes widen at the sight of Sylvia, running along the road, waving her arms as if she's trying to flag us down.

'It's Sylvia,' I yelp. 'She's running down the middle of the road.'

I glance ahead and see a car approaching at some speed. My heart lurches with fright. 'I think we'd better stop or she might get run over!'

Clemmy acts swiftly, looking behind her and braking. She moves over onto the grass verge and switches off the engine.

We flash each other a look of astonishment then turn to see Sylvia peering in through the passenger window, looking red and out of breath.

'Are you going to talk to her? Give her another chance?' asks Clemmy without moving her lips.

I sigh and look down at my hands. 'I suppose I'd better hear what she has to say.'

'Shall I let her in the car so you can talk?'

I shake my head. 'I'll get out.'

'Okay. Come to the house when you're ready?'

I smile gratefully at her. 'Thank you so much, Clemmy. I really don't know how I'd have managed this week without you.'

'Same goes.' My tears seem to be echoed in Clemmy's suspiciously glossy eyes. She laughs. 'What on earth are we like?' Spontaneously, we clasp each other in a big, teary hug.

I glance across at Sylvia, who's standing back from the door, her face tense, patiently waiting.

Sighing, I get out of the car, not knowing what to expect. After the week of shocks I've had, I wouldn't be surprised if she was here to tell me she's not only my mother, but also my sister and grandmother, all rolled into one. (It's likely possible in some twisted, dysfunctional-family sort of a way.)

I close the car door and Clemmy starts the engine and does a twenty-five-point turn in the narrow road. Sylvia and I get involved in helping her, and we just manage to stop her from reversing right into the ditch.

We're both banging on the car, shouting, 'Stop!' and luckily she does, just in time.

I glance at Sylvia and she sweeps her hand over her brow in relief. And despite everything, we grin at one another.

Then I remember her treatment of me the night before and my expression freezes.

'I thought you were at a conference?' I point out, trying to sound confident but shaking inside. 'And you almost got yourself run over back there. It must be something important you've come to tell me.'

She swallows. 'It is. The most important thing ever. More important than a bloody conference.'

My heart does a funny little leap in my chest, but I force myself to remain cool.

'Go on.' I'm determined to make her squirm after what she's put me through. Feeling rejected by the woman who gave birth to me felt like a dagger to my heart.

'I'm sorry, Daisy. For everything,' she says, her shoulders slumped in defeat. 'And I'd be so glad if you would let me explain.'

'Explain what? That you got rid of me because you didn't want me?'

She stares at me in horror, looking genuinely distressed by my outburst of anger.

'So are you really my birth mother?' I demand. 'The girl who scared my poor mum to death by trying to snatch me away?'

Her face is scrunched up with pain. 'I've always hated myself for that. But I was young and scared and my life was in chaos. That's no excuse for what I put your mum through, though. I know that.'

I swallow hard. 'Mum was *terrified* after you tried to take me away. She lived in fear after that, thinking you'd come back again. I don't know how you could have given me away in the first place. But to come and try to get me back?' I shake my head in disbelief. 'I have a dark memory of that night, even though I was so small. It feels like a nightmare, it's so scary. I knew I dropped something and I couldn't for the life of me remember what it was. And it was agony not knowing. *That's* what you put us through!'

She bows her head. 'I'm so, so sorry, Daisy. My mum had multiple sclerosis and I was her only carer. I managed to get the housekeeper job at the Watsons' so we could make ends meet, but pretty soon after, I realised I was pregnant.' She pauses, putting her hands to her face. 'I was seventeen and the father of my baby was five years older and, needless to say, he vanished into thin air when he found out about the baby. Mum was getting worse and I knew I'd have to be a full-time carer. I desperately wanted to keep you with me – you've no idea the anguish I went through, trying to work out a way for me to hold on to you. But in the end, I knew it was useless. My friend, Ella, worked at the adoption agency and it was she who persuaded me I should give you up for adoption. She knew all about the process and she was so supportive at a time I really needed someone's advice. I hadn't told Mum I was pregnant, you see. I couldn't bear to worry her with it while she was getting weaker every day.'

Listening to her story, which is clearly genuine, I find myself softening towards her. What would I have done in her situation?

'Yes, but how could you do that to Mum? Do you have any idea how she must have felt after you tried to snatch me back?'

'Yes. A thousand times yes! I've never stopped hating myself for what I did. Not just having you adopted, but going to your house and trying to get you back. I've wished a million times that I'd done things differently. But back then, I thought I'd done the right thing. I was crucified by my loss. And when Mum died three years later, I lost my mind for a while and I poured all my grief into plotting how to get you back. I look back now and I'm horrified – but at the time, being so racked with grief over Mum, it really felt like the logical thing to do. Mum had gone. But I could get you back and everything would be all right.'

Her words touch a chord within me. In my grief over Mum's death, I set my mind on finding my birth mum. In a way, it was the same thing.

'Anyway, after that terrible night, I tried to forget about you. I buried myself in my work and told myself this was my life. I was a single career woman with no family and I almost convinced myself that's the way I liked it.'

'When did you realise the baby you'd given up was me?'

'Yesterday. At the fayre. I heard you talking to Clemmy about looking for your birth mother and I just knew. I panicked. My head was in a whirl. I didn't know what I was doing. I talked to Arabella, asking her to keep my secret.' She flicks her eyes to the ceiling and adds sarcastically, 'She was her usual accommodating self.'

I feel the tiniest twinge of sympathy for Sylvia. I've been on the other end of Arabella's nastiness and it's not pleasant.

Thank goodness Arabella isn't my mother!

The thought reverberates through me, bringing a pang of relief.

All the time, I've kept trying to tell myself that Arabella's bark was probably worse than her bite and that things would be fine if she turned out to be my birth mother. But now I can abandon that pretence. She's no relation of mine after all!

At least Sylvia feels remorse for everything that happened. It was clearly a huge shock for her, finding out who I was. But she seems genuinely sorry now for rebuffing me at the start.

A memory slips into my head. 'I saw you arguing with Arabella. I thought *she* was ... who I was looking for.' I swallow. 'I'm ... very glad she's not.'

Sylvia's mouth twists into a sad little smile.

'Oh, Daisy, I'm so sorry. For everything. When I realised who you were, I was terrified that, if you found me, my carefully constructed life would just explode around me. Arabella is the only one round here who knows the truth about the pregnancy and the adoption, although obviously she still has no idea that baby is you.' She sniffs. 'I'm *also* very glad Arabella isn't your mum.'

We gaze at each other through our tears.

'You are?' I say at last, my throat aching with emotion.

Sylvia nods. 'Of *course*. You were my baby. I loved you so much. I desperately wanted to keep you but Mum needed round-the-clock care and I knew I couldn't do it. I'd just turned seventeen. I hadn't a clue that I'd spend the rest of my life regretting my decision.'

I smile sadly. 'I'm glad you made the decision you did. Otherwise I'd never have had ...' I trail off awkwardly.

She nods, understanding. 'You'd never have had the mum you did. She ... sounds amazing.'

'She was.'

'Good.' She nods. 'You've no idea how happy and relieved that makes me feel. To know that you had a happy life with her.' She gives a bitter little laugh. 'Perhaps now I can stop beating myself up quite so much.'

'You should,' I say firmly, feeling her pain. 'You were a frightened teenager. You did what you thought was best. And actually, it all worked out fine.'

Sylvia stares at me through her tears. Then her legs seem to give way beneath her and she sinks down onto the grass verge. Covering her eyes with her hands, she starts sobbing as if her heart will truly break.

I watch her for a moment in a daze.

Then I get down beside her on the grass and put my arm around her shoulders.

Chapter 28

TWO MONTHS LATER

I'm on the bus, travelling across Manchester.

It's a special day and my stomach is churning in eager anticipation.

An image of Jake flashes into my mind and my throat tightens. For the millionth time, I wonder how he is. Has he gone for any more solitary camping trips? Is he beginning to move on after Laura's death?

I haven't heard from him since he left the woods so abruptly. His silence probably means he's looked at my manuscript but doesn't think it's good enough and is too nice to tell me that. I'm not going to let it put me off reaching for my dream, though. Stephen King had many rejections before he became a success.

I've checked Jake's website a few times since I got back from the glamping holiday but there's no release date yet for his latest book. Actually, who am I kidding? I check in at least once a day, ostensibly to catch up on book news, but actually so I can look at the photo of him and read the blurb about him over again. I feel embarrassed at myself for doing this, but I just can't seem to get Jake Steele out of my mind, no matter how hard I try. So I've stopped trying to fight it.

I've learned that you can't despatch strong feelings by locking them in a box and pretending you're fine. I did enough of that after Mum died. Trying so hard to put on a brave face and hide my grief just meant my head was filled with confusion and I was never going to be able to see a healthy way forward.

I was lucky – so lucky – to have chosen Clemmy's Lakeside Glamping for our holiday. Clemmy and I are even closer now than we were at uni and I'm going to her wedding in a couple of weeks. I can't wait to see everyone. Especially Poppy, Roxy, Gloria and Ruby.

It was Ruby who made me see things in a different light, telling me that I should celebrate Mum's life by striving for something that would make her proud. I've already started planning another book and my dream is that, one day, I'll be able to leave my job at *Plunge Happy Monthly* and concentrate on my writing. That's obviously a long way off, but I'm determined I will get there ...

I'm living in Mum's house now. It's still on the market and I'm in no hurry to sell it. I thought it would be hard, having daily reminders of the good old days when Mum was still around, but actually, it feels oddly comforting.

My stomach gives an embarrassingly loud gurgle. I didn't eat breakfast this morning because I was too excited. It's a nice feeling, though.

I'm meeting Sylvia at the bus station at ten-thirty and we're going somewhere for coffee and a catch-up. Judging by the last time we met up, two weeks ago, we'll probably still be sitting in the café long after the lunch crowd have gone back to their offices!

I smile, remembering the first time I went back down to Appley Green.

Sylvia and I had kept in constant, almost daily contact via email since finding each other and I looked forward every day to reading her funny tales about hotel life and learning more about her. When she suggested we meet up, I hopped on a train that same weekend and travelled down to Guildford, where Sylvia met me off the train. She'd left the hotel in the care of her very capable assistant manager for the weekend so that she could spend time showing me around. I gathered it was unheard of for Sylvia to take two consecutive days off, and knowing she'd done so for me meant I could relax in the knowledge that our time together was as important to her as it was to me.

The time flew by and, before I knew it, we were standing on the station platform saying goodbye.

Then it got a little bit awkward. Station goodbyes always have a certain drama attached to them. People tend to get sentimental. I felt it and I could tell Sylvia did, too. She was my mum and yet she *wasn't*. I already had a mum who I thought about every day of my life. It didn't sit naturally with me to think of calling Sylvia 'Mum'.

We kept our goodbyes light and friendly, and Sylvia promised to come up to Manchester in a few weeks' time. Since then, I've been down to Appley Green again, and today, a Thursday, Sylvia has driven up from Surrey for a flying visit as she has a weekend conference at the hotel to get back for.

I sway from side to side, enjoying the lulling motion of the bus.

Someone has left a newspaper on the seat beside me and I pick it up and absently start flicking through the pages.

I still have reservations about calling Sylvia 'Mum'. I'm not sure I'll ever be able to, although Rachel seems to think that's entirely to be expected. But things are going well. I can tell that our growing bond is just as important to Sylvia as it is to me, and I've reached that happy stage where I can relax, knowing that – barring catastrophes – we'll be in each other's lives forever.

I suppose it might sound a bit like wishful thinking. But I just know, deep down, that we are altering each other's lives for the better. It's still early days, but I'm looking beyond my grief now to a brighter future. And Sylvia is already transforming into a different person, having begun to shake off the weight of guilt she felt about the actions she took when she was young. She no longer wears black and she laughs a lot these days. She's stopped clinging so tightly to work to fill the vacuum and there's a light-heartedness in her that was missing before.

I get the feeling the future is no longer a scary concept for her. She's got things to look forward to now ...

I turn over a page and my heart lurches.

Looking out at me from a large black and white photograph is Jake Steele.

Holding my breath, I stare at the picture. It accompanies a feature in the arts section of the newspaper, announcing the publication today of his brand-new book. Clearly, he hasn't updated his website, then, because there's no mention there of the publication date.

I swallow hard. Of course. Laura used to do all the technical stuff for him.

Perhaps I should email Jake and ask him if he'd like me to update it for him. He's missing out on good publicity.

My heart sinks. Of course I can't. He'd definitely think I was a stalker if I offered to do that. I need to stop thinking about Jake and wishing, because no good can come of it ...

I fold the paper up and throw it onto the seat in front.

Jake Steele is history. I'm moving forward now.

We're turning into the station and I spot Sylvia standing by the newspaper kiosk, following the progress of my bus. She's wearing a new lilac-coloured coat, belted at the waist, and tan knee-high boots. The scraped-back hair has gone. In its place is a soft blonde bob. It makes her look ten years younger.

She spots me and smiles, and I wave and start gathering my belongings. As I'm walking to the front of the bus, I double back, snatch up the newspaper with Jake's profile in it and stuff it in my bag.

Sylvia looks really pleased to see me.

'I know you're coming down for Clemmy's wedding,' she says, linking my arm as we walk out of the bus station. 'But that's two weeks away and I really needed to see you. I'm so glad you were free today.' Her eyes are sparkling and she seems full of energy, despite having got up at the crack of dawn to drive up here.

I grin at her. 'I was supposed to be at work but I took the day off.'

'Well, I'm very glad you did. Now, let's get a cup of coffee. I'm parched.'

I suggest my favourite coffee shop. It incorporates a glorious bakery and bakes chocolate muffins as good as Poppy's and I'm sure it will be right up Sylvia's street. But to my surprise, she frowns.

'Actually, do you mind if we go to this place here?' She gets out a guidebook about the best eating places in the area and shows me the café she means.

'Yes, of course.' I don't even need to look at it because it really doesn't matter where we go. It's just so lovely to be spending time with Sylvia again.

We walk along, chatting and glancing in shop windows. One of the stores already has tinsel in the window, even though it's still only September, and we laugh about this.

Sylvia pauses. 'What are you doing for Christmas?' she asks casually, turning away to look in a shop window.

My heart tumbles into my shoes. I'm actually really dreading the festive season this year. I'm definitely getting there but all the merriness of Christmas with Mum not here is naturally making me feel anxious and down.

'I'm not sure. Rachel has invited me round for Christmas lunch with her and her fiancé, which might be quite nice.' I say it with a smile but I'm wilting inside. I'd rather spend the big day under the duvet than crash their first Christmas together in their new house!

Sylvia nods and says brightly, 'Yes, that would be lovely.'

'I expect you'll be busy with all your festive guests at the hotel. You won't have time for any celebrating until after the holidays.'

'Well, actually, I was thinking of treating myself to Christmas Day off for the first time in twenty years.' She laughs. 'I'll probably just sleep, eat chocolate and watch TV.'

'Sounds great to me.'

'I mean ...' She pauses. 'If you decide not to go to Rachel's, you could always come down to me and we could eat chocolate together.' She laughs as if it's really not important.

I squeeze her arm. 'I'm not going to Rachel's. I was just trying to be brave, telling you that. I'd love to come down to yours.'

Sylvia smiles at me, her eyes shining.

'There's one condition, though. I always watch sentimental Christmas movies. The weepier the better.'

'Well, that's good.' She laughs. 'Because I'm thinking I've probably got a lifetime of corny movies to catch up on.'

'Oh, you have. And your education starts right here.' A memory flashes into my mind. 'There's a brilliant movie you have to see. *West Side Story*. The musical.'

'Great.' She nods happily.

'Although I think, for Christmas Day, we should aim for cornier than that,' I add. 'Perhaps *The Holiday*?'

'Never heard of it,' admits Sylvia cheerfully. 'But bring it on!'

I'm smiling as we walk along, arm in arm.

West Side Story was Mum's film.

It's time to find out what sort of movies Sylvia enjoys ...

*

'Here we are. This is it,' says Sylvia, and we stop outside what looks at first glance like a bookshop.

We step inside. It's cosy being out of the chill autumn wind and the scent of coffee beans is very tempting, although I think the café must be on the floor above because this area is apparently just books.

'Oh, look, someone must be doing a book signing,' I remark, noticing a queue forming beside a little desk nearby that's piled high with copies of the same hardback book. I start walking over to take a look.

'Ah, yes. I was meaning to tell you—' Sylvia begins, and I turn with a quizzical look. Colour flares in her normally pale cheeks. She smiles at someone behind me, her whole face lighting up. 'Hello, Jake.'

Jake?

I swing round, my heart bumping madly, my legs almost buckling with shock.

Apparently I had no need of a photo in a newspaper as a sad reminder of him!

Because here he is in the flesh. Standing beside a board on an easel that I somehow missed coming in, which announces that best-selling author Jake Steele will be signing copies of his new book, out today. The board has the same picture I saw in the newspaper that I stuffed in my bag.

'Sylvia, great to see you.' He pauses, his eyes locking on to mine. 'Daisy.'

I swallow hard and smile, a flush rising into my cheeks. The sound of my name on his lips evokes all the memories of the time we spent together at his camp in the woods, and my heart starts beating so wildly, I feel quite breathless.

He turns to Sylvia and smiles. 'You managed to get her here. Well done.'

I turn to Sylvia and she's looking a little embarrassed. She shrugs. 'Only too glad to help. After all the trouble you took to have your book signing in Manchester, it was the least I could do.'

I stare at her in disbelief. 'You knew we were coming to Jake's book signing? Why didn't you tell me?'

'Don't blame Sylvia,' interjects Jake smoothly. 'I asked her to keep it a secret.'

'But why?'

He glances down at his shoes and doesn't answer immediately. Then he says, 'I was worried you might not want to see me.'

'I don't know why you would think that,' I say, puzzled.

He shrugs. 'I've had your book for so long without getting back to you. There was a reason, though. I wanted to look into something that I hoped would mean good news for you.'

I stare at him, unable to fathom what he's talking about.

Sylvia nudges me, murmuring, 'If you'll excuse me, I just want to have a look around. I haven't been in a proper bookshop for years.'

She smiles at us both, looking rather mischievous, and wanders off among the bookshelves.

'You ... organised this book signing specially?' I stare up at Jake, still barely able to take in the fact that he's standing right here in front of me.

'I did. I'm sorry I haven't been in touch but it wasn't because I wasn't thinking about you. Quite the opposite, in fact.' He glances down at the ground, oddly vulnerable, not at all like his usual quietly confident self.

'It doesn't matter. You're here now and that's the main thing,' I murmur, finding it hard to drag my eyes away from his, even for a second.

His mouth twists into the gorgeous smile that has been haunting my dreams for weeks. 'So you don't mind?'

I laugh softly. Can he really think that I would?

'No, of course I don't mind. Quite the opposite, in fact.'

We smile at my repetition of his earlier words.

I give a little shrug. 'I thought I'd never see you again and I ... I didn't like it.'

'Me, neither.' His eyes blaze with emotion as he looks at me. Then he glances behind him, at the queue of people waiting. 'Look, I actually do need to sign these books. It won't take long. And then we can talk?'

I nod. 'I'll have a coffee with Sylvia. Come to the café when you've finished.'

I watch him walk away, my eyes lingering long after they should on the breadth of his shoulders, his gorgeous bum and his long, muscular legs, loving every little thing about him. I watch with interest the reaction of the women in the queue as Jake approaches. A few of them stand straighter, flick their hair a little and smile. I'd do the same, I realise, if I was a fan in that queue.

It's so good to see Jake again but I've got to make sure I don't get carried away, thinking I'm the reason he arranged this book signing in Manchester. He could still be hung up on Laura ...

I find Sylvia and we go up to the café and order lattes and squares of iced ginger cake.

When we're settled at a table overlooking shoppers in the street below, I ask Sylvia what's been going on with her and Jake.

She looks anxious. 'I hope you don't think I'm interfering. It's just I knew that you liked Jake, so when I bumped into him at the hotel after you left and he asked if I'd seen you, we got talking and came up with this plan.'

I gaze at her in astonishment.

'Jake was asking about me?'

She nods. 'He had to leave abruptly. His agent wanted him to do an important interview. So he didn't have time to see you before he left and he felt bad. But he came back to the hotel, hoping to see you.'

'Oh. So he felt guilty about me.'

She nods. 'But it was much more than that. He confessed he hadn't been able to stop thinking about you. He wanted to know if you were still with Toby and of course I told him that you'd split up.' She smiles. 'He perked up a lot after that.'

'Really? Did he mention Laura?'

She frowns. 'No, I don't think so. You mean the Laura who died in that tragic car accident? His stepmother?'

I stare at her. Jake's *stepmother*?

If that's true, it casts a whole different light on everything.

'Are you sure Laura was his stepmother?'

'Pretty sure. It says so in this newspaper.' She picks up a copy from the table and finds the feature about Jake to show me. It's the same paper I glanced at and tossed away on the bus. If I'd bothered to read the feature, I'd have found out for myself that Jake's great fondness for the woman called Laura had nothing at all to do with romance.

'I thought he was still pining for a lost love,' I murmur.

'Well, he's not.' She smiles. 'And he really likes you, Daisy. That much is very clear to me.' She smooths a lock of hair back from my brow. 'So why not go and find him and tell him how you feel? Because it's as clear as day to me that you two belong with each other.'

'You think?' My heart is leaping in my chest.

'I do think. So go. I'll wait here.' She makes shooing signs. 'Go, go, go!'

I smile at her. Then I get up, leaving the remains of my ginger cake, and go downstairs to the bookshop.

The queue has dispersed for now. Jake is sitting at the desk, signing books, but when he sees me, he gets up and walks over.

I smile up at him. 'Did you say you had good news for me?'

'I do, yes. Let's go somewhere more private.'

He leads me through to a small adjoining room and stops in the doorway. 'I'm so glad you and Sylvia found each other. I think you're very alike in some ways.'

I smile, delighted. 'You think so?'

He nods. 'You're both independent with a quiet intelligence that I like very much. I can tell you're mother and daughter.'

'I can't call her Mum,' I confess sadly. 'It would seem disloyal to the woman who *was* my lovely mum.'

He nods. 'Give it time. You might change your mind.'

'I hope so. I really want to but ...' I shrug helplessly.

'I'm sure Sylvia understands.'

We walk into the room. It's lined with glass cases, all containing old books.

'First editions,' he says. 'There's *Wuthering Heights* there and *Jane Eyre*, and most of Jane Austen's collection as well.'

I walk along, looking at the titles. 'Wow. They're gorgeous. Imagine owning one.'

'I think this is a pretty good place to tell you that I really liked your book, Daisy.'

'You did?' My heart seems to expand with happiness.

He nods and gives me the smile that always puts my knees in grave danger of buckling. 'I loved it. So I showed it to my agent and she thinks you have a unique voice and that you've written a really heart-warming and compelling book. She wants to sign you up, Daisy. Help you to get a publisher for it.'

I can hardly believe what I'm hearing. 'Hold on, *your agent* likes my book? And she wants to help me find a publisher? Am I dreaming here?'

He laughs softly. 'No, Daisy, I can confirm that it's all true and that you are, in fact, wide awake.'

'You're sure?'

'Very sure.' He moves, bridging the gap between us. 'And I think I can prove it.' His eyes burn down into mine as he pulls me against him.

'And how will you do that?' I manage to croak, his touch sparking off little pulses of desire all over my body.

'Like this,' he growls, lowering his head and crushing his lips to mine.

And there, among the precious first editions of all the famous romance classics, it's finally clear how we feel about each other.

Clinging to this gorgeous man, who I can talk to and who understands me, I steal my hands up over the muscles of his upper arms, feeling the deliciously hard contours of his body against me. Then I wind my fingers in his hair and we kiss for the longest time, until we have to pull apart, laughing, to take a breath ...

Chapter 29

It's the day of Clemmy's wedding and I'm flying around, trying to get ready.

Dropping my lipstick down the toilet, I let out a loud curse.

'It's your fault for dragging me back to bed,' says a voice.

I turn to find Jake lounging in the doorway, giving me that lazy smile of his that always reduces me to a jelly.

I laugh. 'I think it was a fairly mutual dragging, if I remember correctly. Now, stop looking at me like that. You're distracting me. I need to find this book.'

'*Wuthering Heights?*'

'Yes, I said I'd lend it to Clemmy. She's never read it and she's decided she's horrified at her lack of knowledge of the classics!'

'You'd better take it to her, then,' he says, and produces a book from behind his back.

'Ah! You found it. Well done.'

'Where's my prize?'

'What prize?'

'My prize for finding the book. A kiss will do.'

'Okay.' I sidle up to him and he grabs me against him and we kiss as if we actually aren't in any danger of being late for this wedding ...

'Give me the book,' I gasp at last, laughing as he holds it behind his back. 'No, seriously, give it to me. It was Mum's all-time favourite. I'd like it to stay in one piece.'

Something falls out of it. A slip of paper. Frowning, I bend to pick it up.

My heart lurches. It's a letter addressed to me in Mum's writing.

'Are you okay?'

'Yes. But I need to sit down.' Breathless, I move over to a chair and sink down. Then I hold the letter in trembling hands. A memory comes to me. That last day at the hospital. Mum murmuring *Wuthering Heights* and me thinking she wanted me to read it to her ...

Perhaps she wanted me to find her letter.

Taking a breath, I start to read.

*

My darling Daisy

This is a very hard letter to write. Mainly because I love you so very much and the very last thing I'd ever want to do is disappoint you or hurt you. I've thought a million times about how to say this to you so that you'll understand. But in the end, I'm just going to have to write it down and hope you'll be fine.

You've always known you were adopted. But what you don't know is that your birth mother came to find you but I never told you. I suppose I was terrified I might lose you.

Should I have told you? I kept meaning to but then time kept flying by. And now that I'm ill, I don't want to spoil our last weeks together. Please don't hate me for not being honest with you.

My dearest wish now is that you find the woman who gave birth to you.

She must have regretted her decision to have you adopted, and why wouldn't she? You have been the loveliest thing in my life but now I must leave you and it scares me terribly to think of you all alone in the world.

So find this woman, please, my darling.

When she meets you, she will know how wonderful you are and she will love you like I do. I know she will.

Remember that I love you with all my heart and I will always be with you.

And please, please, please promise me you will search for her.

Remember the good times and be happy, my darling.

Your Mum XXX

*

Wordlessly, I pass the letter to Jake to read. Then I slump down on the sofa, so many different emotions crashing through me.

After all my worries that I was being disloyal to Mum by enjoying Sylvia's company, here she is giving me her blessing! My heart feels as if it might explode with love for her.

Jake pulls me gently to my feet and kisses my cheek. Then he holds me so tightly against him for the longest time ...

Chapter 30

The Starlight Hotel looks stunningly beautiful on this crisp autumnal day.

There couldn't be a more perfect venue for Clemmy and Ryan's wedding reception, I reflect, as I step gingerly across the gravel from the car in my high heels. Jake grabs me round the waist and kisses my neck and I give a little squeal of delight.

'Looking gorgeous,' he murmurs in my ear, and I silently thank Rosalind for helping me choose this lovely silky dress.

'Oh, Daisy, the turquoise goes beautifully with your dark hair,' she'd enthused in the shop. 'I won't speak to you again if you don't get it!' she joked.

Thankfully, Rosalind and I have been speaking a *lot* since Toby and I split up. I was so worried our lovely friendship would naturally fizzle out without Toby there as the mutual connection. But, actually, the opposite has turned out to be true.

As soon as she heard the news of our break-up, Rosalind was on the phone to me making sure I was all right, and saying she hoped that I was still free for coffee on Saturday as planned. I said of course I was, and I hung up feeling so relieved.

We don't talk about Toby much but, from what I can gather, he seems happy with Chantelle, although I can tell Rosalind doesn't feel quite the same affection for her as she did for me as a possible daughter-in-law. (I have to admit, I'm secretly very pleased about this!)

'Wasn't it a gorgeous ceremony?' says Gloria at my shoulder, and I turn to find her brushing some fluff off Ruby's sleek black dress.

'It was absolutely beautiful,' I agree.

The interior of the little parish church was decked out with pink and cream roses and lots of greenery, and when Clemmy walked down the aisle, she was a vision of happiness in the most glorious cream silk fishtail-style dress, sculpted to enhance her curves. Poppy, sitting next to me with a sleeping Keira in a sling, leaned closer and murmured, 'Have you ever seen such a delicious bride?'

I had to agree.

'Respect to Ryan for blubbering at the sight of his lovely wife-to-be,' comments Ruby, batting Gloria's hands away. 'Stop fiddling with my dress, Mum. I'm not five years old.'

'Well, why you had to wear *black* at a *wedding* I have no idea!' grumbles Gloria. 'You look like Morticia from the Addams Family.'

Ruby nods. 'Thanks. I always thought she was quite a style icon.'

'It's when people say you look like Uncle Fester that you've got to worry.' Jake grins.

Laughing, we walk through reception to the room where drinks are being served to the wedding guests.

'There's Roxy and Alex!' says Ruby, waving at a couple looking all loved-up in the corner. She turns to me. 'They fell in love at Christmas but Alex was working in Australia. So he's moved back here so they can be together. Romantic, eh?'

I smile. 'Very. And what about you, Ruby? Is there a special guy for you on the horizon?'

She snorts. 'Not for a *very* long time. I'm off to uni in a few weeks. I fully intend to enjoy myself before getting lumbered with a long-term relationship.'

'Very sensible,' agrees Jake, and we exchange the sort of smile that makes my heart leap in my chest.

We've spent every weekend together since the book signing and I've never been happier, although I wish we didn't live so far apart. I already know I want to spend the rest of my life with Jake. But I've no idea if he feels the same ...

'That dress looks amazing,' says a voice and I turn to find Sylvia smiling at me.

'Thank you.'

She's looking smart herself, the efficient manager, organising Clemmy and Ryan's day to perfection. There's a lightness in her face, though, that wasn't there before. She no longer scrapes her hair back in a bun for work. She wears it loose and she looks much more relaxed. And happy.

My mum!

The word bursts into my head, taking me by surprise.

She looks at her watch. 'Time for the wedding breakfast. See you later.' She presses my arm and is swept up in the crowd.

All through the meal, I keep thinking about the letter Mum left me. I know Sylvia would love me to think of her as 'Mum' but I also know she would never, ever ask me to. She's far too perceptive and caring for that ...

Much later, after we've eaten the delicious meal and danced

to the music of Ryan's favourite local band until we're fit to drop, Clemmy and Ryan disappear upstairs to get changed.

Jake is at the bar, chatting to Jed and Poppy, and I'm sitting at a table with Gloria, Ruby and Bob, Gloria's lovely fiancé.

I've never met Bob and, after being introduced, we start chatting. He currently lives and works in London, although he tells me that once he and Gloria are married he's going to wind down his work commitments and they're planning to set up home on the south coast.

'So you knew Clemmy from university days, is that right?' he asks.

I nod. 'And I caught up with her again when I stayed at her glamping site in the summer.'

'And you're here with your boyfriend?'

'Yes. That's Jake over there, at the bar.' Just saying it fills me with a lovely warm feeling.

Sylvia comes over at that moment to give me the key to the room Jake and I are staying in tonight.

'Sorry to interrupt,' she says, laying a hand on my shoulder and smiling at Bob.

I shake my head. 'You're not. I'm just telling Bob how I know everyone.'

I swallow and look up at Sylvia. 'Bob, this is my mum.' My voice cracks but Bob doesn't seem to notice.

Bob immediately gets to his feet. 'Pleased to meet you at last,' he says, shaking Sylvia's hand. 'I know you're the manager here, but we've never actually spoken.'

Sylvia is smiling and chatting away, but only I would be able to detect the glint of a tear in her eye, the slight wobble of her chin.

Before she sweeps off, we exchange a smile that says everything ...

And then, when I think I can't feel any more emotional, Clemmy is coming down the elegant staircase, on Ryan's arm. They look so happy and relaxed, eager I guess to be on their way to the airport and their flight out to the Maldives.

Clemmy is holding her bouquet and when she gets to the bottom of the stairs, she shouts, 'Okay, ladies. Are you ready?'

Everyone gathers round, laughing and chattering, and Jake comes over from the bar to join me. Clemmy ramps up the suspense by making us all wait.

And then she lobs the beautiful bouquet, full of pink and cream roses, over her head.

It soars surprisingly high in the air before coming down inches from my nose. Astonished, I grab it and a great cheer goes up.

'Ooh, it's you next, then,' says Ruby, nudging me and grinning.

I look up at Jake, feeling decidedly awkward, wishing Ruby could be a bit more subtle sometimes.

Jake grins. 'If that's the case, maybe we'd better think about moving in together,' he murmurs, close to my ear. 'Or am I being too eager?'

I smile as a great tide of happiness swells inside me. I reach up on tiptoe to kiss him. 'I can't think of anything I'd love more.'

He grins wolfishly and pulls me behind a handy pillar. And after that, all logical thoughts flee from my mind as Jake kisses the life out of me ...

Acknowledgements

This writing adventure of mine continues to feel amazing and slightly surreal, and there are times I really do have to pinch myself! Lots of lovely people have helped me along the way – but for now, a big thank you to my wonderful agent, Heather Holden-Brown, and the hugely creative and fabulous team at Avon. You set me on the road to achieving my dream and I will always be so grateful. Particular thanks to my lovely, talented editor, Molly Walker-Sharp, who was so supportive (and endlessly patient with missed deadlines!) during the writing of *Summer under the Stars*.

Can love flourish amongst the treetops?

A funny, feel-good read from Catherine Ferguson.

Join Holly as she starts over …

A fun, fresh tale of love, friendship and family from Catherine Ferguson.

Loved *Summer under the Stars*? Then why not head back to very beginning with Poppy and Jed …

Christmas at the Log Fire Cabin

Catherine Ferguson

A hilarious story from the ebook bestseller.

Roxy is hoping that the log fire cabin will help to heal her broken heart …

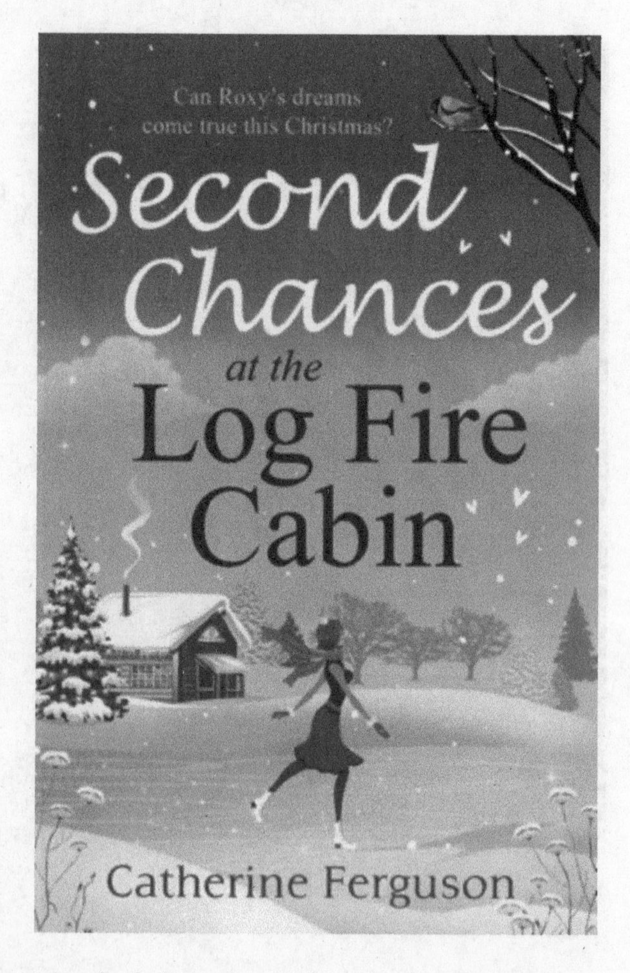

A lovely, feel-good read from Catherine Ferguson.